The Illegal

Virginia Gayl Salazar

THE ILLEGAL

iUniverse books may be ordered through booksellers or by contacting:

iUniverse
1663 Liberty Drive
Bloomington, IN 47403
www.iuniverse.com
1-800-Authors (1-800-288-4677)

ISBN: 978-1-4917-4473-4 (sc)
ISBN: 978-1-4917-4474-1 (e)

Printed in the United States of America.

iUniverse rev. date: 10/30/2014

Dedicated to our writing critique class at Parnell Park in Whittier, California. You helped me retain imprints of my beloved husband Joe, palm tree lover, gardener, landscaper, nursery owner, and friend:

1933 – 2013

Jennie Jaime, Sibyl Farson, Carol Dukes, Iris Zuber, Ann Hardman, Betty Lopez, Piedad Garcia, Dan Delehant, Regie King

FOREWORD

*T*HIS DESERT, THIS VAST *wilderness, rests blanketed with dense mesquite forests, spiny cacti, and giant ocotillo trees growing in the heat. Vultures flying overhead circle dead bones. Bones of many unfortunates splay out near the now dried up wash, not far from rotting flesh permeating the nostrils. As the stench rises up to meet him, José swallows hard to keep from vomiting.*

Animals have scattered bits and pieces of a carcass, not yet picked clean by the raptors José chases away, – over a 20-foot radius – someone, unknown, who recently hadn't made it to America, the land of promise.

SECTION I

The year is 1998

CHAPTER 1

THE THREE BRUTISH CASTILLONE brothers arrogantly marched up and down the main street in the center of town buried deep in the country of Mexico. Descended from one of Cortez' foreign soldiers who settled in the new world, the brothers owned the small village of Siempre, Mexico, through brute force. With their brawn and bullying, they regularly reminded the males of all ages in the town who was boss of the village, and no one challenged them. Many of the older girls and young women fought for their favors – more out of fear of the rough contemptible brothers than desire.

Enrique the eldest controlled the other two brothers, Francisco known as Pancho, and Pedro. Because Enrique was the oldest, he had regularly beaten up the younger two each day of their young lives. They lived in fear of him in spite of their admiration. Even in their mother's womb, he kicked at them. His mother thought he would be pleased to have a brother or sister, so she had told him they were growing within her swelling belly.

But Enrique did not want to share his mother who fed and cuddled him while his anger about the coming baby grew and grew. When they were born, there were two baby boys instead of just one as his mother told him. He raged as only a two-year-old can throw a tantrum. She stopped cuddling him and became afraid of the strange, hostile monster controlling their family.

She said to their father, "Where has such jealousy and hatred come from? I am afraid of him, and he is only a child. What will he be like when he becomes a man?"

After the twins began walking, the child knew he had to have control over them or the two new boys could gang up on him. The habit of ruling the house grew with each day and, as the younger ones aged, they followed him around as if he were king and they were his slaves. They rarely thought for themselves. Obedient, they copied his angry behavior.

One neighbor gave their mother advice when Enrique was ten, "Put Enrique in the corner for an hour."

When told to stay in the corner for an hour for hurting one of the twins, Enrique struck his mother in the chest and shoved her creating anger in her. His drunken father ignored them and gave no help to his wife.

The mother's brothers had all gone to the United States and couldn't care less about their foolish sister's problems. Her three brothers had warned her not to marry their second cousin *el Burro* as Jorge Castillone was known in the village, because of his stubborn hard-drinking ways. They knew Jorge would never support her as a husband should. He refused to go with them to America to earn money to send home as long as he had some kind of alcohol to soothe his cravings. As Enrique grew, he found he could make points with his drunken father by bullying neighbors into giving him their spoiled grain that was easily made into alcohol.

One morning, Juanita commiserated with her drunken husband in front of the young Enrique, "Inez told me to put him in a corner and it does not work. He is now worse than ever. He hit me." Enrique heard enough to know what he would do to Inez.

Three days later the wooden hut of their cousin Inez Huerta Castillone burned to the ground with what few possessions her family owned. Her two-year-old daughter, Cecilia, was scorched as if she were a rag doll thrown too close to the fire. She lived, but no one in the village ever stepped forward when she came of marriageable age. Some even blamed her husband, Dario, who might have started the fire as he smoked his cigarettes sent to him by a relative in Texas. The horrors of the child's burned face, arms and legs were reminders of the dangers of fire. Rumors grew about the kind of person who would do such a thing as to burn the house down.

In spite of the rumors, the fire was an accident Inez claimed, but Juanita knew in her soul it was her son, ten-year-old Enrique, who burned down the home. Two of her treasured matches had disappeared from the box where she kept them hidden under her mattress. She often heard her three sons giggling about the fire and the now disfigured Cecilia. She pondered all those disturbing things in her heart wondering how she could continue living with the knowledge of the evil in her household.

Juanita asked God, crying in despair, *Are bullies born or do we mothers make them? God forgive me. I would have drowned them at birth if I had known the future.* She had no idea what to do to make them behave.

As Juanita complained about her sons to her neighbors to help her with her sons, her husband, Jorge, sank deeper and deeper into the bottom of his homemade brew. He drank daily all day long. Poor Juanita went out into the village to beg for food and coins to care for her young. When she could, she did laundry for a coin or food from some of the neighbors and relatives who took pity on her. The sons, when they hit the teenage years, knew no discipline and deemed it to their advantage to be the masters of the village. They began going into homes to demand food as their right. The locals had very few material items to be coveted, but what they did have soon belonged to the Castillone family. In shame their mother rarely left her home. She lived with the disgrace and walked with eyes downcast while going to pray at the small church set among humble dwellings.

Even radios and flashlights operated by batteries had to be hidden from the brothers. Double A and double D batteries were among the most valued possessions in the community. The small church and their aging priest and two elderly nuns began hiding what valuables they might have. One day, the old priest was discovered dead between two pews. It looked like he had fallen and hit his head. Rumors grew that the three boys, 15 and 13, killed him. Hence no priest would take the position so an itinerant priest showed up occasionally to perform priestly duties and direct the two aged nuns.

As the sons grew into their twenties the Castillone family was feared in the small community of Siempre. The western side lived on fishing from the Sea of Cortez, the eastern side where the very poor dug out a living from the soil the people seemed to be a link to their past. It was like two different towns. Somewhat inbred, the entire eastern village was related to one another. Second and third cousins married. It was good and it was bad for the residents. Everyone helped one another in times of crisis. The youngsters always had adults around looking over their shoulders to make sure they behaved... until the Castillone brothers brought fear to the community. *La policia* from neighboring towns did not have time nor the desire to throw the brothers in jail for the night to teach them to obey the laws.

None of the three brothers had yet taken a wife, because they regularly were serviced by the single females in the community as well as neighboring small towns. The families of the girls dared not refuse. Many of the prettier girls for miles around swelled large with a child of the Castillone brothers.

On the evening of his 25th birthday Enrique Castillone spoke up while carrying three glasses of tequila to the table where they drank in the town's only bar, "It is time I thought about taking a wife. I am sick of looking at you two." He looked down on his brothers in disgust. "None of us is getting on with life as I see José the peon doing."

Pancho replied, "You're right. He seems cheerful enough when all he has is children."

"That's not all he has," said Pedro, slowly raising a thick eyebrow.

"You're right. He has curly-haired Elmira. She must be pushing thirty years old. Why would anyone want her?" asked Pancho. "I would think I was laying with our mother."

"She is only a year older than I am," said Enrique. "She has not started to wrinkle, so maybe she is younger than she claims to be."

"You're right, Enrique. Maybe she would want one of us. Compare us to José and she would choose us," exclaimed Pedro, enjoying the thought of stirring up some excitement.

Pancho spoke up, "The villagers might not like it if we go after someone's wife."

"Who is the boss in this town?" asked Enrique.

"We are," replied Pancho looking at his brother's hands.

"No one dares go against us," added Pedro. "We are the kings for miles around."

His chest swelled with pride.

CHAPTER 2

I N THE SAME SLEEPY village, José turned over in his bed scratching his young, firm *huevos*. He lay with one leg pressed up against his beautiful wife, Elmira, in the darkness of the night. In the cool air she felt wonderful to his touch, but even with the heat of summer he tried to pull her into himself.

José would tell his wife, "Elmira, you are such a comfortable pillow." Her large, shapely breasts had fed all their seven children, and the youngest, two-year-old Joselito was still nursing. So much milk, so much passion. José loved it when plump Joselito nursed on one breast in bed at night. José licked the leaking milk from the other breast as it trickled down the dark areola surrounding the nipple and felt no man had it better than he. When the fat and happy baby was full and asleep, Elmira would slip him over into the homemade cradle beside their bed and turn her attentions to José.

Elmira never told him, "No," when he rolled over and his left knee parted her legs. She was the most passionate woman he knew about. The other men told tales of their wives refusing them. But not Elmira. Elmira loved him and desired his body with all her passionate nature. Her mother had told her on her wedding day never to deny her husband. *You'll never regret it, Elmira, if you please him every time he wants you.* So she never used sex to get her way as is the weapon of many wives.

What man could want for more?

He was happily looking forward to the coming month when the traveling priest would be in town. He set it up last year with the priest

5

to marry him and Elmira in the small Church. It had taken him all these ten years to save up the $50 needed to pay the priest for the Christian marriage. She was well worth $50,000 which he never could have paid in a lifetime of good weather.

He kept scratching until Elmira awoke and reached around and under his leg to help him scratch. He giggled. *What a wife! She herself was an itch he could never get enough of.*

Soon both their desires were aroused and their very early morning ritual became lovemaking in the morning darkness. They didn't want to awaken the children. With Elmira it wasn't sex as the locals talked about. He couldn't imagine life without her. This morning she raised up on him and pleased him in her special way. For ten years it had been this way, since their wedding performed by the *abuelo* grandfather who was the patriarch of their family.

José had always known Elmira. She was his mother's cousin Oswaldo's third child. They were second cousins. She had told him when he was nine and she was five that she wanted to marry him when they grew up. He didn't care back then if he ever married but it was easier to agree with her than to refuse her affection. When she turned seventeen and he was 21, the *village Abuelo* came to them and told them it was time for them to marry. Everyone for miles around made *many* tamales and after the short ceremony by the grandfather, they ate and danced the night away with all their extended family in the village.

Her family had protected her virginity with a vengeance, so José and Elmira came together without much experience except stolen kisses and constant groping of each other during those secret moments when they could slip around a corner. The old gossips had followed them around it seemed, for their mothers often got onto them for being indiscreet and too public in their kissing.

Coming together as virgins gave them the added pleasure of learning from one another. Both were surprised at how good the sexual experience was. They had heard about it, but now were filled with joys they had only dreamed about during the frequent times they had rubbed themselves to climaxes – separately in their lonely beds – they dreamed of marrying and pleasuring themselves as one. Now for ten years it was one to the other.

"Why does it feel so much better when you touch me, Elmira?"

"I don't know, José. It was good when I used to press myself, but when you do it I go out of my mind. It hurt a little the first three times we did it on our wedding night, but now I throb for you. There is rarely any discomfort. Why did God make it so good?"

"My Uncle Miguel told me it would be that way for a woman after the first pain," José told her. "He told me sex would get better and better for you if I did not pressure you to do anything you didn't want to do."

"I can't imagine what you would want me to do that I wouldn't want to. You are my man!" Elmira turned over and spread her legs so they could do it again. She was blessed to be one of those women who climaxed over and over and assumed all women were like her. Soon after their marriage before children, she thought about the days the children would be born and they would have less time with each other. When she complained to her older sister, Alejandra Ortiz Ramirez, about the time children would take, Alejandra told their mother who soon after told her, "The children will be gone to their own homes one day and he will be all yours once more. Like it is with your father and me."

As the children were born, Elmira accepted her lot in life and enjoyed what time she and José had together in the darkness of night. Their union gave them seven children. The village women told the young couple, "God has blessed your coupling."

Elmira longed for the day it would be her and José together, alone again, like it was now with her parents. She recognized the contentment and joy in their lives as they aged, together. She thanked God often for her blessings, especially for José and their energetic children.

CHAPTER 3

AFTER SEEING THE TWO cows and several goats were milked and fed, José Ramirez spent the mornings sweeping and cleaning the general store where he worked from 9 a.m. to noon with Pablo, the small store's owner. He worked for Pablo even at times when Pablo could not afford to pay him either in pesos or flour which was too often.

Pablo sometimes told his wife, "José is a good man. He understands when I can't pay him."

His wife replied, "Good men will give and give but not forever, so don't take advantage of him. He is not stupid."

"It's okay," said Pablo. "José understands. He wants me to have a few things."

His wife would reply each time, "Pablo, José, like God understands, but some day he will see through your chicanery."

Each afternoon José walked his growing area along the two rows of growing safflower stalks pulling oversized weeds. He did the same to the many rows of corn. He looked at the parched, cracked earth where he planted their precious potatoes among the stunted stalks of potential food. Whether barefoot or with his shoes on he moved along dodging the developing potato leaves.

Elmira used the flowers of the safflower to make a red or orange dye for the villagers' clothes. Some safflower heads grew red, others orange. Villagers traded extra grain and vegetables they grew for some of her flowers for their own dyeing.

Elmira taught their young sons, Miguel*ito* and Francisco, to make cheese from their two cows' milk. Whatever the children didn't drink she would let curdle in the hot sun. She pressed the soured curds of milk into solid cheese. She traded or sold the cheese to Pablo for food staples. Pablo in turn sold the cheese to other customers. Cow's cheese tasted better than the goat cheese many of the villagers ate.

Miguel and Francisco, were now old enough to follow José and help him as he directed. Miguel would be ten before long. The laughing, vivacious, older daughter, Alicia, just passed her seventh birthday. Everyone told him she was growing into a beauty like her mother. He was also teaching her to help a little in the small field. More interested in playing with her homemade corncob dolls, she tried to convince him she needed to spend this time in the kitchen helping her mother who let her play.

"Please *Papa*, *mi Mama* needs me to help her," Alicia would say.

José would tease his fingers through Alicia's curly-haired, long tresses that tangled so easily and tell her, "Papa loves you and you love Papa. So you will help Papa, won't you?"

"*Sí, Papa.* I will help." José would kiss her messed up curls that looked so much like Elmira's beautiful curly hair. He thought about the many evenings he helped his wife comb her long hair that curled even with the weight of its length.

José thought about the planting seed that must be saved so it will grow in abundance in good years to feed the family. The temptation to eat the *planting* corn when he saw his children hungry for more food was always there for the poor man. Which is more important: Feeding your child one day when you see him hungry? Or saving corn seed so he can eat many days the next year?

Finally, this spring it rained again. José and Elmira danced in the rain when they realized they would have a little more food this year – and more seed to save for the following year. The children watched their silly parents who were getting wet. They didn't see what was so funny. They watched their laughing and dancing parents and soon joined them playing in the warm rain.

The lack of rain the last four years had created deep cracks two-inches wide between the rows of corn and safflower. Those cracks extended down a foot. Without rain it became foolish to plant a second crop. He had heard how the drought had killed cattle, parched the crops and forced some towns to have to import drinking water. If the people had no pesos, they had no water. They finally resorted to omitting the summer planting season.

Before *Tio* Miguel left for California two springs ago, he told him the canals around the northern Mexican cities now only carried dust.

Tio Miguel said angrily, "California brings in water from their wide rivers through manmade channels to water their crops. Why don't our Mexican leaders spend some of their money to do the same with our rivers?"

José said, "*Tio*, they must be too busy enjoying the good life."

"When I went north last year," added Miguel, "I heard the drought was worse. Three states were declared disaster areas last year, but this year ten states have been declared disasters."

"What does that mean?" asked José.

"It means our *Federales* pledged millions of dollars to help the states."

"*Tio* Miguel, I haven't seen any money helping us here in our village."

"The big cities are complaining they also haven't seen any of the money,"

"Well, where is the money going?"

"You tell me," said *Tio* Miguel.

"Is someone keeping the money?" asked José.

"That always seems to be the case here in Mexico. José, the months of irrigation are now. It is a sad time when canals only hold dust. The birds are hungry. They scratch around and eat the parched *planting* seed before it can take root."

"*Sí*," agreed José. "If there's no harvest, there's no market. The reservoir we dug and cemented in for drinking water for the village is getting dangerously low."

"I will go north to the United States to find work. This drought is killing our village. Some of us must go to California to send back money, to help the family."

"Elmira needs me to help with the little ones. I cannot go," reasoned José.

"I have no wife since Leona died. I will go." Leona had given him no children except for the one who died at birth. He had thought long and often how he might find a widow in America who would have her own house and would bear him children. He had heard stories.

****

José found being a good father was difficult but it brought pleasure. He did his best to show his love to his small sons and daughters. Each morning after he milked the cows and goats, while Elmira fixed a breakfast of corn tortillas, rice, and beans, José wrestled with his sons and then taught them shadow boxing as his father had taught him. He began the morning by giving his older sons his famous bear hug. Even the girls piled on top of them with gleeful laughter as all rolled about on the front room floor.

The toddler, *poquito* Joselito, laughed with belly-laughs and wide eyes as he watched the pile-up. He would yell, "Me, too. Me, too," but just watched. The twins who were five months short of four rolled on the floor wrestling with each other.

Miguelito told his *Papá*, "I will be big one day and then I'll give you the biggest bear hug ever."

"You think so?" said José and gave Miguelito a big bear hug that left the young one breathless. As they laughed, breathing hard. José felt the admiration and energy of his oldest son.

CHAPTER 4

MONDAY MORNING JOSÉ CAME to work at the store and found his employer Pablo cringing in pain and holding his right knee.

"What happened, Pablo? Did you fall?"

"*No, no. Sí,* I'm injured. Enrique Castillone raped my beautiful little Clarita on Saturday night. My poor Clarita. She and my wife Alma are at home crying. I could not bear to watch them, so I came here with my neighbor's help."

José was shocked. "But she's only twelve, though I admit she looks older."

Pablo was pleading and in pain. "*Sí,* she is hurting, and now I am suffering, too. I went looking for Enrique, but he and his brothers cracked my kneecap with that steel hammer they carry. I didn't even get a chance to give one of them a bloody nose. A man in this town can't even defend his family." Pablo slurred his words from the herbs he had taken for the pain.

"Have you been to the *Abuelita*?" asked José concerned and hoping Pablo had sent for the Grandmother who was the healer in the community.

"*Sí, Abuelita* came to my house. *Mi esposa* and her brothers had carried me home from the streets and went for her. Abuelita wrapped strong, tough rags around my leg so it won't move around. She said to leave it like this for two months so the bones will heal."

"Why are you here? You need to be at home," José insisted worried about his injured employer, pale from pain. He did not have to be told how bad the break must be.

"I made the *hombres* bring me here, so I can run the store when you leave after sweeping.

"Pablo, I'll fix things so your customers can bring the food items to you after they have picked up what they want to buy. They can bring you the money. I must get back to my field after lunch."

"Please José, stay a little longer today. I need your help. The pain is torture."

"A little longer, yes. For today." Today grew to two weeks and José got behind in his weeding. Elmira began helping their sons pull the weeds and channeling water from the big cistern José had helped the townsmen build when he was in his teens. She could use only a little water, for it must be saved for drinking by all the community. The recent rain had added some water to the cistern but not enough to fill it. Unless it rained again soon, the crops would be small and stunted.

After a month José looked at Pablo whose knee was healing. José could tell he didn't hurt as much because Pablo no longer complained about the throbbing ache. José said, "You must go to *la policia* in Cruz Grande." Cruz Grande was one village east from their village of Siempre and that village had police.

"But José, I'm afraid of the Castillone brothers. What if they find out?"

"Pablo, I won't tell anyone. They won't know I know. Surely the police will put the Castillone brothers in jail for what they did to your daughter – and to you."

"Will you run the store while I ride over in my wagon? My knee is feeling better. It has been a month, and I have stayed off of it like the *Abuelita* told me."

"Yes, I'll run the store for you," José replied.

The next morning Pablo drove his scrawny horse and dilapidated old wagon to the neighboring town where there was a one-room police station and two policemen. When he arrived, the two men eating lunch noticed him out the window. When they saw he came to see them, they walked out to talk to him in his wagon.

"I need help. I'm from the village of Siempre. My name is Pablo Sanchez."

"We will be glad to help you," the first policeman said. He was short and heavy set, usually with a full grin on his pudgy face.

"*Sí*," said the other. "Tell us what you need."

"We have this bad hombre named Enrique Castillone. He raped my daughter and broke my kneecap with a hammer when I complained," said Pablo.

"Sure we will investigate. Were there any witnesses? Who else saw what happened?"

The other policeman said, "Tell us where they live."

Pablo told them everything they needed to know about the three brothers. And then he returned back to his store in the nearby village of Siempre.

As he rode off, the first policeman said to his partner, "We would help him with anyone but the Castillone brothers."

"They are too strong, too powerful for *la policia* to do anything to help him," said the second.

The first policeman added, "I'm glad he went home. He put us in danger by coming to see us."

The second policeman put his hand on his partner's shoulder compassionately, "Don't you think we would do something if we could? My young granddaughter was fathered by Enrique and not by my daughter's choice. *El Cabron*! I would kill him myself if I thought I could get away with it."

******

Meanwhile back in Pablo's store, José looked up from the shelf he was cleaning to see Enrique and Pedro walk in.

"Where is Pablo?" asked Enrique looking around the store and grabbed some *Corona* beer from the shelves. He handed them to Pedro.

"Oh," said José hesitantly. "He rode out to do some business. He'll be back soon. Do you want me to put the beer on your bill?" Both men ignored his question.

"Where did he go?" asked Pedro. "His leg isn't healed enough for him to be out joy riding. It must be important for him to leave the store."

I don't know," said José lying and trying to look ignorant. "I expect him soon. I'll tell him you were asking for him."

"Do that!" said Enrique stomping out the door with Pedro behind him.

******

José woke up early the next morning. He explained to his wife Elmira he must get to the store.

"Please Elmira, help the children milk the cows and the goats without me. I must check on Pablo."

Some inner fear made him worry about Pablo. The afternoon before Pablo had not returned to the store as José thought he would. He figured Pablo must have been uncomfortable from the long ride. He locked up and went home to spend a little time in his field before dark.

As José walked to work, he kept saying to himself, *I should have gone by his house on my way home.*

Pablo wasn't at the store when José showed up at the door for work, but his wife, Alma Marguerita, was there with the key. She was sitting on the step. Her eyes were red from crying, and there was fear in her voice as she spoke.

"The Castillone brothers are wicked! Mean! They came to our house last night and broke Pablo's kneecap again. He may be crippled and never walk."

"Alma Marguerita, what are you saying?" José was shocked.

"Enrique said he was told by someone he saw my Pablo talking to *la policia* about the brothers raping our precious Clarita.

She continued, "Those Castillone brothers showed up at our house accusing Pablo of going to la policia. Pablo and I insisted Pablo was home with me all afternoon, but they refused to believe me."

"I'm so sorry, Alma Margurita. They probably went by your house and saw the wagon was missing. When they came to the store, I told them he went to run an errand. I should have told him not to go. I feel responsible."

"It is not your fault. How do good people like us protect themselves from evil men?" she asked.

"I will help you what I can," said José ignoring her question. Why ask a question when she knew he didn't have the answer. He tried to hide his growing anger.

"How is Pablo? Is he in much pain?"

"*Sí*," said Alma Marguerita. "I sent one of my children for the Abuelita who gave him herbs for his smashed and bleeding kneecap.

She gave him some of her homemade alcohol to keep him from swearing. "The children don't need to hear those words coming from his mouth. The *Abuelita* says his kneecap may never heal properly."

José gave his broom a wild swing. He was tired of the village fathers who had to be so protective of their sons to keep the Castillone brothers from selling them drugs that trickled into the surrounding villages. Thus far the men had been able to keep the drugs out but for how long? He was tired of the brutality of the three brothers. Right now his anger made him very tired, and he threw the broom across the room.

José had heard rumors that the airport in Cuernavaca, the Morelos state capital, allowed small planes to land. The police would meet the planes carrying Columbian cocaine and under their supervision police vehicles transported the evil drug to sell in other cities.

José did not yet understand how complicated the policing structure of Mexico had become over the decades. The federal, state and local forces operated through the silent code.

Alma Marguerita brought José back to the present by her mumblings. "Pablo is certain *la policia* that he went to see reported him to those devilish Castillone brothers. That's what they are… devils."

José answered, "Someone is going to have to do something about the brothers."

"One person cannot fight three. Perhaps the village will have to meet and plot against them before they do any more evil in this town." Alma Marguerita looked away, not believing her own words.

CHAPTER 5

E ACH DAY JOSÉ RAMIREZ looked at his four sons, three daughters and beautiful, healthy wife, content and satisfied. They had so much love among them. At night, as he lay beside voluptuous Elmira, he knew God had given him everything a man needed in this world. Things were not important. His family was. His children were happy, and he and Elmira continued to be in love.

How he was blessed! Except for enough money.

José and Elmira grew and saved what corn and potatoes they could for the winter. They needed food when the air grew cold and warm weather crops no longer took root. Potatoes taste good with corn or flour tortillas. They never went hungry because of José's and Elmira's planning and days of hard work.

Elmira would whisper to José in the dead of night, "We must hide our extra food from the Castillone brothers. They won't care that we need to eat when it is cold and stormy. I heard they went into the nuns' food last winter and took what they wanted."

José comforted her, "You remember we gave food to the elderly priest and the two old nuns when we heard of the theft."

"Sí, José. That is what God wanted us to do."

José hired out to do gardening in others' yards as well as the two neighbors on each side of him and cleaned the small general store – whatever he could to feed his family of nine. His older children would be teenagers before long, and he remembered how hungry he and his brothers and sisters were as they grew. Nothing could fill them up. He did not want his children going to sleep feeling empty as he had sometimes. He never wanted his children staring at him with hungry eyes as he had looked at his parents. So José worked harder and searched constantly for more work to earn more pesos.

He repaired the few cars in the town even though he did not have one of his own. He longed for the day he might save the money to buy one. But right now, the money they saved was for a real wedding for him and Elmira – a wedding in the church.

******

His mother's brother, Miguel, had come home from California for a visit when José was thirteen. Miguel was his hero who brought home a few potatoes and taught José and the women to cut the potatoes into pieces making sure the eyes were firm and ready to grow. Then they planted them in the ground and soon the eyes sprouted up into sprawling vines, so the buds of the potato pieces grew little potatoes under the soil.

Tio Miguel told them to save extra potatoes in a dark, cool space under the ground and they would be good for winter. In the heat of the summer it was hard to find cool spots under the ground, but José learned to make deep holes under the house to keep them in the cool darkness. He often changed holes and filled in the old holes, because the Castillone brothers took what they could easily find. Enrique, Pancho, and Pedro walked through the fields of corn and potatoes and ate what they wanted. It was easier than stealing at night when they preferred to drink and carouse with the girls.

This year during the winter months, José in the dark of night had dug a secret underground cellar away from the house, so the potatoes were hidden from the prying eyes of the Castillone brothers. In fact, Elmira had another secret, smaller cellar which she reserved for growing seed and the best potatoes with good *eyes* for germinating. José and his family became known around the village as the potato family. They secretly shared much of what they grew, even with the Castillone family, for José and Elmira knew Juanita Castillone was a good, prayerful woman and scarcely deserved the bad sons she bore.

When they needed more sugar or flour from the little store, the storekeeper, Pablo Garcia, was glad to trade for potatoes.

Enrique Castillone walked by one morning and said to José who was working his field near the road, "You always have plenty of corn and potatoes. What is your secret?"

José rubbed his sweaty brow with a large, callused hand and grinned, "Hard work, Enrique. Hard work." Enrique walked on growling under his breath as José called after him, "I have an extra hoe. Any time you want to help me, come on over." José had shared corn and potatoes with Enrique's mother, Juanita, as often as he could. Perhaps that was the reason her boys did not steal much from him. He felt sorry for the woman who had to live with those three monstrous sons. She spent time at the church praying for them every day.

When José had married, he and Elmira continued growing some of his uncle's potatoes for their own eating and bartered with the general store for flour to make wheat tortillas and other items they needed. When they needed more sugar or flour from the little store, the storekeeper, Pablo Garcia, was glad to trade for potatoes.

Tio Miguel visited again last year and went back to California. They hadn't heard from him. There were no phones except in the small store, and his *Tio* did not know how to read or write to send them a letter.

Pablo and his store were controlled by the Castillone brothers, so the one time José's Uncle Miguel called from La Mesa, California, at Christmas, they could not speak to him. They did not have the $15 to pay to talk to Uncle for three minutes. Pablo Garcia charged high prices for the rare phone calls, either out of the village or to the villagers. The Castillone brothers demanded their 80%. Pablo learned to keep his mouth shut, because they beat him whenever he complained.

José's thoughts turned to *Tio* Miguel often. He knew *Tio* would be happy to see him, but José's ties to the village were too strong to go for a better life for his family. He couldn't leave Elmira and the love they had for each other. A shiver traveled along his spine leaving him cold and lonely at the thought of being without his beloved Elmira.

One morning he told Elmira, "I dreamed of *Tio* Miguel last night. He was asking me to come to the United States of America."

He saw fear come into her eyes. "Elmira, I couldn't leave you."

She relaxed and rubbed his face. "I know José that your dreams are swallowed up in trudging the fields with hard, exhausting work."

"*Si, mi esposa*, you are my dream."

In six years his eldest, Miguelito, would be sixteen and old enough to send north to a better job than would be found in their village. José trained Miguel and his smaller brother Francisco to do the many odd jobs he did. His sons must be capable of being good workers to keep the family fed in case José became ill.

The Widow Castro next door to their house was an example. Her husband had been accidentally killed by a falling beam while adding a room onto their home. José and Elmira were helping her raise her two teenaged boys who worked hard growing corn and onions on their small plot of land. It was difficult because the boys did not like to work.

Some hot days while working his fields, José dared to think about sending his oldest son north to California hoping their lives would improve from money Miguelito would send home. He wanted to build a bigger house, but he remembered hearing from his cousins how the longtime illegals were trying to keep new illegals out. The job crunch had hit Southern California.

… The United States encouraged the established illegals to stay in their low-scale jobs by giving them green cards after they were in California six years. The newly-arrived guest workers were pushed out of the better jobs. Many went hungry, became discouraged and returned to their homes in Mexico, disgraced.

Tio Miguel had once told them, "The smart and the lucky make it in the United States. Every migration is rooted in the soil. There are strawberry pickers as well as cotton pickers. The gardeners make more money working for the wealthy."

He told them how it was easier if the undocumented could find a relative to let them live with them while they got established with a job and a place to live. Many piled up in one room and gave rent to the landlords who knew they would put up with insufferable conditions.

Crossing the border illegally had gone on for so many years that few would-be immigrants considered breaking America's laws was a sin. The visiting priests talked about sin but being illegal was not one of the mentioned mistakes man should not do. Instead they just warned the people to make proper preparations so as not to be caught.

José heard some communities collected funds to send three or four of their number, usually young men and boys, to earn money in America. After obtaining menial jobs by standing on the corners where gardeners and construction bosses could pick them up for little money, they would work and send a portion of their money home to be divided among the villagers. But if the Castillone brothers knew the villagers were saving money for anything, they would barge into the homes and take it by brute force.

José and his friends had met in his home one evening last year to discuss sending two or three men across the border. The name of the Castillone brothers came up and the men discarded the idea as not practical.

Elmira joked, "Maybe we should send the Castillone brothers to Texas."

"Maybe the cowboys would take care of them," laughed her father.

José shrugged his shoulder. "You're right. The brothers would take the money."

Only the more educated in Mexican cities understood there were lengthy, legal ways to go to America. There were many papers to fill out and sign. The wait extended many years to those who saw the morality in keeping the law.

CHAPTER 6

LITTLE ADRIANA CASTELLONE HUERTA lived over the short, flat hill from José's family. She began coming to the Ramirez house to play soon after her mother ran away. Nine-year-old Adriana was Miguelito's age but enjoyed playing games with six-year-old Alicia. Adriana's eyes always had that hungry look José was afraid of for his children. Elmira kept extra tortillas, beans and sweetbreads on the table just for Adriana. Adriana loved sweetbread.

Because she found love from Elmira, she soon began coming to their house while the older Ramirez children were at school.

Adriana's father did not make Adriana attend school. An older brother, Marco Andres who was twelve, and her father were all she had. Her brother worked with her father each morning in their onion fields. Marco would often slip away around lunchtime to attend the small school. He was determined to learn to read and write. Their mother had gone north years ago, in the middle of the night, and left her small family's fate to circumstances. They never heard from her again nor did the woman send money. Pablo the storekeeper told them each time any of them went to the store to ask for mail, "Sorry. Nothing has come for you."

Elmira told Adriana one morning after her three older children went to school, "We don't eat fancy food like they do in the big cities, but we eat vegetables and drink milk that God made to build strong bodies." She handed Adriana a cup of goat's milk and watched as the child greedily gulped down the milk in three big swallows.

"Not so fast, Adriana. You'll get the hiccups from drinking too fast." She used the corner of her apron to wipe Adriana's chin and upper lip.

"Adriana, would you like to learn to milk a nanny goat? The next time one of our goats has twins, I will give you the female. They are all expecting babies."

"Would you?" asked Adriana as the unexpected news wiped the sadness from the corners of her eyes.

"Little *Josélito* is asleep for his morning nap and the little ones are playing in the yard. Come out with me right now and I'll show you how to milk a goat." Elmira took her by the hand, and she picked up the bucket near the kitchen sink. They walked to the animal yard and Elmira said, "The boys milked the cows, and it is now time for me to milk the goats."

Along their walk to the goat yard Elmira said, "See that tomato on the vine." Elmira taught her small charge as she picked off a small overripe tomato on the cherry tomato vine. "Watch me as I drop it and crush it into the ground." Elmira stamped on the tomato she dropped near a post of the fence enclosing the animals. "Those tomato seeds will sprout the next time it rains and we will have more cherry tomatoes next spring."

"May I have a tomato to take home to crush into the ground by the back door of my house?"

Elmira picked a fat, small overripe tomato and held it up to the child. "Of course Adriana. Put a little water on the seeds. After a few days some of the seeds will grow for you. Some will wait until next year to grow. God has wonderful plans for seeds."

Adriana smiled happily as Elmira placed the very ripe tomato in the pocket of the child's soiled dress. "Take it out the moment you get home and step on it."

Elmira told Adriana as she put down a short milking stool by the nanny goat who pushed forward to be milked first, "Now watch me as I pull on her teats." Elmira sat down on the stool and tucked the bucket under the goat so the precious milk would squirt into the bucket.

"See how I grab hold of each teat and pull down. It forces the milk out. These goats need to be milked so it comes without much pressure. As I milk the liquid out, it will take more and more pull and pressure to get it out. Now you pull." She had hold of each of the nanny's two teats with each hand. She pulled down on one and then down on the other.

"She won't kick me, will she?" questioned Adriana, not sure and a little afraid. She cautiously put a small hand on the teat and pulled down towards the nipple.

"Now Adriana, use both hands, one grabs hold of each teat and take turns pulling like you saw me do." Elmira smiled as she saw the little girl pull a couple of times but nothing came out. "Pull harder, m*ija*, it will come out."

Pulling harder, some milk shot down into the bucket from one teat. "Look! Look! I did it." She went on milking until her hands became tired from the hard work.

"After you have milked the goat every day for a while, your hands will become strong," said Elmira. "Look how strong little Alicia's hands are. She helps me milk the goats each night."

"What will I feed my goat when you give me one?" asked Adriana.

"Let me think. You have wild grass growing around your house; the goat can eat that. And your father raises onions for your family and the community. Why don't you trade me onions each week, and I will trade you corn? Grass and corn will make a healthy goat."

"I will ask papa. He says we never have enough corn."

"Do you want to help me milk the other five nanny goats?"

"*No, Tia*, I must get home and fix Papa's lunch. May I come back tomorrow and help you milk?"

CHAPTER 7

A T LAST, JOSÉ AND Elmira found their religious wedding day upon them. Their first wedding was before *el Abuelo*, the oldest man in the village. The wedding was secular without a priest as was common in the villages when a couple was young with lack of money. Many in the village would never be married before a priest.

But this time for José and his Elmira, it would be before the traveling priest. It had taken José many years to save the $50 to pay the Church to be tied in holy union before God. Many were never married by a priest, because *pesos* were hard to come by. Every couple there dreamed of being united before God.

José had paid the priest half of the money when he had visited the village at Christmastime, six months ago.

The traveling priest recognized he must be paid before news of the church wedding spread around the area. There were no banks or checking accounts. Thieves would know José and Elmira had *dinero* to pay for their spiritual union. And they might not have it the next time he came to town. As they say in America, *He got it while the getting was good.*

The nuptial bans were sent around to the several towns in the area. Many friends and cousins lived in those villages. Happy voices filled the village of Siempre as everyone prepared for the wedding. The women washed and ironed their very best. The flatirons from Pablo's store were almost sold out. Every pretty dress had to look perfect for that special day. Mamas and wives made their men dress up for this occasion. The men, if they had a few pesos, bought the best shirts and pants they could afford. Some even purchased ties from the store, ties Pablo had been unable to sell before now. The women sewed new dresses for their daughters, dresses made from material from Pablo's store where José worked. Pablo beamed mightily thinking of the *dinero* he made from the occasional wedding.

Many of the women stayed up most of the night baking and cooking. The older women used the wedding for an excuse to relive lives that had faded. Difficult living showed in the lines of their now-smiling faces.

The village children played in the streets pretending to wed.

José and Elmira were kept apart for 72 hours as was the custom. The theory: When they came together after the wedding ceremony, in spite of the seven children, they would feel physically drawn to one another as if love and sex were new to them. The romantics in the village loved the excitement which sent them to bed with their own *esposas* for their own thrills.

It would truly be a honeymoon weekend from Friday afternoon to Sunday morning when they would show up at the small Church for communion before God.

Three days prior to the wedding, Elmira went to stay with her mother and father. The six younger children stayed at their house with José and his visiting sister who came to attend the children. Elmira took along a large *robosa*, a wide scarf, and in it bound up little *Josélito* and the clothing they might need. She wrapped it around her shoulders and walked proudly to her parents' house about six houses down from theirs. *Josélito*'s bright, dark eyes studied the world around him as he bounced up and down repeating over and over, "Bah, bah, baaah."

At night alone with her two-year-old *Josélito* and feeling lost without her husband José, she planned and dreamed about the coming Church wedding. They would truly belong to each other in God's eyes. "What an honor!" she thought.

José and Elmira were loved and respected by their family and neighbors. Loved because they were family and friends to all of them. Respected, because José and Elmira offered a helping hand to any who truly needed help.

Friday morning her mother, Alejandra Alejandra Contreras Gonzales, helped Elmira wash and then brush out her long curly hair with aloe vera juice and precious oils. Then Alejandra piled the partially straightened hair on top of Elmira's head. The beautiful hand-me-down family veil that once came from Madrid in Spain, brought out the shiny blackness of her hair. She made a gorgeous bride. The white gown handed down from mother to daughter for four generations fit her tightly, perhaps too tightly. That Friday afternoon her mother went ahead of her to the church with the baby. She stopped by José's home to get the other children.

José was to come alone without Elmira. He would see his bride for the first time in three days as she walked into the Church. He wished he could go to her mother's house and walk proudly down the street with Elmira to the little church. But that was not the custom.

The day was the perfect, planned and dreamy day every bride asks for. The trees heavy with spring blossoms, sent many drifting aimlessly with the lazy, waffling wind. Those blossoms collected on every surface. Warm breezes carried the white and creamy orange petals from one plot of ground to its neighbor creating snowy thatched roofs among the desert palms and spiked agave cacti.

As planned, José walked to the church building with his male cousins. They arrived first before his bride.

Elmira, as was the custom, walked from her parents' home towards the little Church. She came to the small outhouse behind the church. She pulled the door toward her to look at her face on the small, cracked mirror hung on the outside of the outhouse door. One of the neighbor men hung it there years before when his wife complained she didn't know if her hair looked proper for worship services. It was not broken when he had hung it there, but years of the door slamming had taken its toll on the looking glass.

Elmira fancied having one of the long mirrors hung on the back of her bedroom door. The big catalog at the store advertised short and long mirrors. She was a woman, and she needed that last look in a mirror to make sure all looked as she wanted it to. *Who could be a luckier woman than I? José is right. God has blessed us beyond words.* She pinched her cheeks to make them rosier.

Hearing a noise behind her, thinking it might be José, she turned around planning to tease him that he should not be here but to wait inside.

But it was Enrique Castillone whose home was only yards behind the Church. He was amazed at how beautiful she appeared in the white wedding gown. Her long, black curls were pulled up tight on her head and flowed around her face like a picture frame.

"Excuse me, Enrique, I am a little late. I must get inside for the wedding." She began moving to the side.

"How about a little kiss. You are more beautiful than the young girls in the village. Much more woman."

Enrique was surprised at her shocked look more than if she had slapped him, as one of the girls in the next village had. He had slapped that *punta* back, and pulling her into her parents' bedroom, he raped her. He dared not get the reputation of letting a woman slap him. His two brothers had stood guard with knives drawn listening to the girl scream and scream. Pedro grinned taking pleasure in her agonizing cries, but Pancho frowned. He was angry and ashamed. Yet he had not dared confront his older, stronger brother in years. Enrique hesitated with those memories.

Elmira stepped around Enrique quickly, dashed up the gravel walk to the front of the church and in through the open doors where friends and relatives were waiting. He had not expected to be turned down or he might have prevented her from entering.

He called after her, "I'll get that kiss. You wait and see." And he stalked angrily through the church door after her. During the next hour her vows before the priest rankled Enrique to his very soul. Rejection without words was no less rejection. Rejection was something he would not tolerate.

******

Elmira walked up the aisle alone toward José and the visiting priest. What should have been one of the happiest moments of her life was marred by Enrique's threat. Enrique did not know what "no" meant. She knew she had attracted attention to herself because she looked especially voluptuous in her grandmother's wedding dress today.

What am I to do? Will the priest help me? Can anyone help me? If José tries to defend me as Pablo did his daughter, José will be hurt. Pablo Garcia still walks with an incredible limp and pain. Since the

Castillone brothers had broken Pablo's knee twice with a steel hammer, she knew they might also injure José.

Following the wedding service, all of the village celebrated with food spread out on wooden tables with long boards. They were laid on pieces of wood nailed together to form an X, called trestles – built especially for this occasion. The smells from the food the village women had marinated and cooked, fried and baked throughout the night permeated the warm air for miles around. As a breeze blew through the town the odors wafted along reminding everyone the wedding was over, and now the eating would begin. Tortillas and boiled beans, refried beans, rice and all the meat prepared for today were in hot pans with covers still on. Onions, home-grown cilantro, and rosemary flavored many of the foods.

Three young goats had been slaughtered, barbecued and cut into small pieces for their *carne asada* to be eaten with fresh tortillas. The double stacked cake baked with imported chocolate was mixed and baked by three of the cousins' wives, not fancy like those in America but beautiful and luscious-looking nonetheless. The sweet breads in long, flat trays were too numerous to count.

Everyone ate hungrily and happily... except for Enrique Castillone. He was too angry to feel hunger. He kept drinking on a sour stomach.

José said, "Luscious food, luscious woman." He glanced excitedly into Elmira's bosom happy to know she was all his.

"You say that," she responded giggling, "after all these ten years."

Grinning like a school boy with his first crush he said, "I'll never stop saying it."

Then José and Elmira danced. For hours they danced in happiness in the street in front of the Church. The men of the villages soon danced and twirled Elmira in her wedding dress that was designed for circling out toward the partner who needed long arms to prevent touching it. Her full breasts spilled over the medium cut neckline.

Enrique leaned against the wall of the small church watching her dance. His brothers came to him several times to remind him he could dance with the prettiest girls, but he could not get his mind off of Elmira. He irritably told them to leave him alone which they eventually did.

Enrique glared. He wanted to make Elmira uncomfortable so she would never snub him again. Pretty Maria Salasar slyly walked over to him. She was still a teenager and figured she could do worse in picking a husband. She saw how others groveled before the brothers. She figured their wives would do well after the young men moved out of their parents' home. Enrique had used her many times since she was fourteen. Maria thought, "He owes it to me to marry me." God had been good to her by not letting her get pregnant. He married none of the girls he had given children, so she knew that would not be a way of catching him.

Today, Maria chose to wear a low-cut dress against her mother's advice not to attract the men in that way, especially Enrique. She took Enrique's hand and pulled him to her without a word. He started to pull away, changed his mind and took her out into the street with a bounce to his walk.

Enrique led Maria near to where José danced with his Elmira.

"Look, José," Enrique yelled loudly, "can you do this?" He picked up Maria and threw her into the air as he danced around her, catching her and tossing her into the air, over and over.

"Please Enrique, be careful," pleaded Maria. "Don't drop me."

"You mean, like this." Enrique burning with rage at all women, threw her even higher into the air, turned around and let her fall to the earth. He stalked off angrily behind the church to his home, muttering loudly, "Women must respect their men." There he drank himself into a sleep-deprived stupor with his father's homemade agave brew.

Shocked onlookers rushed to help Maria. She had caught herself by her feet and hands as she fell. She heard her left ankle snap as it twisted beneath her, and she screamed in pain. Her father and two younger brothers carried her off to their home hoping not to interfere with the wedding celebration. And their fear of Enrique Castillone.

José and Elmira were in shock. "How could a man purposely hurt another person like that?" asked José thinking of Pablo and his daughter.

Elmira ran up and asked Maria's mother who was following her husband and two sons. "Can I help her?"

"No, Elmira. It's not your fault. That evil Enrique must be punished for the many things he has done to *mi muchacha*. I told her not to wear that revealing dress. I will cut it up!"

Another woman nearby whispered loudly so all could hear, "I wish someone would kill him. Hell is to be his just end. God tells me it will be soon." Later Elmira remembered it was the village *Abuelita*, the healer, who predicted the end to Enrique Castillone.

Darkness was beginning to cover the village, so José soon took his Elmira to the empty house the villagers reserved for the *matrimonia*. The *matrimonia* was a hammock hung in the house for the marriage bed. The hammock was large enough for two – with room to spare to cover them with the netting to keep the mosquitoes off them. They would be alone for the next two nights. They had spent two nights here in the hammock when *el Abuelo* married them ten years ago. They were sure Miguelito was conceived during that cherished weekend.

It had taken them the first part of that first-time-night to learn how to use the *matrimonia* to their benefit. Others had told José how to rock and ride the hammock, but doing it was not that easy without practice.

The room was decorated by the village women with fragrant flowers and vines of honeysuckle that grew behind their homes to attract the honey bees. A large candle was lit on the table.

Elmira sat on the chair in front of the table taking down her beautiful, long curly-black hair. José finished undressing first. Then he watched, as he had so many times in their bedroom, the shadows blend with the dark of her hair as the curve of her breasts invited his memories to repeat all that was so good between them. The shine from the aloe vera juice and oils rubbed into her hair brought highlights into the room as if romantic moonlight had invaded the house. The pleasant odors permeated their every pore when she slowly came near him as he waited for her in the hammock.

Neither said a word but began the preparations for her to climb into the *matrimonia*. They would lie east and west in the hammock for they could rock, could ride, or lie very still – whatever they wanted, not north and south as the unknowing foreigners often did.

José and Elmira thought only of one another during the coming hours as they rocked and moaned in the m*atrimonia*.

CHAPTER 8

E NRIQUE WAS INCENSED AFTER being rebuffed by Elmira behind the small church before her wedding. A kiss, just a kiss was all he asked her for. Enrique was embarrassed that a woman had rejected him and he hated that feeling. How dare she turn down his advances! He was glad she was the only one who knew about it and feared she would tell others.

"Lucky for Elmira I am too drunk to get out of bed," Enrique raged on and on. He drank as much that weekend as his drunken father. Enrique had not seen him sober in years. Jorge Castillone was so wasted in the mornings that he drank again in an attempt to get over his perpetual hangover.

Enrique knew José would come after him when, and if, Elmira told him. He felt confident of that. Enrique knew he himself would have been a raving, wild man if José made a pass at his wife – when he got one. Right now, however, Enrique wanted José's wife.

What if she tells others how she sent him on his way? Others would shame him. He was actually doing her a favor to look at her with desire. And to turn him down showed she was like an American bitch he had seen on the small colored television they kept at Pablo's store. Only the store had electricity and the phone and the TV. One day the rest of the community might have the money to hook up and string their own wires to the government-installed telephone and electric lines. In the future the villagers would have the sophistication to purchase battery-operated televisions, but not yet. Enrique envied

Pablo his television, and thought how to get electricity to his father's house where they all lived. He was impatient.

Angrily Enrique plotted what he could do to get even with Elmira. He did not confide in his brothers, Pedro and Pancho, because he was ashamed to let them know he had been turned down by a woman.

"She is an old hag by my brothers' standards. They prefer those under twenty years old," thought Enrique. He was confused also. The young girls wanted him, but when he wanted the older, most beautiful woman in town, she refused him. She preferred to get married in the church to the town worker, José.

Humiliation ate away at Enrique's very bones. They ached. His muscles tensed and his gut knotted from the tightness, so he did not sleep well at night. Tossing and turning kept him awake. When he fell into a light sleep he dreamed tormented images of José and Elmira hitting and tearing at his face.

He wondered when José would come to him to start a fight after Elmira told him about Enrique's pass at her. "Yes, that is it. Beating José with my fists might make me feel better," Enrique reasoned. "With a crippled husband Elmira will prefer me."

However, during the next week José continued to be his cheerful self. It made Enrique more livid but hesitant with angry thoughts of revenge.

"It would serve José right," he said aloud in his bed, "if I take Elmira away and make her my wife." *But would God get even with me? After all, they have been married in the Church by the priest. And she might bring her children to live with us, and I would not want her pesty children around.*"

Enrique was afraid of no one, except God. Where he got his fear, he did not quite remember. Yet he did recall his mother on her knees praying to God, over and over, to help him when he was small. Those prayers had made an impression on him and his fears.

Those brats will have to stay with José. I will not allow them in my house when I take Elmira to be mine – for a while. I'm not sure how long I will keep her.

CHAPTER 9

F RANCISCO "PANCHO" CASTILLONE FELT guilty. He had urged Maria to dance with his brother Enrique. Pancho, now 23, had danced two dances with Maria Salasar at the wedding. Four years earlier his brother, Enrique, had picked her out as one of his *puntas* when she was still thirteen. At the end of the second dance at the wedding, Pancho had suggested she ask Enrique to dance with her. She had meandered around the dance floor and walked up to Enrique where he was leaning against the Church wall glowering at the dancers. He had already had too much tequila.

Pancho was not sure why Enrique had been acting so unhappy, perhaps angry. Rare was it for Enrique to act so. He was the confrontational type. The twins, Pancho and Pedro, had found that out all of their lives. Enrique never let anything slide that upset him. Sooner or later whatever bothered him became known in the community, especially to his brothers.

After Enrique threw Maria into the air during the dance, and she had hit the hard street unprepared to catch herself, Pancho was shocked. He was used to his brother's cruelty, but injuring Maria was more than Pancho could tolerate. Pancho had always been attracted to the innocent, pretty Maria. In fact, he knew he loved Maria. For some time Pancho no longer felt joy or pleasure in the village girls.

But Enrique let his brothers know Maria was one of his, so Pancho had kept his distance. He continued to tag along with his brothers out of habit and some fear.

Pancho knew how much it hurt when he heard the bone snap in her ankle. Once when Pancho was about eleven, Enrique had thrown him out of a tree and dislocated his shoulder. He still remembered the extreme pain. It took that shoulder a long time to heal because Enrique shoved him often and kept that shoulder muscle torn for over two years. Pancho still was not sure if that shoulder healed correctly. His parents could not protect him from the cruelty of his older brother. The town *Abuelita* often told him, "Hold up that shoulder so they will be even." Pancho knew the dull pain made his shoulder droop. When he was fourteen, he finally was able to make that shoulder level with the other – after the pain stopped – through exercises taught him by the healer. It took effort and determination and years more to strengthen it.

The morning following the wedding, Pancho showed up at Maria's family's door. He wasn't sure what to say or if he would be welcome. He knew of the fear the community felt for him and his brothers. Usually he did not think about others, but today he cared.

When Maria's mother, Ramona Salasar Ramirez, came to the door, her mouth fell open in fear. Her hands went to her throat as if trying to protect herself.

Pancho saw the fear and flinched.

"Please, *Señora*, don't be afraid. I came to see how your daughter is. What can I do to make things better for her?"

She paused before answering, "Pancho, I appreciate you coming." He still could see questions on her face.

"May I see her to tell her I'm sorry?" he asked.

"Of course. If she will see you. She has cried many tears since last evening. Her ankle tore through the skin when it broke. It will take time for it to heal. I fear she may walk with a limp forever."

"That would be terrible. Enrique must have been out of his mind."

"His temper has made this a town of fear," said Maria's mother. "Let me see if Maria will see you." She went inside and told a surprised Maria that Pancho had come calling. The herbs *la Abuelita* had wrapped around her foot to stop the pain were beginning to wilt. Her pain was building again, but her emotions pushed the pain away.

"Yes, I will see him," she said to her mother. "Perhaps Pancho will be a way to get back at Enrique."

CHAPTER 10

T HE SATURDAY FOLLOWING THE church wedding and their second honeymoon, Elmira finished her morning chores. The older children were in catechism. She asked her mother to watch the four-year-old twins and the baby *Josélito*, while she talked to the visiting priest at the Church. She knew he would be going to another village soon.

"I am going to ask for prayers for my young ones," lied Elmira.

Her mother, Alejandra, was pleased that her daughter was taking an interest in prayer, so she eagerly said "*Sí*, I will do it."

Elmira walked the few blocks to the small Church. She saw the small outhouse where she had looked in the mirror that morning before the wedding. *Can I tell the priest and ask his advice about Enrique? What will the priest say?*

She had never confessed to a priest before. Life had no pressing problems until those few minutes with Enrique. She had never expected a lot, and life had given her so much.

"What are you doing here, little one?" She turned as she heard the frightful, familiar voice behind her.

"Please Enrique. I have an appointment with the priest who...."

"I don't think so," Enrique interrupted in nasty tones. "I haven't seen you come past my house to make an appointment."

"He is expecting me," she lied.

"Let's complete our unfinished business. I want my kiss!" he demanded as he grabbed her and pulled her close.

"I am a married woman. I can't kiss you, Enrique," she moaned as she struggled with him.

He grabbed her by her long curly hair practically dragging her behind the outhouse. "You can kiss me and do much more. I see how José smiles a lot. You must please him." As she tried to scream, he kissed her roughly. She spit at him when she was able to pull loose from his clutching lips.

Violently he threw her to the stony ground and pulling at her skirt, he yanked it up over her head, "Now please me as you please José." He straddled her forcing a piece of her raised skirt into her mouth until she could scream no more. He felt her go limp.

Soon Enrique finished with her and pulled the skirt from her mouth. He couldn't believe she did not enjoy it but had fainted. The other girls often cried at first but begged wanting more. He didn't realize many pretended hoping he would not hurt them again.

This Elmira is a strange one. She spit at me before I threw her to the ground.

He felt her begin to stir beneath him, but her movements no longer aroused him. Enrique left her, threatening, "You will not tell anyone, or I will do it again and again." She waited until she could no longer see him. Then she clumsily and painfully ran to the door of the old, small Church and throwing the door open, she went inside.

The elderly priest was lighting candles as she rushed up to him. "Father, Father, I have been raped."

"Elmira, my child, what are you saying?"

"It was Enrique. He raped me behind the outhouse."

"Enrique? You must stay away from him. He is bad, a demon. You must keep it secret. He will return with his brothers and hurt all of us."

"You must tell *la policia*. He hurt me. I am cut. I am bruised. I am bleeding."

"Child, child, there is nothing I can do. I am an old man." He knew of the dangerous Castillone brothers, descended from one of Cortez's soldiers from Italy. He knew he would be leaving the next day to go to the next village for two weeks. What could he, an old man, do against brutality?

"I am leaving for the next village. I will be there a while and then on to the next. There is nothing I can do," he repeated. "I will pray for you."

CHAPTER 11

E LMIRA PAINFULLY LIMPED HOME wanting the safety of her bed and bedroom. *Is there no one who can help me if the priest himself is afraid of Enrique and his brothers?* What did she dare tell her mother who was there caring for her little ones? She washed her face in the bucket of water on their small back porch.

Then she walked quickly through the kitchen into the shadows of the front room to her bedroom to change her torn and dirty clothes.

Her mother was making tortillas for the evening dinner, tossing them from hand to hand. Not looking up as Elmira walked by, she said, "How did the prayers go?"

"I forgot to say them after talking to the priest."

"Forgot? How could you forget to pray?"

"*No se, no se.* I want to lie down for a while before I make José's dinner. Please go." Her mother, puzzled about her daughter, left at Elmira's words.

For the first time in their marriage she pushed José away from her night after night when he reached for her. José was confused. What had he done to make Elmira refuse his love. It was as if she had crawled into a box and closed the lid behind her.

Elmira did not tell José or her mother about the sores that soon began plaguing her private area. She did not associate the painful blisters with the brutal rape that left her depressed and wanting to be alone.

"My dear one," he would ask, "What have I done? I love you. I want you."

"José, you have done nothing. My heart is full of tears. I cannot love you until I have done away with my grief."

"But why are you grieving? I would give my life for you."

"I know, José. It would be better if you hated me."

"I could never hate you. You are the love of my life. My treasured one."

"I am the one who is the ruined vessel." She sobbed and sobbed.

"Ruined? You are beautiful. The one I long for." He pulled her close, rubbing her hair and eyebrows as she cried herself to sleep, her back to him. After a long while, he slept – fitfully.

In another house, on the hill behind the church another man slept as if in a stupor. It was Enrique, satisfied. *I have gotten even.* He smiled in his sleep.

******

Adriana came to help Elmira milk the goats each morning. She was sad. Elmira did not hug her with enthusiasm as she used to. She would hold Elmira's hand as they walked out to the goats, and Elmira would cling tightly to her hand as if she were the one who was the child.

When they finished, a very weak Elmira suggested they have a glass of goat's milk at the kitchen table.

"*Tia Elmira* you look sad. Have I done something to displease you?"

"*Hija,* you are one of my reasons for living. You and my seven sunbeams. Your mother Socorro was my dearest friend when we were growing up. Her going to the U.S. was a disappointing day for me. I was sad most of all, because she didn't tell me, 'Goodbye.'"

"She did not tell me goodbye. My father says she told him she was going to work in that far country. She just left one evening. Why would she leave without telling us she was going?"

"I don't know, child. I don't know."

Elmira felt tired all the time. She often forgot to eat and rarely combed her now-tangled curly hair. Adriana pleaded, "Please, let me comb your hair."

"Thank you, *hija*. Be gentle." And Adriana combed her hair, stroke after stroke, before she would run home to fix the evening meal for her father and brother. Elmira was the closest person she had for a *mamá* during the past four years since her own mother disappeared. The empty part in Adriana reached out to fill that void in Elmira left by Enrique's violence.

CHAPTER 12

T HAT FATEFUL MORNING, ELMIRA's and José's three older children were in the small school, so José went alone without his eldest son, nine-year-old Miguelito. He must clean the store for the few pesos Pablo the storekeeper could afford to pay him each week. He felt depressed. He was sweeping the floor near the heavy flat irons and ironing boards, when Enrique walked in.

"Oh, it's you," said Enrique scornfully. "Go get me some *Corona*. We need more beer at our house."

"Pablo ordered more, but the shipment has not come in yet. We'll let you know when the *Corona* comes in. You'll have to drink *Dos Equis* or *Sol*."

"I'd rather drink my father's agave brew. How is that *gordita* of a wife?"

"Elmira is not fat. She is beautiful," declared José continuing on with his sweeping not wanting to argue, much less hear a human voice. He had been depressed far too many days to pretend cheerfulness for this bad man.

"She is fat! If I say she is fat, she is fat!" Enrique screamed in rage.

José was stunned at Enrique's attitude. Surely he was upset about the *Corona*. Enrique had never paid much attention to him but ignored him as some people ignore servants.

José kept silent, not wanting to stir Enrique's wrath. He often thought about the bad limp Pablo walked with because of defending the rape of his daughter. Because of the discomfort, Pablo hired José more and more often to clean and do the things he could no long do without pain.

Enrique had become irritated since raping Elmira. Elmira looked at him with disdain the two times he had seen her milking the goats when he walked by her house. *Does she have something better with José?* His ego deflated and he felt hurt. Now he thought, "*I must put José in his place.*"

"Your wife, Elmira, is fat. In fact, she is lousy in bed. Since that day I had her, I have been disgusted. You can keep her. I was thinking about making her my wife, but she is not worth it."

"You beast," said José glaring at the taller man. "Elmira wouldn't waste her time with you. She is an honest woman, and you are a spoiled brat. The whole community knows it. She is my wife."

"So, she has not told you about the wonderful time we spent with her pleasuring me," Enrique couldn't believe she had said nothing to José even though he had ordered her not to. Enrique was disappointed. He had at least expected José to avoid him in shame.

"She would not soil herself with you," insisted José.

"Oh, yes, she did. Elmira bragged how I turned her on. She wanted me. She told me what a good lover I am. She wanted to leave you and come with me, but I wouldn't let her."

José finally was beginning to question what had happened to Elmira. She was different; definitely things were not the same in their marriage bed. Out of the bed she seemed the same yet quieter and never laughing. Had Enrique raped Elmira as he had Pablo's daughter? That might explain the change in her.

Enrique put his unshaven face close to José's so that their short, black mustaches touched. José backed up into the ironing boards and a couple of them clattered to the floor.

Enrique kept coming closer, and José in self-defense pushed the broom he used for sweeping between them. Suddenly anger overcame the fear José felt in his heart. His free right hand reached out flailing around when Enrique grabbed him by the neck. José's strong hand grasped the nearest flatiron, and he raised it to fight off Enrique. With all the strength he had in his wrist he brought the iron down at an angle on Enrique's head.

Enrique made a little whimper like a kicked puppy and slid to the floor, blood spurting from his split skull.

José looked at what he had done to Enrique. Dropping the flatiron to the floor beside the body, he bent down to see if Enrique was breathing. He saw no movement. Blood collected on the floor around Enrique's white face and bloodied hair. José ran to the door and looked both ways. Seeing no one there he dashed down the street and up the hill to his home.

"Is it true, Elmira? Is it true? Did Enrique rape you?" José cried with emotion.

"Yes, José. I didn't want you or anyone to know. I was afraid what you might do." She began sobbing. Finally she said, "Who told you?"

"Enrique himself. He told me. Enrique attacked me at the store, and I hit him with a flatiron."

"Oh, José, he will be coming after you. He will kill you."

"No, Elmira. He is dead."

"Dead? Enrique is dead?"

"Yes, my love, Enrique cannot hurt you anymore. He's dead." He cradled her to him.

"You must run away. He will be after you soon," Elmira whispered, still not understanding the gravity of his predicament.

"You're right. But it will be his brothers after me. I am sure Enrique is dead."

"Then you will be put in prison for the rest of your life if his brothers don't kill you. The government will have you shot. José, you must leave."

"What about you and the children?" he asked.

"Our families will help care for us. We'll keep growing the potatoes. In the U. S. you can make money to send for us."

"Yes, I must go to America, and I will send you money when I can." Already José was tying up his clothes into a ball so he could carry them with him. She stuffed some tortillas, several raw potatoes and a bottle of water into a small cardboard box and pushed it into the center of the ball of clothes.

He kissed Elmira's trembling lips in desperation and said, "My heart will be with you wherever I go."

"And mine," she said, tears streaming down her cheeks. The last she saw of her husband were with his tears joining hers as they kissed goodbye. He ran out the back door and over the hills behind the town on his way north to the Mexican-American border.

CHAPTER 13

ONE THING JOSÉ LEARNED about life in the coming months. Life is full of change. He called his years with Elmira, *My Happy Years.* He would lie silhouetted in moonlight and shadows watching the somber landscape wherever he slept at night. He relived wonderful moments with Elmira as he fantasized in an effort to keep in touch with her. Like prisoners during wartime, his memories saved his life.

SECTION II

CHAPTER 14

J OSÉ SPENT THE FIRST three miles running in a long trot from his
home and away from the dead body of Enrique Castillone. Then he
slowed to a fast walk while dodging huizache and mesquite bushes in
the almost lifeless terrain. For the next two days he rationed the food
his beloved Elmira had pushed lovingly into the bundle of clothing.

He ran at first from fear knowing that in Mexico a man is
thrown into prison, guilty until proven innocent. He had heard of
too many people who were still in prison or who had died there:
Tales of prisoners who had to eat the lice off their own bodies and the
cockroaches crawling out of worn mattresses to squelch their hunger.
His village often talked about fear of prison that kept the uneducated
people in Mexico under control.

It had not occurred to José or Elmira to stand and fight. No one
in the village ever fought back except Pablo when confronted by the
Castillone family. Self-defense was the last thing that passed through
his mind until Enrique's hands were around his neck.

He only knew that Enrique lay dead in the general store with
blood on the floor around him.

And soon people would be looking for him after searching the
store for clues to the murderer of Enrique Castillone. Everyone knew
he should be there cleaning the store. Could he have stayed and lied
saying someone else did it? But he was not a liar, not even a bad liar.

And he knew it was his fault. It did not occur to José if he hadn't
fought back, he might be the one lying there strangled, or worse.
As he had worked for Pablo, the owner of the small general store,

he was reminded daily of the violence of the Castillone brothers. He winced whenever he thought of Pablo limping around on the smashed kneecap the Castillone brothers gave him, not once but twice.

As José walked along he often kicked a rock that bounced noisily along the pathway not far from the road he took. An occasional reddish-brown scorpion scurried away to find another rock where it could find shade. The heat beat down on all. Used to the hot sun from hours he spent working in the fields with growing corn and potatoes, José knew to keep his shaded hat low over his face. The sweat running down his forehead and temples cooled him, but the salty perspiration burned his eyes.

The wide rim of his hat gave shade enough to protect his eyes from the glaring sun that reflected up from the rocks and hard ground beneath his burning feet, overheated even in his sandals. The thick calluses on the soles of his feet protected them from the burning, but he could feel the terrible fire of hot rocks that didn't crumble when kicked.

His feet were used to many hours of walking and standing to work, but not in the extreme heat of the desert floor. The heavy temperatures scarcely went away at night. Only an occasional breeze helped him. He prayed for the dew of the morning that dampened the ground. Many mornings there was no dew.

He slept the first night behind the broken trunk of an ancient tree stump. He folded his well-worn jacket to lay his upper body on and put his rolled belongings under his head for a pillow. He kept a large stick handy for the occasional *coyote* looking for a meal. The few he saw kept their distance – they were afraid of man.

At the end of the third day he knocked on the door of the poorest, rundown house in the small village seventy miles northeast of his hometown. His feet were sore and tired. He rubbed his left heel where it felt like another blister was forming from the rubbing of his old sandals.

"What do you want?" asked the poor, old woman who answered the door of her aging adobe home.

"I need something to drink and to eat. I'm willing to do work or repairs in exchange for a tortilla or two." His tongue felt thick from the lack of moisture in his body.

"You work first and then I feed you. I don't have much but if you will help me I will share with you what little I have."

"What do you want me to do?" asked José, while his stomach growled.

"More than repairs, I need someone who will get water for me. I am old and my back cannot carry enough water to bring to my kitchen. It has been a long time since I could carry enough for a bath. I can get enough to drink and to mix flour for my tortillas and some to cover my beans for cooking. If it weren't for neighbors who bring me flour and rice and beans, I would die."

"Your neighbors are kind to help you."

"But not enough to make me comfortable. I'm sure they will give you water to drink."

"I am sorry I don't live in your village. I would help you," said José.

"It is easy to speak words. It is more difficult to do. Won't you stay with me for a few months to help this old woman?"

José's thoughts told him he was too close to home to stay in this village. He must move on.

"I'm sorry I can't stay, but I will see what I can do to help you before I leave," he told her.

"Follow me." Stiffly on aching bones, she walked behind the house with José tagging along where she pointed to an old bucket which he picked up and started to walk toward an old well.

"No, no. That well does not have water any more, not for years. Go that way to the neighbors' house. They will let you get water for me. Knock on the door and tell them I sent you."

"What is your name?" he asked. "So I can tell your neighbors who sent me."

"Rosa Ramirez Gonzales." He briefly wondered if she might be related to his family from centuries ago.

José walked to the neighbors' house where he found a woman outside beating her clothes in an old tub with a long, round stick.

"Rosa next door sent me over to get her some water. She is too old to be carrying water." He stood watching her a few moments as she beat the clothes up and down.

The woman stopped and said, "I know she is. She falls sometimes. *Mi esposo,* my husband, and I help her how we can. All her family is

49

dead except for a son in the United States of America. He has never returned to see how she is. Maybe he thinks she is dead by now. Maybe he is *está muerto*. All I know is he left when his father died."

"It seems this world is a hard place," said José.

"What is your name, and what are you here for?" asked the woman.

"My name," he said stalling for time to think of a name, "my name is Manuel Garcia." He knew a Manuel and a Garcia so he put them together.

"My last name's Garcia, too. Maybe you and my husband are cousins."

"Could be. Sure.... Oh, sure. Call me Manny. I better get the water." He walked over to the well leaving the woman shaking her clothes in the water. He took the rope attached to a bucket and lowered it into the well. He pulled it up and twice filled Rosa's bucket. He took the empty cup tossed aside beside the well and filled it with water. He drank hastily and filled it twice more until his thirst was quenched.

"Do you mind if I return several times to get Rosa enough water so she can bathe?"

"Please do. I am sure she would be glad. I feel badly that I have not taken her more water for baths. I do what I can to keep her alive."

José looked at her, "I am sure she appreciates the food. Food keeps her going. A clean body helps a woman feel alive." He thought of Elmira how she loved it when he washed her back, how he felt when she washed his. How they teased one another. Each time he always had made sure the tub was full so he would be covered above the waist when it was his turn. He did not want his sons and daughters to see his nakedness.

Their children had always crowded around laughing and trying to help with scrubbing when it was his turn to bathe. The more Elmira pushed them away, the more active they became. He and Elmira always felt so loved at those times. When it was Elmira's turn, once a week, they put the children to bed early, and then the parents played. The children never argued about *Mamá's* and *Papá's* time together.

The woman's words brought him back to the present. "I will try to be more helpful in the future. My name is Maria la Madrid de Gonzales Garcia."

"Thank you, Maria. You are a good woman," added José.

He walked back to Rosa's house with the bucket of water. That bucket of water he poured into the larger bucket in which she kept water for cooking. Five more times he returned to get more water and each time poured it into the short tub in her small kitchen. He doubted if he could fit into the tub. Somewhere along his travels he had hopes of finding a river to take his bath.

When he was finished, he sat down to rest a moment in her kitchen on the only chair that still had four legs. He looked at the other two that were broken. He must not leave until those chairs were fixed. There was much she needed to have done for her.

"What is wrong with your well? Did it dry up one year?" he asked Rosa.

"No, several years ago there was a big earthquake and the sides of the well filled in. There is probably water under all that dirt and rotting wood."

"While you are fixing our food, I will look at the well." He let the door weakly slam behind him. While looking in the well he saw the old ropes used for pulling up what probably once was a bucket. When he tugged on the ropes, they appeared to be strong enough to hold his weight.

He looked behind the old, dilapidated house and saw a rusty shovel. As he walked through the house he saw doors and windows that needed to be fixed and replaced, but he knew water was the priority. It would keep the old woman alive with the food the neighbors brought to her.

He dug about thirty minutes when Rosa called to him to go to eat. He washed his dirty hands in some of the water he brought to her. He ate hastily at first, then slowed as his thirst and hunger were satisfied.

"How deep was the well before it caved in?" he asked.

"Too deep for me to get the dirt out when I had the strength to do it. None of my neighbors would help."

"Well, I will see what I can do."

"*Gracias*, I will be forever grateful if you can do it. It is the love you show for an old woman who never forgets. God will praise you."

"I need God's forgiveness, not praise." With tears glistening in his eyes José turned and walked out the back door to the old well. He lowered himself again with the ropes to the dirt level and the shovel.

After working an hour throwing dirt up onto the ground around the well, he heard a male voice above him.

"I am Maria's husband from next door. We can do more if you let me raise the bucket full of dirt so I can dump it."

"*Sí*, two work better than one," said José. The two men took turns filling the bucket and the other dumping. Occasionally they had to spend time removing old wood. "Rosa will use this to burn in her wooden stove," suggested Maria's husband.

After two more hours José struck water. He kept digging until there was water up to his waist.

"That should be enough," said the neighbor man. "My name is Jorge. You are a good man for helping *Señora* Rosa."

"I would do as much for my own mother. Her son is not here to help."

"You shame those of us who have let Rosa suffer. I thought we were being helpful by letting her use our well. My wife Maria gives her food every few days so that she can cook and make for herself. Other women bring her food when they have an abundance."

"Rosa is getting too old to work long and do heavy work. She needs to be included in someone's family."

"I will see what the nuns will do to help her," suggested Jorge.

"Do you think they will take her in to help her?"

"I don't know. I will ask Maria to talk to them, for we do not have the room for her. We are raising our six children in two rooms. Two rooms for eight people. Where would we put her?" (José knew the man felt the burden of a neighbor who could not fend for herself. Yet he did not want to make her burden his.)

The two men hammered in the metal bars to tie the ropes so Rosa could pull up her own water.

He stayed there three days and fixed much of what Rosa needed done in her home to be more comfortable or until a place was found for her to live. José reinforced her one good chair and repaired the other two. With chairs to sit in, perhaps kind neighbors would be encouraged to visit her.

Rosa insisted, "I want to die here in my house as I saw my husband die in our bed. That is God's gift to the good and happy man."

José's last gift to Rosa was cutting up one of his potatoes and planting the pieces in the soil he tilled for her near her back door.

There the sun hit the hottest. He dug a four-inch trench for water to go from the well to her back door. He showed her how to plant with one or more eyes in a section he planted.

"Be sure to allow water in the trench and it will water these plants. You will have potatoes grow under the soil. You can boil them and then eat them when they are soft. With a touch of salt and butter fat from your goat's milk, boiled potatoes are delicious."

José knew he was too close to home to stay in this village very long. The Castillone brothers must be after him. Surely they knew by now he had run away. Would they put up a picture of him on one of those papers that said, WANTED. He knew his parents and Elmira's parents would help Elmira with the children. None of them had ever harmed Enrique, but Pancho and Pedro might not care, only wanting vengeance.

But José rationalized they would leave his family alone. José was the one who had killed. He was the one *la policia* would be after. And the wicked brothers, who knows what they might plan.

His imagination frightened him. In the morning he must leave.

CHAPTER 15

THE NEXT EVENING AFTER walking all day, José wearily limped towards another village. He stopped at one of the more prosperous farms along the road and asked for some beans and rice in exchange for some work. He had eaten the two tortillas Rosa had given him when he left her poor hovel, because she was so poor he would not, could not take the beans and rice she offered. He had the satisfaction of knowing she would have potatoes to eat from the potatoes eyes he planted by her backdoor steps. Now he was hungry and wished he had kept one of them to eat, even if it were raw.

The husband of the house looked at José observing the sweat from the day and the soiled pants legs. The water and the dirt from the well had dried on his pants. José had tried to wash it out with Rosa's help but some of the grime remained mingled with the dust from today's long walk. Because he was in good shape, he walked quickly in spite of the newly-broken blisters and was able to travel by foot about 20 miles a day, even in the heat. He tried not to think of the pain knowing that soon those blisters would harden and callous over.

The man said, "I will be going north to La Managua in two days. Would you be willing to help me load my wagon with vegetables? Out of my field."

"Oh, yes, I would indeed be willing. May I accompany you to that city? I'll help you unload when we arrive at the market." *José was pleased with his good luck.*

"I will pay you five pesos if you will help me. Wait in the shed where you can sleep tonight, and I will have my wife bring food to you."

José volunteered his new name, "Manuel Garcia. That is my name. Call me Manny."

"Garcia?" said the man slowly. "That is a good name. My name is Juan Garcia."

"You are right Señor Garcia. Garcia is a good name. Perhaps we are cousins."

The second morning after a breakfast of goat milk, tortillas and rice, José helped him pull more vegetables from the soil, wash them and put them on the wagon.

José's host peered at him with sharp eyes, "I hear some men are looking for someone from the south. He must be a bad man who has murdered an important man from their village. Be careful. You never can trust strangers. I can tell you are a good man, but we never can tell, can we?"

"No, we never can tell," agreed José.

"I am a good judge of people. I've never been wrong. I could tell I could trust you the moment you opened your mouth to speak."

"God has given you the gift. I am glad you trust me." José was confused by the man's conversation, but he sensed he could trust this man.

On their way to market Señor Garcia drove the wagon with José sitting beside him. "You know, I knew you were the man they were looking for. You fit his description. It was when you were eating that I saw you pray. I knew you could never do something against your God."

"It was a mistake. I did not mean for the man to die. He was choking me, and I feel guilty for what was done. My wife and my children will suffer for what I did. I will suffer forever for what my family will do without. My prayers are that He..." José pointed to the sky, "will comfort them and guide me to find a new life somewhere else so I can bring them to me."

"Are you sure they are not in danger back in your hometown?"

"I would return to help them if I thought there was danger. Our families surely will not let harm come to them if they can help it," said José.

"You are right. You must continue on your way. You can send money to help your family. Are you going to the U.S. of America?"

"I thought I would go to Mexico City to see if I can find work." José did not think it best to tell Señor Garcia that he planned to hunt for his uncle who might live in San Diego, across the border. The Castillone brothers had much power for miles around their village. Who knows what influence they might have this far north if they tortured José's new friends he met along his travels.

Early the next morning they directed the donkeys pulling the wagon toward the Farmer's Market on the main city street. They had driven the donkeys all night with one man dozing while the other held the reins. Señor Garcia paid for a section, and they began unloading his numerous vegetables on benches they set up in order to sell the healthy produce.

Even on damp mornings stalls are filled with baskets of sweet red strawberries, cacti called *napolitos*, long, thin carrots, potatoes, yams, cilantro, even blood oranges had made their way into the groves of oranges, lemons, and grapefruit trees raised for sale. The occasional pretty pomegranates were sold, not only for their sweet taste but their medicinal value to the women.

It was still early, and not many customers were milling about the stalls.

As three school children walked by, one took an apple. Señor Garcia gave the other two boys apples without charging them. "Tell your *papás* and *mamás* to bring their *dinero* to buy my food," he said.

"Why didn't you yell at el *muchacho* for stealing?" asked José.

"Because he was hungry. By giving a little to these poor urchins, their friends and families will come to buy this evening, and I'll make more money."

Near them José noticed three women making tortillas for the hot beans and rice they had to sell to hungry customers. José was longing for Elmira's cooking. Her food always had filled that hungry spot within him.

Señor Garcia saw him staring at the tortillas, "You're hungry, or is it the women you're eyeing?"

"The tortillas, *hombre*, the tortillas. I miss my wife's cooking. My mind and body ache for her."

"Bring your wife to you soon. You need her," Señor Garcia advised.

José nodded.

Señor Garcia walked over to the women and ordered two fat burritos, goat cheese and the cool goat's milk. He and José ate and talked.

"We will stay here until all my produce is gone. If I have trouble selling some, I will take it to a market and sell it for a small amount. If they paid me what it is worth, I would not need to take time here selling to street customers.

"Manuel Garcia, I wish I had the time and money to take you to Mexico City, but I must get back to my own home. *Mi esposa* becomes frightened if I am gone for too many days."

José thought to himself, *I wonder if mi esposa Elmira is frightened?*

CHAPTER 16

T HE VILLAGE HAD A big funeral procession for Enrique Castillone – the likes of which few people could afford. Pedro and Pancho, his twin brothers, demanded each family, especially Elmira's and José's relatives, to give money to pay for the wagons and cars used in taking Enrique's family to the small cemetery. And to pay for the funeral. The other families paid what few pesos they had, but their hate doubled for Enrique when Elmira told them why José had to flee.

"*Papá*," she fell on her knees before him, "please forgive me my beauty. It attracted Enrique and he raped me. And now my husband has killed the evil Enrique. José has run away to North America to escape the revenge of Pedro and Pancho."

Her father replied, "Elmira, this shame will be the death of me. It is not your fault God gave you beauty."

With some of the money that Pedro, the stronger of the twin brothers, strong-armed from his community, they had paid for a huge tombstone that surpassed all others in the church cemetery. On it their mother had inscribed:

Enrique Ricardo Castillone
1976 – 2001
*May God rescue your soul
from Hell*

Juanita's two younger sons, Pedro and Pancho, could not discourage her from using those words.

"But *Mamá*," said Pedro, "I want to tell of the brave deeds of Enrique." He turned around and glared at Pancho who had refused to help him steal the money from the villagers.

"Yes," said Pancho. "It will shame our family if we don't put something about the courage of Enrique. We know he was not loved by the villagers, but we don't have to leave your words for grandchildren to read."

Juanita was adamant and said, "I have written what I have written." She turned to the tombstone maker and gave him 50 pesos. "My sons will pay you the rest when the job is finished." She walked out the door with her sons reluctantly following.

CHAPTER 17

TWO MONTHS LATER IN Siempre, Elmira huddled in her kitchen, shaking. She did not understand why she had the chills. No flu or pneumonia ever had affected her this way. If José were here, he would have made her go to *el Abuelita*, who would have made her drink some local herbal medicine. She feared what her parents would say if they found out. The miserable pain in her lower abdomen made her ashamed, not knowing what was wrong.

So one Saturday morning Elmira dragged herself from her bed. "Miguelito, you must take care of the little ones while I go to see a friend. Send your brother Francisco to the store to do the easy sweeping, and Pablo will understand if you are late. You're never late." He nodded and fed the smaller ones some leftover corn and rice. His mother had not made tortillas in several days. In his fear for her health he dared not ask her to do more than the little she tried to do.

The oldest three children, ten, nine and seven, had become adults in mind long before they would be adults in size. They accepted the responsibility without question, especially Miguel.

Miguel had not only taken over working at the General Store for Pablo, he had taken over many of his mother's duties. His tenth birthday passed unnoticed. Miguel dropped out of school but insisted Francisco and Alicia continue their studies at the school. Alicia celebrated her seventh birthday shortly after Miguel's tenth. She took over the cleaning and helping him with the feeding of the twins and the youngest one, *Josélito*.

The neighbor girl, 10-year-old Adriana, came over in the early mornings to help Alicia milk the goats. Elmira told her older children, "Adriana is to get the next nanny goat that will be born." The last two born were billies so they will be raised for eating.

Adriana said to Elmira, "I am afraid for you. You are getting too thin. You are the closest person I have for a mother. Please get well."

"Adriana, I cannot get well. When I go to be with God, please help the boys with the little ones. Alicia is too young. You are too young. What must God's plans be for my family?" She stared vacantly out the window into the ragged clouds defined by a sharp wind.

This particular morning Elmira forced herself down the street and over to the house of *la Abuelita*. She was not only an older, respected female in the village but a *curandera* and *yerberas*, healer and herbalist. Thus *la Abuelita* was respected in the village for her knowledge of folk medicine.

In the short time of three months Elmira had lost weight. Even though she tried to make herself eat, she found it difficult to swallow. Her eyes were swollen from too much crying. Her children clung to her skirts worried and helpless. The swollen eyes would soon become sunken from the sexually transmitted disease that ravaged her body. Enrique might be dead, but his evil lived on in her uterus.

Although the Mexican culture is considered Patriarchal, the women are the main caretakers of the family and are the major source of health for them. Not only are they the health source but the ones through whom the property is passed down to the children.

The priest often reminded his parishioners, "The women know who the father is for each of their children. We men too often pick up and leave, so it is more difficult to know who created each child. That is why the land passes through the mother."

La Abuelita took one look at Elmira when Elmira opened the curtain to her house and said, "Child, what has Satan done to you? I know José has fled the village, but what's happened to you?"

"I am cursed. My husband is gone. And my body is ravaged. At first I had horrible sores in my private areas and now I have fevers."

"Ooooeeeiiiiii," moaned *la Abuelita*. "What haven't you told me?" She was used to knowing the problems in the village before anyone else knew. "Who gave you this sexual disease?"

"Sexual disease? I don't understand."

"Did José give you this disease?"

"How could he get a disease? For always, it was just we two. Then Enrique Castillone attacked my body and raped me. I would not sleep with José any more. I felt revulsion to have any man touch me. God forgive me, I would not give my true husband his due. God must be punishing me for telling him, 'No.'"

"He is not punishing you. You may have saved José from this terrible thing you have by *not* having sex with him. You may have saved his life."

"His life? If he does not have it, he will live? Thank God!" Then the horror of what was going on in her own body invaded her mind so deeply, she fell to the floor. "Please give me some herbs, something to help me. I don't want to die. I want to see my children grow up, to see them marry."

La Abuelita sat beside Elmira on the floor and cuddled her to her breast as a mother nurtures a small child. "I will give you herbs to ease the pain. We will make your last days as good as God will provide." She walked the younger woman back to her house and put her to bed. She made some soup with herbs and spoonfed her. Then she went to the parents of Elmira and told them their daughter was dying of a bad disease, that Elmira needed their love and care, that the children needed their help to raise them to adulthood.

******

Early on a Saturday morning, the children rushed into Elmira's small house with the good news. The lead nanny goat was giving birth to a kid. They pulled their mother by the hands out of her bed.

"*Mamácita*, please come. Please come," begged five-year-old Leon, one of the Ramirez twins.

"Yes, *Mamá*," said the other twin, Valeria. "A little goat is coming out."

Elmira pushed back her pain and forced herself to go with the children to the goat yard. She knew she must form good memories within the children and for them.

Miguel, now a mature ten years old, was rubbing the small wet creature with an old, clean cloth. "Look Mama. We have a healthy male goat. He will be good to eat next spring."

"I don't want to eat him, I want to play with him," said Valeria.

"You can do both, silly," said Miguelito.

"Look Miguel," said Francisco, "another kid is coming."

"No, Francisco, that is the afterbirth. The mother will eat it to give her energy for the coming months of nursing," said Elmira softly. They watched as the nanny goat did as she predicted.

"*Mamá* there really is another kid coming now. I see its hind legs," said Francisco. The children as well as Elmira looked at the mother goat and gathered around.

Elmira explained to her children, "The second twin often comes hind legs first. Help her Miguel, so the kid can find air soon." Miguel carefully pulled on the hind legs as the second kid was born.

Alicia happily exclaimed, "It is a nanny. This one belongs to Adriana."

"You are right, Alicia. This one belongs to Adriana. You must run to get her so she can see the goat that will give her family milk one day." She turned to Miguel and Francisco and told them, "Be sure you teach her where to take her goat for good grass around her home. Her family has never had goats before."

Francisco spoke up, "I will go with Alicia to get Adriana to show her the new kids."

******

The morning of the goats' birth was the last time the children remembered their dear *mamá* respond with enthusiasm and spontaneity. It was as if she had given in to her illness.

Elmira always smiled a faint half-smile when any of the children walked into the room. They were all she had left of José until he would send for her.

CHAPTER 18

Spring turned into summer.

LOOKING FOR ANONYMITY IN his travel northward, José finally found himself in the largest city in his country called Mexico City, an endless metropolis. The southern sprawl of the city lay before him. Without a car to ride in, it was difficult to get from one place to another quickly. It took money to ride the buses, and José was saving what money he could earn for the *coyote* who would eventually sneak him across the border into the United States.

He decided to walk, to learn of the city and the people. Perhaps that way work would find him.

José walked along a wide boulevard, San Juan de Letran. Staring in the super-large windows in amazement he found the large supermarkets and banks were a world he had never seen. He observed people eating on fancy dishes when he walked into the Sanborns Restaurant but left when the waiters stared oddly at him.

He slept in an alley behind trash cans the first night.

On the second day of walking José found a group of people sitting in the quadrangle park across from the Bella Artes. They were near busy markets and the hub of big-city politics. He joined them quietly when he saw several men and women listening to a strongly built middle-aged Mexican male who was speaking in a low voice. He must have wanted to be heard but only by those crowded around him. José soon learned people dared not talk out against the government.

The man was saying, "Do you know what would be going on in Mexico if so many of our poor were not going to the United States? I'll tell you what. We would have the poor marching on the Casa Blanca, our *Presidente's* home, on the west side."

He looked around and saw the response written on their faces.

"You're right. Some would be arrested, maybe killed. But when it is thousands marching on his home, *el Presidente* would listen, out of fear. What is *el Presidente* doing for our people? Nothing. It is all talk. What do we want him to do? I'll tell you what I want. I want him to create jobs for our poor. Our people should not have to be going north and leaving their families. Sometimes they are able to take some of the family north, but if they do they usually don't return. The grandparents suffer. I watched my parents grieve and die from missing my two brothers who headed north across the border."

A young woman sitting near José spoke up, "I remember how it was under the former *Presidente* José Lopez Portillo. He was an ignorant coward who allowed the oil boom to plunge Mexico into a terrible financial crisis. He was loved by his relatives and close friends because they got rich off the oil. *Presidente* Portillo was an intellectual, not a politician who knew what he was doing. But look at the problems this new *Presidente* has inherited."

The first speaker interrupted, "The ministers under Portillo threw out Portillo's moderate spending plans. They inflated the spending far beyond the country's means. Nepotism and graft ruined our country. Then the new *presidente* made his mistress, Rosa Luz Alegria, minister of tourism. His son José Ramon was Assistant Minister of Programming. Everyone of his family made money it seems at the expense of the common people. After Portillo left the government, he went to Europe and put himself into self-exile and... luxury."

The young woman said in a lowered voice, "He should have exiled himself out of shame and given his riches to the poor."

Another man also spoke in a lowered voice, "I hear investors sent $9 billion out of the country. Pemex owes one fifth of the country's foreign debt. That is why we Mexicans are hurting. If those with big companies and stores cannot hire the poor, then the poor will always be with us."

A man standing in the back complained, "Portillo got us in this mess. He changed his women faster than he did his undergarments.

When he left office he divorced his wife, Carmen, moved in with his mistress in Spain, and then married a film star and had two kids with her."

"Well, at least he is dead now and can do no more damage," another man said.

The man standing next to him grumbled, "Well, Portillo had no political experience. He just wanted to please his friends and make money for them and himself. He was a figurehead for his political friends who used him to bankrupt our country. Greed. That's what it was. Now, what are we going to do?"

An attractive bleached-blonde with dark skin said, "Our government tells us they lose half their money from taxes that people don't pay. They accuse us of evading taxes. It is our money and the *federales* want what we have."

"*Si*," said the man sitting next to her. "They are overpaid and still want more."

The woman near José again spoke. "The presidents rob the treasury blind. Our poor have little reason to stay in our country. Hunger is pushing them north across the border."

"But *Presidente* Fox wants to have open borders. The Americans are too smart to open the borders to us," said the first man who had started the harangue.

"You're right," said a man with auburn-red hair. "One day the Americans will close the borders so no one can get through. I hear about the Arizona borders being so tight that people who live in Arizona kill any immigrants who try to sneak across their farms going into Arizona."

Another man spoke up, "If the borders are closed, it will hurt our country. Family members send millions of dollars back home here to families in Mexico. Closing the border would kill us. Our economy would crash. We must get more jobs here in Mexico City to keep more of our young men at home... and working."

"But our new *Presidente* sends out encyclicals stating that the U.S. must keep our borders open between us."

A woman added, "I like tourists to come here, but if the borders are open both ways, will we want what gringos do to our land? Too many are retired and living here in tourist communities."

"Tourists bring money."

"Tourists try to tell us what to do and how to act. I don't like it," said one clerk on his lunch break from a nearby market.

"Remember the Treaty of Guadalupe Hidalgo. I challenge *el Presidente* to call for no walls between us and the United States. The Treaty called for peace between our two countries. Where are *el Presidente's huevos?*"

"Be quiet," said his wife sitting next to him. "The trees have ears."

"*El Presidente* has his own wall along Guatemala's border," interrupted the clerk. "He allows no one to come in from the south. That is wrong when he wants our people to go north."

"It's the poor he wants to send north. He wants to get rid of the poor."

Suddenly they heard shrill whistles from *la policia*. "Someone has turned us in. Run!" said a young woman sitting near José. She grabbed his hand and dashed to a very old, dilapidated restaurant across the street.

"Here. Sit with me at this table. We'll order a chocolate drink."

"I am sorry I have no money with me," José said, feeling ashamed he did not want to pay money from that hidden in his shoe.

"That's okay. I'll buy. If *la policia*, the police, come in, we need an excuse to be in here." She waved to the waiter who eagerly dashed over to serve his two customers. There were no other customers in the room.

The attractive young woman with short, dark hair told him what they wanted, and he brought them hot chocolate drinks and gave them each a cookie.

Curious, José ate the cookie and drank the chocolate drink. He had never had such chocolate mixed with sugar, even though he had heard about chocolate. It tasted bitter even with sugar in it. He wrinkled his face at the taste.

"Do you use cream in your chocolate?" the young woman asked.

"I didn't, well uh, I haven't had chocolate like this before, so I didn't know about it." She leaned over and poured cream in his hot drink.

He tasted it, a little bit at a time because it was so hot, and licked his lips. "You are right. It gives it a better, a good taste."

"Yes, a distinctive taste. You're from the farm, aren't you?" she said grinning at him.

"We have a small piece of land. Very small. I guess you might say I have a farm. We were able to raise some potatoes and vegetables so the children can eat."

The door was thrown open wide, and two men in police uniforms came in. The young woman took José's hand and lovingly looked into his eyes. He tried to pull his hand away but she held it firmly.

She turned to look at the policeman when one asked roughly, "Were you at the dissension rally across the street?"

"No, *mi dulce corazon* and I have been sitting here planning our wedding."

The other policeman turned to the waiter and said, "How long have these two been here this morning?"

The waiter said, not wanting to lose his only two customers since early breakfast, "A long time. They've been here all morning. I wasn't listening to what they were saying."

The first policeman, his hand on his night stick, yelled at the waiter, "You had better not be lying to me." He turned and left the restaurant with his partner following behind him. The waiter returned to the kitchen trembling.

The young woman saw the questions on José's face and said, "Thank you for helping me. My friends and I want to change our government. We want our *Presidente* to make more jobs to help the poor and working class. Some people might call me a socialist. But I call myself someone who wants everyone to have a job. I am one of the Leftists one of the speakers was talking about. I follow in my father's footsteps. He teaches at the University here in Mexico City.

"By the way, my name is Elena Veracruz. Since we are planning our wedding, I need to know who you are."

"I am, uh, Manuel Garcia. I have a wife. I can't marry you," he said using the name he had told all the others.

She laughed loudly with a howl, "I don't intend to marry you. Calm down. Where are you from?"

"From a small town you wouldn't remember tomorrow morning. I am unimportant and the town is unimportant."

"Manuel, you are important. You helped save me from jail just now."

******

Elena took Manuel/José to her apartment.

"I am a journalist with one of the newspapers. It's sad that I cannot write the things I want to write, but I keep an eye on the pulse of Mexico City with my job. I will write about the Central Park meeting to let everyone know there are people who are dissenting. The only thing I will not be able to write is that I agree with what the rebels want to do."

"You have a job and money to feed yourself. Why do you care?" asked José.

She peered at him sternly. "You really mean what you say, don't you?"

"Yes," he said, puzzled that she questioned him.

"Don't you care about what others think and want?"

"Yes, I care about others. But should I care to make them think the way I think?" He struggled trying to gather his thoughts.

"If what you think is important. Yes. You should want them to think as you do."

José nodded. "That is strange. I always thought everyone thinks much alike."

"Do you know wicked men?"

"Yes, I do," he said, remembering the Castillone brothers and Enrique lying there in a pool of blood.

"You don't think like those bad men, do you?" she asked.

"Never! I could never think like they think," José said.

"So, how can you change the thinking of evil men?"

"With my fists?" he offered.

"No, you can never truly change someone's heart with force. Fists are out."

"Well, how do we change another's thoughts?" he asked.

"Through education," she said and added when she saw puzzlement on his face, "You tell them reasons why they need to think like you."

"That is too much thinking, I think," José said.

"Not so. Thinking can be enjoyable," she said, becoming bored with the conversation. "I'm going to bed. You sleep on the couch," she pointed.

CHAPTER 19

I T TOOK ELMIRA A long, hard year to die. Her heart kept waiting for her beloved José to walk in the door to her bedroom. Some days she would hallucinate. She would hear *José's* voice telling her how much he loved her. One day slowly faded into the next day, full of pain and the herbs *la Abuelita* gave her to numb that pain.

In some villages *la Abuelita*, the dear grandmother, was known as the *Curandera* – the one who cured. Out of respect they called their healer, *la Abuelita*.

Miguel complained to Elmira, "*Mamácita*, you are not the *mamá* I once knew. The herbs *la Abuelita* feeds you takes your mind away."

"I know, I know, *hijo*. Please rub my back." And Miguel and Francisco took turns rubbing her back. She often would whisper, "José, don't ever stop rubbing my shoulders. What would I do, if you weren't here?" The boys would look at each other with tears raining down their cheeks unashamedly. They knew she confused them with their beloved *Papá*.

Each morning after the cows and goats were milked, Elmira sent Miguelito to clean the small general store and always said, "Please Miguelito, bring me a letter from your *Papá*."

Each evening when Miguelito came home, he told her, his heart flooding with sadness, "There was no letter this time. I'm sure there will be one soon." His heart filled with sadness for his mother and the little ones. Occasionally Pablo, the store's owner, sent several pesos home with him to buy some extra food from the store. Pablo got the pesos back when they bought flour for tortillas.

As summer turned to fall, the twins began school. Elmira's mother, their *Grandmamá*, showed up each morning to care for the two little ones not yet in school. She made tortillas for the evening and the next morning. If there was not enough flour, the *Grandmamá* brought flour from her own meager supply. Hard times were coming when the coolness of winter bore down on them.

Before Elmira's death in the winter, *la Abuelita* cried many tears, "These seven children will inherit the disgrace of their dead mother and their father who are not here to protect them."

After a while she came up with an idea. "I will issue a warning that anyone who touches these, Elmira's children, will have *the curse* upon them. I will not be able to protect them from hurtful words, but my curse will protect them from fists and bruises." She immediately went to see the nuns who would give the information to the villagers.

She arrived back at her house satisfied. She knew the superstitions of the villagers and tapped into those fears. The children would be safe for a while.

CHAPTER 20

ELENA VERACRUZ TAUGHT JOSÉ or Manuel Garcia many things while he stayed with her.

One morning she told him, "My friend, Oswaldo, works at the airport. He will get you a job there hauling baggage."

"*Gracias.* My thanks will be forever if you can get me a job. I must save money or I will never be able to send for my family." *Or cross the border to find mi Tio Miguel.*

The next morning José went to the airport and asked for Oswaldo Garza Rosales who worked for Mexicana Airlines. In his hand he had the fake identification papers Elena bought for him, so he could get the job.

"I am Elena's friend, Manuel Garcia. I appreciate your helping me to get a job."

"I owe Elena several favors. Glad to help you. Call me Lalo as my friends call me."

Oswaldo took him to the baggage supervisor in his office. "This is my friend Manuel Garcia. He needs a job. He is strong like a bull, not too smart, and will do what you say."

The supervisor said, "We need strong workers. Lalo, I will hire him because you vouch for him, and I see here he has all the necessary papers." He shuffled through them page by page.

He gave Manuel some more papers to fill out. Oswaldo had to help him read them because Manuel could not read but a few words. José printed his name M A N U E L as Elena had shown him the night before, over and over. Then Oswaldo told him to print an X beside Manuel since José did not know how to write Garcia.

The supervisor, Señor Perez, told both men, "You must not let anyone who does not work with Mexicana Airlines get near your baggage. If you see anyone trying to leave strange baggage with your deliveries to the planes, you must detain them and notify me immediately."

Manuel looked puzzled.

Señor Perez said, "Since the terrorists blew up the bottom tower in New York City, we have been ordered by *Presidente* Vicente Fox to watch for terrorists. We have not found any as yet, but we will be heroes the day we find some to turn in to the authorities."

"You mean we look for bombs?" said Manuel, looking frightened.

"Yes, bombs. They could even be in packages of food. If you are afraid, someone else can have your job."

Oswaldo said, "Of course Manuel is not afraid!"

"No, I am not afraid," said Manuel, swallowing hard to push down the fear.

"And look for strange-acting people," said Oswaldo as they walked out of the supervisor's office. "Some people will use the planes as if they are bombs themselves."

"How could a plane be a bomb?" asked Manuel not understanding.

"It is full of gasoline and will explode if it flies into a building."

"Oh, *mi Elmira*. I am afraid."

"No need to be afraid. FBI agents from the United States work among us and they fly on the planes. Flights are cancelled if they become suspicious. They let nothing happen to us." Oswaldo hoped he could cause Elena's friend to calm down before Manny lost the job and getting to prove he could work.

"Lalo, what is an FBI agent?" asked Manuel.

"They are like *la policia*."

"Oooeee!" worried Manuel. He followed Oswaldo in a daze and copied him as he threw suitcases, carrying trunks, cases and crates on the large carts. Soon Oswaldo took him to another department where he was expected to read tags and match them to air flights. Oswaldo noticed Manny could read a little which helped him match the tags. Then he had Manuel load the luggage onto the large carts. By lunch time Manuel was so tired he had almost forgotten about his fear.

Through the local post office at the airport José, or Manuel, began sending $50 or more home to Elmira in care of the village store that his friend Pablo owned.

"Why do you insist on sending cash?" Elena Veracruz asked.

"Because our village is a small village and checks and mail orders are difficult to make into pesos." How could he explain to Elena he was afraid *la policia* might trace him through receipts.

"And why do you want to sign the name José instead of Manuel?"

"Because that is the name she says when she loves me." José blushed, not wanting to say more.

He sent the pesos and a small gift, each time, in one of the big thick envelopes. Elena, his new friend he met in the Central Park, taught him to copy the address she wrote on the envelope. And she showed him how to print a note inside:

MY BEAUTIFUL ELMIRA,

I LOVE YOU.

JOSÉ

José felt happier than he had in a long time. He knew his family was getting fed and buying things they had not been able to get since he left Siempre. But he no longer felt safe in Mexico City. In a few months he must move on his way to California, money and anonymity.

Chapter 21

José never dreamed he would be riding a bus back and forth to his airport job, but here he was waiting for a bus.

He had argued with Elena, "Bus money is money I can be sending to my family in Siempre."

Elena became exasperated. "Don't you understand? You can make more money if you ride the bus instead of getting up so early to walk. Ride the bus. If your health breaks down, you won't be able to work."

"But I have good health. I don't get sick."

"José, you try to save pennies when you can make dollars. You can work overtime or get a second job during the time you walk to the airport. Two hours is a long time to walk, and each way at that."

"A second job. I had not thought of another job. I will ride the bus. Thank you, thank you, Elena."

He paused and asked, "And what is overtime?"

"Overtime is what you work after it is time to get off. They will pay you for it," she explained.

"I will work overtime." He grinned his big grin that lit up his face and hugged her.

"Now Manuel, you know you are married." She kidded him. He jumped back as if she had slapped him.

"You are right Elena. I must keep myself for my Elmira. Besides I just wanted to thank you. Not love you."

******

During the next month in Mexico City, José waited for the municipal bus that would take him to his job at the airport, there he met Diego Munoz. Diego appeared to be his age, around 30.

Diego said to him, "I saw you at this bus stop yesterday morning. Where are you going?"

"To work at the airport. Where are you going?"

"I work for the City."

"Oh." Jose blinked questioningly.

The bus came at that moment and the two men climbed up the steep steps, paid their fares and found seats on different parts of the crowded bus.

The following morning as Jose walked up, Diego spotted him. "You must live near here."

"Yes, I do," said José. "I'm renting the couch of a friend."

Diego said, "My wife and I and three children live two blocks away in a house with her parents. It's my desire to save up enough money to buy our own house."

"I have my own house in another town, but I am making money to send to my family."

"You could make much more if you go north to the United States. But here you can make some money and go home to see them occasionally."

José paused and cautiously said, "I have thought about going." He didn't trust this man enough yet to tell him he couldn't go home because he was wanted for killing Enrique Castillone.

The bus came and they climbed on, but this time they sat in seats across the aisle from one another. There were fewer people riding today.

"When are you going to the USA?" asked Diego.

"I'm not sure. I have a good job at the airport right now, and I want to send much money to my family. And my former employer sees they get the money."

"I have thought about going to Texas myself, but I went once and couldn't make enough money. They say I am clumsy and not too bright." Diego looked downcast. "At least here, I have a job."

José started to answer when Diego jumped up and yelled to the bus driver, "Stop! This is my stop!" He ran up the aisle to the front door and got off.

José looked out the window at his new friend as they drove off. He kept watching and saw Diego start running after them yelling something. José was puzzled. He looked on the seat where Diego had been sitting and there was a gun. He must have left it. José moved from his seat and sat by the gun wondering what to do with it. Finally he put it under his shirt and stuffed it inside his pants. He had never handled a weapon before. He was nervous.

He muttered to himself, "My friend must be a crook. Why else would he have a gun?"

He hid the gun in his locker at work. What should he do with it? He would get in trouble if the airport officials caught him with it. He decided to take it home and find out what Elena thought he should do with it.

That evening he told Elena about the gun. She laughed, "I would like to have been there to see that man chasing the bus. It must have been comical."

"I did not think it was funny. I was wondering why he was chasing us. When I saw the gun, I dared not turn it in to the bus driver."

"You need to give the gun back to him tomorrow. It isn't your gun, and you don't want to be caught with it on you." Elena was matter of fact.

"You're right. He will be at the bus stop."

"Goodnight Manuel, I must finish this story I am writing about our emigrants who are dying in the deserts of New Mexico and Arizona. My editor wants it turned in tomorrow morning."

"Why are our people dying in the United States?"

"They cross the desert during the brutal heat of summer. Some walk. Others are placed in vans by *coyotes* who don't give them water," Elena said.

******

The next morning José looked for his friend at the bus stop. He was relieved when he saw him sitting there. He handed his friend the gun wrapped in José's jacket. Diego's eyes widened in delight.

"Oh, José. Am I glad to get this gun back. I was written up at work yesterday for not having my gun."

"What's written up?"

"Written up means I have a black mark against my name."

"You have a gun. What do you do?" asked José.

"I am a policeman. I direct traffic and any other grunt work they can find for me."

José sat silent. *La policia. Of all the people in the world and I have to find a policeman for a friend. He may be dumb, but he may be smart enough to turn me in.*

It is time for me to leave. I must go to California and safety – from those who would keep me from sending money to my family. I must go to the Airport and pick up my last pay.

******

That next day while delivering baggage at the airport, he watched as several hundred men with dark mustaches like his own disembarked from a Mexicana Airlines jet plane. There were officials guarding them as they got off.

His friend, Oswaldo, who had gotten him the job said, "I have heard these are the illegals that are being sent back to our country. It is called 'The deep repatriation' program. The U.S. doesn't dump them at the border any more. They want them to return home."

José shook his head not understanding, "I thought the Americans kept them and made them citizens."

Oswaldo replied, "That was last century. This century is a whole, new world."

José said, "I hope you are wrong."

At lunchtime he walked into the terminal and saw his friend Elena Veracruz from the Mexico City newspaper interviewing some of the illegals.

He walked up in time to hear one of them proclaiming to her as she took notes, "I will return to the United States in 15 days. I work construction and nowhere in the world can I make more money than in Riverside County. Big, beautiful houses, that is what I build. They need me in the USA."

The illegal next to him said, "I will visit with my wife and children for a month and then I will go back. I made it across successfully on four other occasions. I will probably make it next time. I was unlucky enough to be caught in that undocumented sweep of the neighborhood. I have to return – jobs in Mexico don't pay anything."

"Even *el Presidente* understands that," said another man.

Another spoke up, "We all agreed to come here rather than stay in that detention facility in Arizona. They gave us spinach pasta and soft drinks on the three-hour flight here."

The first man said, "Please don't call us wetbacks in the article. Very few of us swim across the Rio Grande anymore."

Elena answered him with a sweet smile, "I understand. Wetback is an old-fashioned name and rarely used by anyone anymore."

"Oh, hello, Manuel," said Elena to José when she saw him listening. "What do you think about the border brothers being sent back to Guadalajara and Mexico City?"

"I heard that 422 people died last year trying to get through to Arizona, Texas and California. Isn't that enough to discourage people from going over into the U.S.?" José flushed, not sure what he should be saying.

She replied, "Isn't this going to make it more expensive for our people to try to go across the border? Ultimately, will it save lives as the Border Patrol hopes?"

José said, "I don't know. If someone is determined to cross the border, he will go across the border, no matter how many times it takes."

CHAPTER 22

H E LEFT MEXICO CITY that night by taking a bus to the edge of the city – Elena Veracruz insisted he ride. Then he walked. He was fearful about catching a ride like a hitchhiker.

The next two days José walked many miles deep into the night until he felt faint. His water was gone by the evening of the first day. In the middle of the third day, he saw a well and dragged his weary, blistered feet to the side of the well and dropped on the edge of the cracked wall. The old bucket was broken, but it still would hold a little water. He dropped it into the well and brought up about half a cup of the life-giving fluid and clumsily drank from the bucket. He lowered it again to get another half-cup of water.

A heavy, almost masculine voice called loudly, "Don't you drink our water!"

He looked up to see a young manly-looking female who appeared to be younger than he.

"Sorry. I am very thirsty. I have walked many miles." The small amount of water had given him new life.

"You know you oughtn't steal. This well belongs to our neighbors and to my family."

"Let me assist you in getting water for your pitchers." He looked at the woman and the younger women who walked up surrounding her. He remembered the story the priest often told his parishioners of Jacob and his love story of Rachel and Jacob. Jacob loved Rachel from the moment he saw her, but her sister Leah was said to be dull of eye. Here was a litter of five young women who were lacking in beauty as

Leah must have been. The younger ones were still not yet in their 20s. And they were crude though young.

His wife Elmira would never have denied a thirsty man drink. Her beauty showed to her very core. "Inside and out, she is beautiful," his mother told him when she realized José and Elmira would one day marry.

The girls interrupted his thoughts. "Yes, why don't you fill our pitchers. When you have finished, we will let you have more to drink," said the oldest of the girls who had told him not to drink.

When he had completed the job, one of the five girls who all turned out to be sisters, took his elbow and said, "Come home with us for dinner. Our father is hungry for conversation with another man."

"Thank you, I would like to," José said cautiously. The girls all giggled. Then they took turns touching him on the back and arms. Even the youngest who was about twelve took her turn. Shocked at their familiarity he followed them.

After dinner the father sent his daughters to the other room to clean up the dishes and pans. José and the man leaned back in their chairs around the dinner table picking raw vegetables from between their teeth with sharpened twigs.

"The meal was very good for an empty stomach," said José.

"Oh, my daughters. They aren't bad cooks. I have five of them. You are welcome to choose one."

José looked at the man and explained, "I have a wife and children back home. I cannot marry another woman."

"That's okay. I won't tell them or anyone around here that you already have a wife. I want grandchildren and you can understand by looking at my daughters that it has been hard to marry these girls to anyone. I have little money. We scrape the soil to grow what food we can cause to sprout. I have no possessions to tempt a man into marrying even one of my ugly daughters."

José replied, "I have a homely sister, but she is such a good woman and an excellent cook that her husband does not notice she is unattractive. Teach your girls good manners and perhaps they will someday find husbands." He hoped he was not overstepping with his advice.

"I think it is that there are so many of them. I love them like I would love an ugly pup but they exasperate me." The father put his head in his hands to show his sadness. "I want grandchildren. I need a grandson to help me till the soil to grow food. With no sons I have had to make sons out of my daughters. They can do anything a man can do."

"Perhaps that is the problem," said José. "A man does not want a woman who is as much or more of a man as he is."

When it came time to go to bed, the father sent José to the barn to sleep. "I will not be offended if you sleep with one of my daughters before you go on your way. At least one of them will come to see you tonight. Please help an old man out."

José frowned, but took his belongings and rolled them back into a bundle of clothes, climbed the slatted stairs to the loft and lay down in the hay soon to be used to feed the two old donkeys.

Just as he began drifting off to sleep he heard noises below. "Manuel, where are you? My sisters and I pulled sticks to see which of us would get to sleep with you. I won. And aren't you lucky! Where are you?" He recognized the masculine voice of the oldest sister.

I would like to help their father out. But my love and my seed belong to my Elmira and my children. My God would not be pleased. He whispered his thoughts as a prayer.

Surely the Ugly One would find him soon. Hairs on his neck and arms stood up straight in fear. How could he get down from the loft without her hearing him? He walked to the open window and felt some ropes hanging there. Would he dare to climb down the ropes to the ground below and find escape that way?

He tossed the ball of clothes as hard and far as he could and listened. He heard nothing, so he began making his way down two of the ropes. As his feet hit the ground, strong arms wrapped around him.

"I knew you would come down the rope. You are so anxious to make love to me."

José was silent as her hands began fumbling with his clothing. He decided to be honest with her. "Dear woman, I have a wife. I have seven children. I am on my way north where I can make a home to take them to."

"Seven children! Oh God, my prayers have been answered! Another child for you. You wouldn't even miss one. But I want you to stay with me and help me raise the child you can give me. My sisters will be so jealous."

José kept backing up until he tripped over his ball of belongings. He grabbed them in the blackness and began running in the direction he presumed to be away from this strange family. He heard her footsteps behind him. She must know this ground as no stranger could know it. He crouched down like a trembling hare and heard her rush by him huffing and puffing with grunting noises. Staying still for many minutes, he heard her running footsteps disappear in the distance. From memory he slowly walked over to the road he had used to get to the well. From there he again headed north.

Nothing he found in the future could frighten him more, he thought, than these young women and their father who would steal his seed without thoughts of what he wanted.

CHAPTER 23

A LBERTO HERNANDES BERMEJO AND his wife Alma were driving along in their old jeep he had purchased for a couple hundred dollars at a used car lot in Mexico City. They saw José walking along the road going north in the opposite direction, and Alma yelled, "Stop! Stop!"

As he pulled over to the side of the road, he protested to his wife, "You already used the restroom back there."

Alma retorted, "Let's pick up that man to help you drive." She could see José running along the road to catch up with them for the ride they must be offering him.

"*My* beautiful one, I can drive all the way there," said Alberto, irritated.

"You will see Alberto. You will see I am right." Alma pulled her long, brown hair over and around one shoulder so the stranger could see how beautiful she was. Jealousy proved to be a strong aphrodisiac for her Alberto. It had been a few days since Bermejo had satisfied her passion. Making him jealous was often her method of getting her way.

As Alberto made a U-turn in the road, Alma threw the door open.

Huffing and puffing, José caught up with them and took hold of the open door, "Thank you, Señor and *Señora*. My feet and legs are very tired, very sore."

"Where are you going, tired one?" asked Alma.

"I am going to California. The border is a long way to walk."

"We, too, are going to the border," said Alberto. "We are visiting relatives near there."

"*Gracias*," said José and promptly went to sleep, snoring lightly.

"Isn't he handsome, Alberto?" asked Alma of her husband. She reached over and put her hand on José's knee hindering Alberto's making another U-turn.

"Stop that, Alma! If I were a woman and not particular, perhaps I would think him to be handsome." Alberto finished the turn and kept driving.

"Why did you tell him we were going to the California border?" asked Alma.

"Well, we are going near the border, but I didn't say what border."

******

When José awoke, Alberto asked him to help drive. For two days, they drove during the cooler early mornings and in the cool of the evenings. José noticed the weather was getting hotter and more humid.

He wiped his brow. "I didn't know it was so miserably hot in northern Mexico."

"Yes," said Alberto.

The end of the second day it was late and the moon was not shining. The darkness kept José from seeing his hand held before him. Alberto stopped the car and told him to get out. "This is as far as we are taking you. The border is not far from here."

José thanked them and found a tree to sleep under until light surrounded him as insufferable heat and moisture punished his every movement. He was used to the dry heat of the desert area of Siempre and not the tropics as found near Guatemala.

CHAPTER 24

THE NEXT MORNING JOSÉ awoke to find himself near Tuxtla Gutiérrez, Mexico. He had never seen so many trees and shrubs. It reminded him of stories of the jungle.

He asked the men in the squatters' camp near where he had been dumped, "Which way is it to the border?"

"The border? It is not easy to get across the border."

"Well, some strangers picked me up outside Mexico City and dropped me off here last night."

"You cannot always trust strangers. This border may not be where you would want to go."

"Please direct me to the California border.

"The California border? You are confused. You are near the Guatemala border not far from Tuxtla Gutiérrez, Mexico."

"I want to go to the border, where California is."

"Ha ha. You are south, not north. Someone wanted to play a big joke on you."

"It is no joke. It's my life they are playing with," said José.

José didn't realize he was in the last jungle in North America. The Lacandon jungle is a 1,290 square-mile Montes Azules reserve where squatters live on farms which environmentalists claim are hurting the jungle ecosystem.

One of the settlers told José, "We believe the environmentalists are mere fronts for corporations who want to exploit jungle resources. They tell us there are jaguars and many species of birds and some endangered plants with other animals living all around us. We just want to grow our corn around our dozens of squatters' camps. That is what our enemies call us: squatters. The birds eat our corn. These people must leave us alone. We believe they tell lies to get us out of here. They don't want to share the land and we have to live somewhere."

José shook his head and said. "I fear there are many dangers in the world outside my village."

The friendly settler suggested, "Take your *siesta* here in the heat of the day. When it is cool you can walk to the next village, or perhaps a passerby will give you a ride to get you there."

He told the settler who let him sleep on his porch, "Wherever they take me could not be any farther away from the California border than where I am now.

He slept for awhile under shrubs during *siesta* time and was awakened by the sound of trucks and screams of the families in the settlement around him.

The hard-voiced leader of the military tried to explain to the people, "We must relocate you to the El Caracol area. Please cooperate and no one will get hurt. This is our job and we mean no harm to any of you."

"This is our land!" screamed one of the women.

"*No, Señora,*" he insisted, "this is government land. You are not to grow your plots of corn on government land!" His voice grew harder.

José obediently climbed onto the truck along with the many Indian farmers who would be relocated miles away.

An hour later he was dropped off with the others in a new political area 35 miles away, he looked for a person willing to give him a ride going north. It took him two hours of asking others for help before a soldier going to the next town said, "Get in. I'll take you to the next village where you can get a ride going to Arriaga. Many migrants ride the roofs of railroad cars to take them north toward the United States."

José prayed as he went, he asked questions and learned what he could from them.

CHAPTER 25

A S JOSÉ HEADED NORTH once again, he became more confident in his own decisions about people as he learned to ask questions and listened carefully to their answers. He felt the train was unsafe, so he asked for rides from common people. He now believed riding by vehicle was a good way to make better time.

After passing Mexico City again, he hitched a ride from a country farmer in the farmer's oxcart. The farmer took pity on him and let him ride and sleep in the back with the cheap wheat he had bartered for behind the mercado in Samalayuca. He planned to sell his produce and the wheat at the market in Juarez.

Juarez is miles north from the main center of Chihuahua state. It is across the border from El Paso, Texas. People drive and walk back and forth from Juarez, Mexico, into Texas. Identification has not been easy since the 9/11 attacks in New York City. Both sides of the border are clamping down and demanding proof of residence for either side of the border and two forms of ID.

The farmer woke him and explained to José he must go on and leave him at the small park outside of Ciudad Juarez. José got out somewhat refreshed from the morning's sleep in the oxcart and found a water fountain with water slowly coming out of it.

He tried to drink water but it took him a long time. His thirst was so great it was worth being patient.

A high male voice said, "You don't have to put your mouth on the spigot. Turn the handle below and more water will come out." José obeyed and drank deeply of the warm water that flowed heavily as he turned the handle.

When he was finished he looked up to see a short bear of a man. The voice did not fit, but José did not care.

"*Gracias.* I needed water."

"Don't we all!" said the other man.

"Do you have work I can do for you?" asked José.

"Perhaps, if you know how to help me fix my broken down van. It is obvious from your clothing you are uneducated, so I may be asking too much of you."

"No, you are not asking too much. I never owned an automobile, but I helped fix a few of them in my small village where I come from."

"And where is that?" asked the man.

"Many miles on the other side of Mexico City," said José.

"Then you must be heading into Texas."

"No, I want to go to San Diego."

Joaquin laughed. "You are a long ways from Tijuana. Well, you must go many miles west to cross over into California. You would be wise to go to Baja California along the border and try to get in there. They're the most lenient of all the border crossings. But the *coyotes* who take you fellows across without green cards charge a lot of money."

"It's taken me well over a year to get this far." José looked depressed, and the man felt sorry for him.

"Why don't you help me get my van running and you can ride with me a ways. Just call me Joaquin the Prepared." He walked toward his van with José following. He handed José some pliers and screwdrivers. José peered into the open hood at the engine and checked the wires he could see but found they were all attached. The hoses, too, were in place and appeared to have no leaks.

"Here it is. The points on these old vehicles need to be sharpened. He took his pocketknife and whittled around until he smiled in satisfaction. Then he returned it to its place above the upper left of the engine.

"Now get in and see if it will start," José said. Joaquin the Prepared started the engine and smiled broadly. "You are a true mechanic."

"*Gracias*," José replied.

"Climb in and I will share tortillas and beans with you and then you can help me dump this old rug that I have in the back," said Joaquin.

"*Gracias, gracias,* Joaquin the Prepared," said José as he crawled into the front passenger seat. He wrinkled up his nose in disgust for the rug and other contents in back all smelled of age.

After eating their lunch Joaquin drove out to the desert and José helped him dump an old rug that had had many years' use.

José said, "This is a heavy rug. One man would have had much difficulty pulling it into the desert and leaving it. You're lucky I came by."

"Not really lucky. I was waiting for you," the man said.

"You didn't know I was coming, did you?"

"I knew someone would come. They always do. You know José, we must be careful. There are many roving bands of rich señores' sons we call 'Juniors' who kill their enemies and dump them out here. And drug dealers whose drug projects go awry will dump their victims out here. Have you ever killed someone?"

Shocked, José answered, "I don't know. I could never kill someone without good reason."

"Do you know the excitement of forcing a woman to go against her will? Have you ever raped a woman?" asked Joaquin.

"Oh no. I respect women. I love my wife. I love my daughters. Never would I...."

"I am joking. You are too tame and too-small-village to know about such things."

"I don't want to think about it," said José.

"You must think about it. Did you know more than 250 women have been sexually assaulted, strangled and dumped out here in this desert?"

"What evil gang would do such a thing?" asked José in anger.

"Maybe one man who hated his mother would do it."

"But his mother would not make him kill other women," José tried to explain.

"Don't you realize, José? All women are alike. They take advantage of us men. They pretend to love us, but then one day they go off with someone else. Just like my mother. She betrayed me time after time. She would bring strange men to her bed and push me away. I hated it."

"But you were her little boy," said José, "and mothers don't sleep with their little boys when they have a new husband."

"He was never her husband."

"Where was your father?"

"My father disappeared before I was born."

"She must have loved you," said José.

"She did until I was 23, and then she got a new boyfriend and disappeared with him. Then I was alone in her bed. She was not there to rub my back and all the things a woman does to show a man she loves him," said Joaquin. "And then one day they found her in the dump. She had been strangled."

"Who killed her?"

"We will never tell, will we?" Joaquin the Prepared smiled evilly. "I still sleep on her pillow."

José's hairs on the back of his neck raised up. His senses told him something was not right with this man who called himself Joaquin the Prepared.

CHAPTER 26

JOAQUIN DROVE THEM BACK to the small park with the slow-running water fountain. José declined Joaquin's offer to sleep in his old van alongside him after they ate dinner beneath the starry heavens.

"I will sleep outdoors with a rock for a pillow. I am getting almost used to such sleeping conditions," José exaggerated. Anything but sleeping in that smelly van.

"That's up to you, Manuel. It is warmer in here."

He found a flat rock and placed his clothes bundle on top for his head to rest on. Wearing the strong jacket he bought in Mexico City at Elena Veracruz' advice, he tried to sleep. He felt nervous just being near this man who told him of his mother being strangled by her lover. He wondered if a man could take pleasure in having his mother killed and dumped in the desert as Joaquin appeared to enjoy. He thought out loud to himself, "Can a man love and hate his mother at one and the same time?"

Out of the shadows he watched as Joaquin walked over to a girl sleeping alone. He kneeled over and appeared to stroke her long hair as she slept. Suddenly his hands grabbed the girl around the neck. José heard a bone crack and the girl's eyes popped open in terror and shock. Joaquin was moving on her as a husband moves on the woman he loves, but Joaquin was watching this one die as he moved. She made several convulsing movements and stopped breathing.

José awoke moaning.

"What did I dream?" He thought a few minutes and remembered he was in the desert seeing a woman crawling out of the rug he had helped Joaquin dump on the dry, hot ground. Soon there were rugs all around him and women crawling out.

"Does my dream mean Joaquin rapes and strangles women? If so, I helped him dump that last one in the desert. Will the police think I am guilty, too?"

Does Joaquin really hate women that much? I must be sure if it is true. Then I must notify la policia. How do I let them know and not be thrown into prison along with him? If I stay with this man, will I be safe? José felt nauseous thinking of the police and the poor women who no longer enjoyed the warm rays of the sun on their bodies.

When light from the dawning sun brought José to a sitting position, he was tired from lack of rest. He wasn't sure what he should do. Stay with Joaquin or find someone who would get him into town where he could find some odd jobs to do for some money?

"Manuel, get up. I need you to go into Juarez with me and get more rugs." Joaquin ordered José to help him.

Obediently José climbed into the passenger's seat of the van. He spoke little as was his custom when he was unsure of his thoughts.

"You are wondering where I make my money, aren't you?" asked Joaquin.

"I thought of it," said José.

"I buy for less and then go door to door and sell for more. I buy many sizes of rugs to save the ladies a hard trip to the *marketa*."

"I thought you didn't like women."

"I don't. Rich ladies are not like other women. They are special with glittery jewels and refined painted faces. They buy my rugs, and I carry off the old ones for them. Sometimes the old ones are good enough to sell to the poor families along the border towns. The children are very happy when they get a rug in their shanties. It is the closest to a bed most have ever known."

They spent several hours going through the rug factory in downtown Juarez, picking out the rugs Joaquin pointed out to the salesman. After loading two dozen rugs into the van, Joaquin treated José to a bean and rice lunch. They sat outdoors under the large umbrella of the taco stand, eating and talking.

"After *siesta* time, we will go to Generosa Street to sell some carpets. I will show you how a real salesman works," said Joaquin proudly to José. "I am the greatest salesman in Mexico. You will see."

"I always worked hard with my hands to get money," said José.

"These men don't know how to make their wives feel beautiful. I do. And then they will buy anything I have." Joaquin ignored much of what José said. He was preoccupied with himself.

"Manuel, don't ever let anyone know how much money you have. They will always think you have more. When people think you are rich, they will want to take it away from you. I know, because I want to take it away from these wealthy families by selling them my rugs for more."

The taco maker came out to bring them more *Corona* beer. He was in a chatty mood.

"Have you heard the latest about the woman killer?"

Joaquin answered, "What is the latest?"

"They found another woman in the desert this morning. It has run through the gossip mill of the city in a matter of hours. I don't know how much is true and how much is not. It was in the newspapers that the Juarez police mishandled this case, because they left the documents for the investigation in an abandoned office. Last winter the homeless were cold and went into the office and used all the materials they could find to burn to keep warm. So much of the evidence has been destroyed. My brother is a policeman and he knows about these killings." He was proud he had such interesting information to tell these strangers.

He continued, "They suspect one man does it, and my brother tells me this desert killer does not make his victims bleed."

"How do they know it is only one man?" asked José. He finished drinking his second beer but noticed Joaquin had not opened his. Joaquin was listening intently.

"Because of the evidence. My brother tells me an international human rights group called Amnesty International from England is now delving into the investigation. They say there are over 400 victims from here to Chihuahua. At least 100 are similar. They are women and there is no blood."

"How would they know?" asked Joaquin the Prepared.

"He only strangles them as he is raping them. What kind of man does that to another human being?"

"A man who doesn't like the way those women live. They must be evil women who don't love their families enough," said Joaquin.

94

The taco maker asked him puzzled, "How would a man like that know when a woman doesn't love the family like she should?"

"Perhaps when she is willing to give her body to a man who doesn't love her," Joaquin said.

"Only the man would know if he doesn't love her. She might believe he cares for her. She certainly couldn't read his mind," said José.

"Families love each other. Strangers don't love them," Joaquin stood up and paid for José's beer and the *Corona* in the bottle which he carried back to his van. "Come on, Manuel, it is time to sell our stuff."

"One more thing," said the taco maker, "*Presidente* Fox has set up a special prosecutor to investigate all the killings." He lowered his voice so only the two men could hear, "He has set up a database to identify victims to match DNA with the relatives. My brother thinks *el Presidente* should ask foreign forensics experts to come and widen the DNA database. Guadalupe Morales, Juarez commissioner on women, wants to hire Argentine forensic authority Luis Fondebrider who worked in the mass-murder cases in Rwanda and Guatemala."

"What about the man? Do they know what he looks like?" interrupted Joaquin.

"Nah! It could be one of us. Who knows!" The taco maker tried to look wise.

******

The next morning José got up early and walked to a nearby park to learn the news of the city. He especially wanted to know if the information was out about the murder of Enrique Castillone.

Everything seemed quiet in the park. Few wandered around among the trees in the middle of the park until a group of women gathered in the mild sunshiny morning. He noticed they carried signs of some kind of protest. José, now Manuel Garcia, wished he could read.

"What are you protesting?" he asked.

One older woman replied, "Protesting? We are protesting the deaths of our daughters. My granddaughter was killed in 1995."

One woman looking almost young enough to be her own daughter said, "We are grieving the murders of our daughters. My daughter had just discovered she was going to have her own child. Some brute raped and murdered her. He ended two lives. Today is Mother's Day, May 10, in Mexico."

A long, dark-haired woman with blue-green eyes and her hair piled high on her head reminding him of Elmira on their wedding day said, "When my daughter was killed by that savage beast, my Mother's Day ended forever. She was my only child."

Another said, "Mother's Day and her birthday are the most difficult days of the year for me. I am raising my daughter's children. It made me a mother again. I have to go home soon to get ready for Grandmother's Day at my house. It is a bittersweet time for the children."

The blue-green-eyed woman angrily said, "For me it is Mother's Day and Christmas. My daughter loved to help me make tamales for festive dinners. The mariachis would play their music. It was our custom. All the family would come to help us eat. Now I just cry and no one wants to come to dinner to watch me cry."

"I believe the police must be paid off by the murderer. They lose evidence. Some of the evidence is destroyed they claim. Mother's Day reminds us of what they're not doing to find the evil one who did this to our children."

"When another one dies, there is just more finger pointing and much paperwork."

"They give us counseling and expect us to get over it. We wait the return of our daughters."

"I hate the authorities. They lie to us. They say our daughters are 'Bad girls.' My daughter was a virgin until this evil man raped her. She was covered in blood because it was that time of the month for her. And then he strangled her."

José knew he must do something to find out if Joaquin the Prepared was guilty. But what?

Then he came up with an idea.

CHAPTER 27

A FEW DAYS LATER JOAQUIN picked up two young women of the street. They insisted on working together. José refused to be included in a sexual liaison to Joaquin's confusion.

He explained to Joaquin, "My wife is waiting for me. I must not look at another woman." He stayed in the red, rust-colored van and watched the three laughing, hugging and walking into the building. Soon after, José got out of the van to go for a walk to carry out the plan he had thought of. He asked people at the street corner for directions and walked to the library in Juarez. He had learned about the wonders of a library when Elena had taken him to the library in Mexico City.

"I need someone to help me write a letter."

"I will assist you," said the grandmotherly Mexican woman behind the desk in the adult section of the library. "I will have to charge you a few pesos." José looked at the kindly woman and knew he could trust her.

"I can afford three pesos. Will that be enough?"

"Yes, Señor."

The woman pulled out an envelope and a piece of paper. "Now what do you want to write?"

"I want to write a letter to *la policia*."

The woman said surprised, "What do you want to say?"

"Please help me. I don't know what to say, but to explain to them they must arrest a man in this city who hates women. He kills them, rapes and dumps them in the desert. He refuses to turn himself in, and I want to save more women from being strangled."

She replied, "I was just reading in the newspaper about our first lady, Marta Sahagun Fox. She is calling on authorities to solve the killings of hundreds of women over the past ten years in Ciudad Juarez. She has asked all of us to give the commissioner any clues we might have in order to solve these murders."

José said, "*El Presidente's* wife is interested in these murders? Thank you, God."

"Let's see," the woman said. She wrote in her best typing:

"To: *La Policia,*

"Please investigate" she typed and looked up as she asked José, "What is the man's name?"

"His name is Joaquin the Prepared."

"The Prepared. That is what Joaquin means, *prepared*. My two-year-old grandson is named Joaquin."

"That is what he calls himself, Joaquin the Prepared."

She typed exactly what he told her and handed it to him to read.

"*Señora*, I cannot read or write."

"Then I will read it back to you." She read calmly hiding her nervousness.

"*To La Policia,*

"*Please investigate Joaquin the Prepared. He may be involved in the murders of several hundred women who have been strangled and raped and dumped in the desert. He dumps them in old rugs. He sleeps in his green van. You can find him in the small park outside Juarez: The one with the drinking fountain that runs slowly and needs fixing.*"

She looked up and asked, "Do you want to put your name?"

"Please no. Just sign what you think."

She wrote, "Signed, Anonymous."

Then she said, "The three pesos will pay for the stamp and stationery. I will send it out in today's mail."

"*Muchas gracias, Señora*, many thanks madam. My conscience will be clear when he is in prison and cannot hurt any more women." He walked back to the apartment building where Joaquin was being entertained by the two women. By the time José returned he could hear Joaquin snoring loudly from his exhausting afternoon's pleasure.

José sat on the front steps to wait for him to awaken.

Meanwhile Camila Domingo, the elderly librarian, had folded the letter and put it in the envelope, stamped it and in front of José put it in the box on her desk to go out for the day. After José left, when her lunch hour came, she took the letter out of the box and rushed to the police station in the next block.

"I must give you this letter," said the librarian to the police lieutenant who spoke to her first. "A young man who seemed sincere came in and told me to write this to you, because he wanted his conscience to be clear."

He tore the envelope open and read the letter. His eyes widened as he said, "*Madre mia.*"

Turning to the librarian, he told her to come with him.

They went into the back office where the Captain read the letter and then looked at her, asking, "Whose handwriting is this?"

"Mine."

"Where'd you get this information?"

"I'm a librarian at Mar Vista Street one block over. A young man came to the library to ask me to write this letter – over an hour ago."

"An hour ago? Please tell me more… how you wrote this letter. Do you know you said things in this letter that only the killer or killers would know? Who told you this?"

"I told you. A young man came to the library. He paid me three pesos. I didn't know it would get me in trouble." Camila Domingo trembled.

"I don't say you're in trouble. I'm attempting to find all the details for the report I must write."

"I understand, but I am afraid."

"You need to be afraid… if the person who had you write this letter is an accomplice of the murderer or the murderer himself." The police captain spoke in a loud voice but ended up in a whisper.

"*Madre mia!*" Camila moaned. "He didn't look like a murderer."

******

José sat down on the porch steps of the apartment. He heard Joaquin awaken inside demanding more from the two women. He then listened to Joaquin inside having sex again with the two. The sounds both frightened him and aroused him, for it had been a long time since he had felt his woman's arms around him.

José looked at the van in front of the house. It was a rusted red vehicle Joaquin had picked up the day before from an auction near the border in Juarez.

"How long will he continue with them? Does he intend to kill them? Isn't it more difficult to kill two women than one?" he asked himself. He needed to get back to the park where the other van was with his belongings locked in the front passenger seat.

An hour later Joaquin walked out laughing, "I am the greatest! I made them both happy, and they knocked some money off the price. I call myself the four-hour man. No other man can compare to me."

José wanted to say, "No other man would want to," but he bit his lip.

"Well, say something, Manuel. Am I not a great lover?"

"You must be a great lover."

"Let's stop over on Miramax Street. I want to sell a rug or two before going to the park for the night. I feel great!" He walked taller and straighter to the rusted van. He was calm and eager to work. He even whistled while he worked.

At the third house he sold a mottled-green carpet. He returned to the van and had José help him carry the new rug to the house and they moved furniture and laid the rug in the front room of the house. Before they left they placed the old rug in the back of the red, rusted van.

As hours passed, José noticed Joaquin the Prepared acting strangely. He was no longer calm but seemed nervous, shaky and irritable. If José had asked him what was happening, Joaquin might have told him he would shake until he killed again. Then he would calm down until another day his body again became irritable and shaky.

Joaquin drove José back to the small park with the leaky fountain. The sun was still high in the sky. José wondered if the police would get the letter the next day. He planned to be gone in the morning, and Joaquin would be arrested. The world would be a better place without this dangerous man running loose.

"I'll be back in a few hours. Wait for me," said Joaquin.

"*Sí, Señor* Joaquin," said José. "Where are you going?"

"I must thank the women I saw this afternoon." José watched Joaquin's bottom lip quiver as he spoke.

CHAPTER 28

J OSÉ WAS ASLEEP ON the ground outside the green van when the police crept up to the van and stumbled over him.

"Please, I am not the man. He'll be back soon. Wait!" José yelled at the police as they took him to the police station.

Just in case this man told the truth about there being another man, the captain left two of his policemen to wait in the back of the van.

"This van sure stinks," said one of the officers as they waited to see if there was a partner.

"Smells like death to me," said the other officer.

"It stinks too much to sleep, even if I felt like it," said the first one.

Soon they heard the engine of another vehicle drive up and park beside the van.

"Shhh, be quiet," said his partner.

They heard the door of the other vehicle slam and footsteps come towards them. From outside they heard a high-pitched voice say, "Manuel, I knew you would start sleeping in the van one day. The coolness of the night was bound to get to you eventually."

As Joaquin opened the driver's door, the police held their guns pointing at him but he could not see them in the darkness while they moved toward him.

"You're dead if you move," said the first policemen.

Joaquin froze, said not a word, and raised his hands. He had prepared for this day. The pills were in his pocket.

******

José was surprised to find a bed in his cell. He lay on the hard cot in the Chihuahua jail. The holes in the cot were large and sank in the wrong spots for his strong, stout body. He had trouble getting to sleep. He tried to sleep on the floor but the guard yelled at him, "Up, get in your bed."

José was covered with bruises. When the police had come that night to arrest the killer of many women, Joaquin had killed not one, but both of the women he had been with earlier in the day. He had returned to the Park expecting José to help him dump the two old carpets in the desert. It was nice to have a helper. This man, Manuel Garcia, an ignorant farm worker, was strong.

Most of the prisoners were crowded into cells where they had to sit on the floor or stand. Each protected his space with his elbows, feet or fists. José did not know the police kept him apart because the captain suspected the other prisoners might injure or kill him if he had killed or even helped the serial killer of the 400+ women found dead in the desert. Experts were coming from around the world to study him and Joaquin *the Prepared.*

On the third day in the jail, a man and a woman waited in a room to speak to him. They were lawyers sent by the government to interrogate José.

"Your partner is better now. He took the small pills in his pocket and nearly died. He planned for you to take credit for the murders."

"Mercy! I would never kill a woman."

"Why did you write the letter?" asked one of the lawyers.

******

Three months later the lawyers released Manuel Garcia onto the streets of Juarez after he testified for them in the Joaquin the Prepared case. He had not told them he was actually José Ramirez who was wanted for the murder of Enrique Castillone of Siempre, Mexico.

The government paid Manuel/José more than enough money to fly to Mexicali.

Chapter 29

J OSÉ FLEW TO THE border town of Mexicali on *Aero Mexico*. He feared going across the border into Arizona, New Mexico or Texas. That fear came from stories he had heard in Mexico City about the two rival *coyote* gangs shooting it out over who would collect the money. Four had died in the gunfight. José was frightened, so he had spent more days to get to Tijuana which made him closer to San Diego in California where *Tio* Miguel would be.

He lay on the cot in the home of a family who wanted to help him in exchange for repairs on their home. He thought back about the people he had met. To the young woman, Elena Veracruz, who told the police she was planning their wedding in the small restaurant in Mexico City. Elena may have been right. The past century the millions of poor who migrated into the United States was Mexico's way of keeping the poor from marching on Mexico City and its leaders. Elena had told him she wanted American leaders to help Mexico as they had Germany after the World War. José had asked her where Germany was. He had never heard in his small village of the country of Germany. He only knew there had been a great war across the waters many years ago.

There is so little I know about this vast world, he thought.

But he had asked her, "Elena, you say our leaders rob the treasury, won't they steal the money the Americans send to help the poor?"

"You are ignorant of so much Manuel, but you are also smart."

"What do you mean?"

"I mean there is much you don't know but when you once learn something, your brain kicks in to figure things out. You remember I told you how crooked the government is."

"*Gracias,*" José said. "They are taking money out of my pay at the airport to give to the government. It is my money. They never took money from me when I worked for Pablo in his store."

Elena Veracruz replied, "Pablo should have paid taxes and made you pay taxes. It is probably so little money he would pay that it would cost more for the government to go after it. And Pablo didn't send it to them himself. We call that tax evasion."

"It costs less doesn't it, if taxes are not on food or furniture?"

"Yes, it does cost less. But some claim we cannot compete with the U.S. and other countries if we can't sell for the same prices."

"I'm not sure I understand."

"I don't either. They put royalties on items and tax gasoline at the pump. The oil is owned by the government so they get theirs. Our government spends $150 billion in federal spending."

"I don't understand a billion. What is a billion?"

"It is $10 hundred million. I can't fathom it either. My newspaper keeps showing ads of smiling children and the crippled who urge taxpayers to help Mexico by filing their returns by the deadline of April 30."

"You mean I have to send in money?"

"Yes, the government wants you to. They guess that half of the money the government should get never gets paid."

"I don't understand. Please tell me about your family." José was bored.

"My family lived in Magdalena de Kino, Sonora. They had to leave because the citizens in Sonora were covering the streets with their dead bodies as revolutionaries rode through the town on horses. It was the time of the Revolution. No one dared stand up to the ones taking over. My grandfather slipped out of the town in the dead of night with his new bride. They left to save their lives, not for economic reasons as most leave today. There were few guards along the border between Mexico and the United States in those days. So they slipped into the U.S. with no documents. Their son, my father, worked hard to attend the University. When I was old enough he worked hard to send me to the University. He made sure I kept the Spanish language and learned fluent English. He came here to Mexico City to teach and to help in any uprisings that might take place. I work to make this country better as Americans constantly improve their country. We can do it, too."

"You will do much to help this world. I can see that. God will not let harm come to you." He thought of the goodness of Elmira and remembered how an evil man harmed her.

"Manuel, I hope you are right. If they throw me in prison, they may let me rot there."

******

Another thing Elena had taught him. She said, "Go to the California border of Tijuana. Both sides of the California border are safer than Texas, New Mexico or Arizona. I read last week how American officials go quickly to close down the safe houses where illegals stay. And they arrest them and send them back here to their hometowns. Many bad stories come back to us and we don't know if they are true."

"I would be afraid to be sent back to my home," said José.

"But Manuel, you would get to see your wife and children."

"For how long? I did a bad thing and the authorities might come for me before I had a chance to see my wife and young ones." José put his face in his hands.

"What did you do?" asked Elena.

"You would be better off not knowing."

She spoke in worried tones, "I won't pry into your business, but if you are running from the law, all the more reason for you not to be arrested. You must blend into the crowds of people who every day cross over into San Diego County from Tijuana."

José sat, still without speaking for fear he would divulge all his problems if he once began talking.

Elena continued, "Don't go through to Phoenix in Arizona. I read that 18,000 illegals were returned by the Border Patrol out of Phoenix each year They pick up illegals in large swoops and send them back here to Mexico. The newspapers say lawyers don't even show up to help them as they do in California. California is full of lawyers. Everyone there knows that lawyers will help them, so that is where the lawyers live."

"A lot of people," said José. "I had never seen 18,000 people until I came to Mexico City. By the way, where is Phoenix?"

"Phoenix is a big city in Arizona and they are tough on our people. To work there, you must have a green card."

"A green card? What is that?"

"A card that is green. It says you can work legally in the United States, but it is not easy to get one."

"Can I make my own? I saw green cards at the drugstore."

Elena had laughed.

CHAPTER 30

J OSÉ THEN CAUGHT A ride from an old farmer to ride to the farmers' market in Tijuana, Mexico.

José set foot in Tijuana in the summer of that year. It had been over two years since he left his family in Siempre. He found numbers of hungry people. He rationed himself to 15 pesos a day for food. On Mar Vista Circle he found someone who told him to go across the street to find food with the Scalabrinian missionaries. After eating a filling meal of beans, rice and tortillas, they gave him temporary shelter as they do to travelers migrating through the Tijuana border crossing.

José had prayed, "Please God, I must find a good *coyote* to sneak me across the border."

After a hot shower the missionaries gave him a place to sleep. He thought of the other 40 or so migrants who were going to sleep around him in the same building. Are they good men and women? Or are they criminals like I am? Will God forgive me, or am I destined only to wander this earth? He fell asleep praying.

******

José climbed out of the trunk of the car. His lungs were deprived of air, and it took him a few minutes to begin breathing normally. He swooped up pints of oxygen by gulping deeply and extending his diaphragm like a baby does at birth to suck in the life-giving oxygen he needed. They had been riding in cramped positions for five hours.

"Never again will I ride in the trunk of a car," José said to one of the four men who rode in the trunk with him.

"We risk our lives each time we come to America," answered Diego, an 18-year-old. "Last year, my brother, Enrique, died in a trunk because, they claimed, the fumes from the exhaust leaked into the trunk from a hole in the pipe under the back end of the vehicle."

"Is that why I saw you make a hole around the wires to the taillight?"

"Oh, you noticed. I was hoping no one would."

"I was glad you did, because we got a small amount of fresh air," agreed José. "Hardly any came to where I was riding, but it was enough."

The driver of the car came back around to where the men were and said to them, "I am taking you upstairs to apartment B4. You will stay with the men in that apartment until you have finished paying off what you owe me. If you try to leave, I will come after you and break your little finger. Don't mess with me. I will come by every Friday to get my share of what you earn. I expect you to work hard and eat beans and rice until I'm paid off. *Comprende*?"

The five men answered, "*Sí*." They understood.

Their *Coyote* walked ahead of them up the outside staircase. A dark-haired man with a short mustache like most of them wore answered the door when the *Coyote* knocked on B4.

CHAPTER 31

FOR FIVE DAYS JOSÉ stood on the corner of La Mirada Blvd. and Leffingwell Road in Whittier, California, and waited for work. There were about fifty men waiting, praying for any kind of job. The ones who pushed themselves out to the street were chosen first by the gardeners and construction drivers who needed helpers for that day. Some used body language and called to the bosses to choose them.

By Friday, José eased his way to the curb when he saw a gardening truck pull up. The agreeable looking gardener appeared to be searching in the crowd for someone.

José pointed to himself and caught the gardener's eye. "Please, hire me," José said knowing the man probably couldn't hear him. He just hoped the Hispanic-looking man read his lips.

The gardener driving along the curb put up one finger. Then he responded to José by motioning to him to get in.

"Get in," the gardener said in Spanish. "I'm Yucca Joe. I speak Spanglish. What Spanish I don't know, I sneak in English words. I'll help you learn some English this way."

"*Gracias*, thank you," said José climbing in on the passenger side of the truck. José found he could understand much of what Yucca Joe said, and he guessed at what the strange words meant.

"Tell me about yourself," said Yucca Joe.

"I have been standing here all week and not one job. More men than jobs. I am newly arrived in Whittier."

"What are you called?" asked Yucca Joe.

"They call me Manuel. Manuel Garcia."

"Manuel, do you have a wife and children?"

"*Sí*, in Mexico. Seven children and a beautiful wife wait for me."

"You and your wife were busy getting that many *hijos*? You look too young to have seven children. Why did you leave them?" asked Yucca Joe.

"We needed more money to live," said José lying, wondering if Yucca Joe would hire him if he knew he had killed a man.

"My wife has been bugging me to hire a family man so he can help his family. The man who has been working for me gets drunk and sometimes doesn't show up for work. Then I waste time trying to get a substitute for the day."

"Please, *Señor*, hire me every day. I am a hard worker. I am a good worker. I will not get drunk and let you down."

"Slow down," laughed Yucca Joe. "I can't promise, but we'll see. You will meet my wife, and she will bug me to keep you permanently I'm sure. You sound like the kind of person she has been asking me to hire."

That Friday José helped Yucca Joe mow ten yards, front and back, and edge all the lawns.

About noon that day, Yucca Joe said to José, "You are right. You are a good worker and what is better, you are fast and thorough. I tend to get in a hurry and am sometimes sloppy. *Mi esposa*, wife, will be happy I found you."

"It is hard work, and I enjoy working hard."

"On Monday, I will pick you up and take you to my two commercial accounts where there is a lot of trimming. I will see if you can pick up the art of trimming. Trini, my longtime helper, starts trimming and doesn't stop. If I don't keep watch over him, he will trim a bush to the ground. I have lost several accounts because of him."

"Perhaps he was drinking and doesn't see correctly when he's drunk," offered José.

"Manuel, he just doesn't have the mind to know how to trim properly. At least Trini can mow a straight line. One time I hired a fellow who couldn't even mow a lawn straight. I took him up to the one where we are heading now—a rich home at the top in the Friendly Hills area. The lines of that lawn looked like a drunken sailor had mowed that grass, but the man was not drunk. I didn't have time to see if I could retrain him. I just told him to get a job in a restaurant. Any place, but not mowing lawns."

"I would like to meet Trini. He sounds like a nice man."

"A nice man, but a drunk. I know where I might find him. He'll be in a bar on Washington Blvd. so drunk he's falling off the stool. I don't know how he walks across the street safely."

After the two men finished the last account that day, they piled all the equipment into the pickup. José noticed Yucca Joe threw the rakes and hoes down in the truck. He had seen some gardening trucks drive by with racks to separate the rakes and hoes and brooms.

"I'll pick you up Monday morning here at your apartment. Trini works for me on Saturdays," said Yucca Joe. He handed José the $50 he had promised him for the work.

****

The men in José's apartment slept around the apartment on pillows and blankets thrown on the floor. Those who had been there longer slept on the two couches. An old outdated color TV sat by the door on a small table. They cooked rice and beans and bought homemade tortillas from the women who came to the door selling them each night. Everyone shared the food in the old musty refrigerator. No one complained when a new person like José came in to the group. They remembered what it was like to be hungry and frightened.

Some of the men went to the nearby *Marketa* that sold food, drink and other necessities for more money than the regular markets. José was disappointed to see how many of them bought beer and drank themselves into a stupor.

"Aren't you aware that you are spending money you could send home to your families?" he asked them.

"Do we care?" several answered him, so he learned to keep silent.

Late that first Friday night he was there he heard a knock on the door and a young woman in a low cut bright yellow blouse greeted him in the hallway when he answered the door.

"Hi, honey," she said in Spanish.

"Who do you want?" José asked.

"I want you or anyone else who has *dinero*, money the Americanos call it."

111

"*Como?*" asked José, not understanding.

"Hi Carmelita," said Dario, one of José's housemates. "Come in. I have $10 for you tonight." Dario pushed José aside and brought the woman in by the hand.

"Dario, $20 is what I'm worth? Come on you can afford more. I have something special for you tonight." The two went to the bedroom and shut the door behind them.

After 20 minutes Dario came out of the room and asked, "Who's next?" One of the other men went in the room and took his turn. Soon he came out and another followed him. Gregorio, an older man, was so drunk he could hardly walk. He went in the bathroom and came out with toilet paper hanging from his soiled jeans. He took his turn going into the room with Carmelita.

The door of the bedroom opened and José could hear her screaming at Gregorio in angry words, "You insult me coming in here with toilet paper dripping from your behind. You can keep your money!"

One of the men told José to speak up if he wanted to go in to Carmelita. "But you have to have money. She will not take an IOU."

José shook his head horrified, "I have the best at home in Mexico waiting for me. I do not want seconds from a woman who will do such things for anyone with money."

Suddenly the door opened and there stood José's *coyote* looking at him with his hand out. He looked around the room.

"Where are the others that I brought with you?" the *coyote* asked.

"They went down to the store. They'll be back soon," said José.

"Give me your $500," he demanded of José.

"Today was my only job. I have $50." José reached in his pocket to show him the money.

"Good. I'll take that." The rough-looking *coyote* snatched the money from José's hand.

"Hey!" said José. "I need money for food."

"Borrow money from your friends here. Tell the other four I'll be waiting at the bottom of the stairs in front. If they make me wait, I'll break their little fingers. And you...," he glared at José, "you better get more work next week. I don't like lazy men."

CHAPTER 32

EARLY MONDAY MORNING YUCCA Joe picked José up at his apartment and told him the bad news about Trini.

"I tried to find Trini on Saturday. He lives in an old trailer in Pico Rivera. The trailer is parked in someone's driveway, and they let him pay $50 a week for living in that junky substitute for a house. Well, the man he rents from tells me he is in the hospital. Trini was walking across the street to his trailer. Yes, he was walking in the crosswalk from the neighborhood bar and some man ran him down. Trini was drunk, but it looks like he can sue and get some money from that jerk's insurance. People got the car's license number."

"How badly is Trini hurt?"

"Both legs are broken. The man must've been speeding and his front bumper threw him in the air. The bumper hit his legs and broke them. He has a bump on his head where he hit the hood of the car. Luckily the car didn't run over him."

"I feel sad for Trini," said José.

"Look at it this way, Manuel. My wife will be happy because you can work for me six days a week, not that she wishes bad luck on Trini."

"I will work hard and make sure you are happy to have me work for you," assured José.

"Don't thank me. You're strong and this gardening is burro's work. I need you so I won't break my own back."

****

José's new boss, Yucca Joe Mosqueda, sprayed insecticide on some of the plants while José pulled weeds in a nearby flower bed.

The new customer, homeowner Hazel Jones, came running out. "No, no insecticide. Organic gardening. I use a diluted mild detergent in a sprayer. It gets rid of most of the bugs. Please, organic gardening."

Yucca Joe laughed, "Okay, I'll do it your way. Do you want me to spray for you?"

"No, just weed, mow and edge. I'll spray the bugs." She looked at the ground and saw some black ants crawling around near their nest. "See those black Argentine ants. I use cayenne pepper along the baseboards in my kitchen. They track the pepper back to their homes. They don't come back again until the next rain and then I pepper them again. They ingest or eat it and get super indigestion and die. It may be mean, but I don't want them inside my house. Outside's all right but not crawling over my food and silverware."

Hazel Jones trotted back into the house.

Yucca Joe laughed, amused, and spoke to José, "Manuel, if you want to keep a customer, always say, 'Yes,' and do what she wants. It's their yard, so let them enjoy their garden their way."

"What if your way is better?" asked José.

"That doesn't matter. If they are happy with ugly, let them be happy. We're not married to them. And sometimes there is more than one solution to a problem. So let Ms Jones have her way. She's happy, and I will get my check the first of the month."

"That is true," said José. "But it still looks better the way you do it in other yards."

Yucca Joe laughed and said, "Another thing. You'll find a lot of our women customers are happier with organic gardening more than they are with using Roundup to kill weeds and insecticides for whitefly and fire ants. They worry about chemicals injuring their pets. She is right about cayenne pepper. Pepper is pet friendly. Dogs and cats don't like the pungent smell and only once will they smell it up close. Not a second time."

****

Yucca Joe was the friendliest fellow José had ever met. And he liked to talk. He spoke English but also spoke Spanglish as he called it. If he had worked as hard as he talked, he could have been rich.

Yucca Joe spoke enough Spanish he and José could communicate. The gardener had worked with the Hispanic population long enough he had learned the naughty words of the street in both English and Spanish.

"Did I tell you the one how I sent a dog to the psychiatrist? This little dog was a pest. He'd "Yip, yip," at me all the time. So I began teasing him. I would chase him back to the garage and he would lie there with his teeth chattering in fear. At least he began leaving me alone. He barked only at a distance.

"One day I got to the house to mow the lawn and the owner came out to tell me, 'Please Yucca Joe, don't chase my dog any more. I had to take him to a psychiatrist to calm him down.'"

José asked him, "What is a psychiatrist?"

"A psychiatrist is a doctor who doctors your mind for pay. So she took him to a pet doctor who worked with the dog's mind."

"Americans," mused José shaking his head in disbelief, "they have money to go to mind doctors for their pets. That is strange."

****

"See those illegals working out in the field," said Yucca Joe pointing to a strawberry patch full of brown faces hidden under hats. "I call them the Round Backs."

"Why?" asked José.

"Because when they pick strawberries in that position long enough, their backs curve to round. They don't have to get old to have round shoulders. The strawberry fields are dying off around here. Once was, we could buy flats of fresh, ripe strawberries back there right off the street. Now we have to hunt over in Orange County to find a place to buy fresh vegetables out of the field. These days I just go to the supermarkets to get what I want."

José was puzzled about the workers. "Why do they hide under hats and wear hot bandanas?"

"It not only protects them from the hot rays of the sun and the fertilizers, but it hides their faces from the authorities, the INS, to you, Manuel, they are *Migras*. Look closely next time and you'll see many of them wear a band around their foreheads to keep sweat out of their eyes. Their hands are dirty and they don't want to wipe dirt into their eyes."

"They are like me," said José remembering his plot of ground in Siempre. "They keep their backs to the sun. I always work faster when my back is to the sun."

"I always work faster when I have to pee," said Yucca Joe. "So I can finish and rush to a gas station."

"We always peed in the fields at home," said José.

"With homeowners peeking out the windows when we mow their grass, we don't dare give them a thrill. They might call *la policia*."

José was embarrassed. It took him a long time to get used to Yucca Joe who talked about bodily functions so easily. "Where do many of my people go to work?" asked José.

"Manuel, many go north to the San Joaquin Valley. Those are the best fields in America, the most productive farm belt in the world. The San Joaquin lies in the shadows between Los Angeles and San Francisco. It is only a three- to five-hour drive by truck from Whittier. But growing cotton and corn and wheat and alfalfa is the most back-breaking work God ever handed to mankind. Except for stooping to pick strawberries. The Valley is built on the backs of farmworkers – it first started with the Okies who came here during the Dust Bowl in the last century."

"Okies? Are they my people?"

"No," laughed Yucca Joe. "They were poor white people who came from the Midwest of America when they couldn't make it farming the land where they lived. Sort of like you and your people who couldn't make a living in Mexico."

"Then I am a brown Okie," said José.

Yucca Joe laughed uproariously. "That is a good description of the problem."

"What is a bowl made of dust, the Dust Bowl?" asked José.

"Well, the best I can explain it, the middle part of America did not get enough rain, so the soil dried to dust. Newspapers called it The Dust Bowl."

"Yucca, if I want work as a farmer, where is the best place to go?" asked José.

116

"Manuel, listen to me. Don't go north to Bakersfield and Fresno unless you want to live in small over-crowded cabins. I get upset at the crowded apartments you have to live in until you illegals start making enough money to move into someone's house. But cabin living is worse. Tiny bathrooms that barely take care of one person, and they may have a dozen or more dependent on it. They get clogged and the odors are horrible. And then how do you sleep? And no baths for those sweaty, perspiring bodies. And the heat is often over 100 degrees. Yep, don't go north."

"But money, are they paid much money?"

"Yes," said Yucca Joe. "Because of brave men like a man named Cesar Chavez who fought for union wages fifty years ago, the ones who have green cards get paid minimum wage."

"What is minimum wage?" asked José.

"Minimum wage is the least they can pay them by American law, except for those of you who will work without green cards. They work you like a slave who will work for food and a place to sleep. Not often do you find someone who will pay more than pennies."

CHAPTER 33

Yucca Joe and José stopped in to see Trini after he returned home from the hospital to his trailer. He had his casted legs raised on sofa pillows someone had taken from the couch and placed on his bed.

"Hey Trini," said Yucca Joe in Spanish. "This is Manuel Garcia. He's helping me while you are laid up. We came by to sign your cast." He saw a red pen on the table and signed his name and drew a picture of a yucca, similar to the ones that grew in the desert.

He handed the pen to José who signed Manuel in crude square letters on the cast. José proudly remembered how Elena Veracruz taught him to print and write:

MANUEL

"When will you be able to work for a day or two to give you some drinking money."

"Tomorrow I will work," said Trini.

"That is a joke. I won't let you work until you can walk," said Yucca Joe. He handed Trini a twenty dollar bill.

"*Gracias,*" Trini grinned widely showing the space where his front teeth were missing. He told Yucca Joe when he first met him and now repeated the story for José, "I think I lost them in a fight in a bar when I first came to this country from Mexico. I was so drunk I don't remember what happened. When I woke up out on the street and could feel, I found no front teeth. Just gone. I looked in the street and no teeth. Maybe I swallowed them."

José commented, "That would be enough to make me stop drinking"

Trini laughed, "Drinking is my only fun. I can't get it up with women any more, food doesn't taste good, so there's not much that gives me pleasure. And my drinking buddies are fun to be with. The taste is the cure for me."

Yucca Joe laughed also, "Trini, you probably can't get it up because you drink too much. Have you thought of that?"

"One is in my mouth and the other is between my legs. That doesn't make sense."

"Okay Trini, believe what you want to believe. It's your body and your life."

"Didn't you bring me some beer?" asked Trini.

"Trini, you know my wife would kill me if I brought you alcohol." Yucca Joe and José watched disappointment spread across Trini's sun-dried face. José was fascinated as he watched Trini's small, dark mustache which twitched for a moment uncontrollably. "But I did bring you a six-pack of Pepsi."

"I like the burning as Pepsi goes down my raw throat, but it doesn't numb me like the alcohol," said Trini who long ago realized he was an alcoholic. The neighbors around his old trailer called him *a drunk*.

****

One month grew into two and then three.

Yucca Joe had a problem. He had two workers now, Manuel and Trini. He could only afford to have one permanent helper. His wife was happy about Manuel being a family man who was sending money home to his family in Mexico.

One afternoon Yucca Joe and José dropped by the Catholic Church, St. Gregory the Great, on Telegraph Road in South Whittier. The Church where Yucca Joe sang in the choir each Sunday morning. St. Gregory's was a busy parish for the working class.

Yucca Joe spotted the priest, Monsignor Ruddy, a kind and compassionate man, who was walking along the wide parking lot.

Yucca Joe drove his white Ford pickup beside the priest and called to him, "I was looking at your flower beds, trees and the hillside. It looks like you need a gardener."

"You are so right," said Monsignor Ruddy. "I have been thinking about getting a full-time gardener who likes to pull weeds and will keep the place attractive."

"I have just the man for you."

The priest asked, "And who is that?" He expected Yucca Joe to be asking for himself and his workers.

"I have a former worker who was hit by a car and is unable to do some of the heavy work I need him for. But he is just perfect for this place."

"Send him over next Monday, and I will see if he will work out for us."

Yucca Joe took Trini over to apply for the job, and Monsignor Ruddy feeling compassion hired him on the spot. Because Trini did not speak English, Yucca Joe explained to the priest about *aquí* for here and *ahí* for over there and to point as he said the words. Trini knew the ins and outs of gardening so without speaking English and pointing with *aquí* and *ahí* they could communicate. And everyone would like him because he smiled much of the time.

After Trini had worked for the Church for a month, Yucca Joe and José dropped by to watch him as he was watering the hill behind the Church – by hand.

Monsignor Ruddy noticed them talking and walked over to speak to Yucca Joe. "Hey, Yucca Joe. Trini is a great worker, except for one thing."

"What is that?" He expected the Father to complain about Trini's drinking.

"He waters all the time. Sure he keeps down the weeds, but he is constantly watering. Just why did you want me to take him?"

"Because the customers complain of his constantly watering their plants."

Father Ruddy chuckled and said, "Yucca Joe, for that: You're going to have to say five Hail Marys and an Act of Contrition. I'm not sure that can be forgiven." Both laughed.

And José asked later what was so funny and Yucca Joe tried to explain, but José could not understand what could be humorous about saying Hail Marys and the Act of Contrition. To him religion was serious business.

****

"Yucca, why are you taking beer to Trini today?" asked José.

"Because I want to prove a point. Trini says *Corona* is the best beer. I took the cap off and poured Coors into this bottle. But watch Trini drink it as if it were *Corona*. I don't think he will be able to tell the difference."

They walked up the hill behind St. Gregory the Great Church where Trini was watering and watering.

"Thank you, Yucca, for the beer," said Trini when Yucca Joe handed him the bottle. Trini proceeded to pull off the cap with a flip of his thumb.

They both watched Trini drink it down in two long swallows. "*Bueno*, it is good," said Trini. "On a hot day *Corona* quenches my thirst better than any beer or water."

"You're right," said Yucca Joe winking at José.

CHAPTER 34

The year: 2007

A TALL, SLENDER YOUNG MAN walked into the office of Alberto Luiz, a worker for the Mexican Consulate in San Diego.

"I am looking for *mi papá*. How do I go about finding him?"

"What is his name? And how long has he been gone from home?"

"He goes by the name of Manuel Garcia. I'm his son."

"And how long has it been since you last saw him?"

"He has been gone for seven years, since 2001," said the young man.

"I will need to go through the Mexican agency in Tijuana. My friend works for Mexico's Secretariat of Foreign Relations, and she is good about finding family members who have crossed over here to the United States. Sometimes she finds they settle near the border and never quite make it over. Or they simply start a new family. He may not want you to find him."

"*Mi papá* would never do that. I fear something has happened to him."

"Mira Sedano is good. In the first part of this year she has resolved over half of the cases taken to her. She was telling me the other day over lunch about a case she had solved last month."

"What happened?"

"A mother came to her because her son did not return home to her as he did each night. He worked on this side of the border in Chula Vista on a visitor's visa. He drove over here to work as a

122

mechanic each morning and returned home to Tijuana each night. One night he didn't show up."

"Was he injured?"

"No, he was in the habit of buying a car occasionally for a little money at an auction and then selling it for more money to buyers in Tijuana. Ms Sedano found this one time he had bought a car at the auction, and when it was searched at the border it had concealed drugs under the gas tank. He couldn't prove they were not his drugs. Authorities threw him in jail. So he could go home to his family in Tijuana, he finally pled guilty. He swears he never took drugs and didn't know about them. Mira Sedano believes him. He proved to her satisfaction he had no prior history of drugs nor friends who did drugs. He was too busy working and driving back and forth to work to get involved in such nonsense. The *Mexicana policia* made him plead guilty and took away his visitor's visa. He told them he didn't ever want to return to the U.S. when he felt he had to plead guilty just to get back home."

"The police made him say he was guilty when he wasn't?" The young man was amazed.

"You would be surprised the things people will say and do to remain free. Come back tomorrow, and I will list the things you will need for *Señorita* Sedano to help you."

****

The month before in May, 2007, Miguelito son of Jose Ramirez alias Manuel Garcia, drove as a co-driver into Tijuana with a Mexican truck driver carrying produce to the USA. The driver stayed over a few days so Miguel could find out information. He was pleased Miguel had helped him drive to the border for he needed his help to carry and unload the produce in San Diego.

"Mi Amigo Miguel, I am happy to be your friend. It is a long ride from Queretaro on Federal Highway 15 to Highway 2 to Tijuana. The drive is long when I am alone. I am glad you can help me drive to San Diego."

"*Bueno*, my friend Arnaldo. I am more happy than you are. That would be a long way to walk or hitchhike."

The city of Tijuana has many undocumented workers pass through by finding men called *Coyotes* who will transport them for thousands of dollars to the land of dreams, California. The undocumented search for the *coyotes* but not so much as *coyotes* look for them. *Coyotes* are men willing to risk prison knowing they can become rich on human cargo if not caught. How often they are in cahoots with law enforcement is not a well-kept secret. The five billion or so dollars sent from the U.S. to Mexican relatives helps the Mexican economy survive.

The city of Tijuana has come of age. It is now the metropolis of border towns.

Tijuana has become an artist's haven, a reformation of artistic tradition. Centro Cultural Tijuana, founded in 1982, as well as inSITE where their art exhibitions have been attracting artists experimenting in all forms of media since 1992.

Once known as a tourist trap where the poverty-stricken converge on the compassionate Americanos to buy their cheap prizes, where quickie divorces and equally rapid marriages could take place, it now shows artists from San Diego and other cities distributing their wares of canvases, sculptures, literature and dancing and partying at the Jai Alai Palace.

Miguelito arrived in Tijuana just as his father had before him more than five years before. He and Arnaldo, too, found numbers of hungry people on the streets. He rationed himself to five pesos a day for food. On Mar Vista Circle they found someone who told them to go across the street to find free food with the Scalabrinian missionaries. After eating a filling meal of beans, rice and tortillas, they gave them temporary shelter as they do to travelers migrating through the Tijuana border crossing.

The missionaries gave him and Arnaldo a place to sleep after a hot shower.

"Will I find *mi papá* in California?" he asked himself as he fell asleep praying that his father was safe.

SECTION III

SECTION III

CHAPTER 35

J OSÉ CONTINUED GOING BY the alias Manuel Garcia. He worked hard for Yucca Joe and paid off the *coyote* who had brought him to La Habra, California, from Tijuana, Mexico. Yucca Joe had helped him write a letter to Elmira explaining why he would be able to send her only a little money until the greedy *coyote* was paid off.

José told Yucca Joe many things about himself and the death of Enrique Castilone. So many memories he had buried. It was easy to talk to the Yucca. He felt relieved to have a friend he could confide in.

When talking about the cruel *coyote*, who got a kick out of threatening to cut off little fingers, Manuel admitted seeing one of his former housemates with a missing little finger. Yucca Joe advised, "Manuel, I think you need to turn this *coyote* in to the Border Patrol."

"You're right, Yucca, but I accidentally killed the man who raped my Elmira. If I turn in the *coyote*, he will turn me in. Then I will be sent back to Mexico City. I will not be able to bring my family here to be with me. You must understand I need to get a place to live and plan for our future. After they are established here, I will make other decisions to redeem my taking of a life."

After that conversation, Yucca Joe helped José find an apartment in a triplex in nearby Whittier where other illegals lived until they found work, paid their *coyotes* and found better places to live.

José rented the extra bedroom of his apartment to two other undocumented young men who worked with other gardeners. He complained that they drank too much at night and kept him awake. Now he was looking for better renters.

One morning he called Pablo in Siempre once more. It had been a year since he talked to him on the phone. He often felt upset after talking to the man who owned the general store in Siempre.

"Please tell Elmira I will soon have the money to send for her and the children. Be sure to tell her I love her and think about her every day."

"I will tell her," said Pablo. "Continue sending the money to me by mail in cash and I will make sure she gets the money. I'll help her contact a *coyote* to help her get to the border."

"Thank you, Pablo my friend. How big are my sons now?"

"Big. You would be proud of them. They help me in the store. And your oldest daughter is the village beauty. She looks like her mother did."

"Elmira, must still be beautiful," agreed José. "She is beautiful, isn't she?" His voice was demanding.

"Of course she's beautiful." Pablo shivered, thinking of Elmira lying in the nearby village cemetery.

****

A few months later on a Sunday morning.

José was sleeping when a noise at the front door of his apartment in the triplex awoke him. He slipped on his long trousers and opened the door. There before him stood a tall, strong-looking young man, a stranger with a short, black mustache. He reminded him of someone.

"Are you José Ramirez?" the young man asked in a familiar Hispanic dialect. The hairs on the back of José's neck bristled. He was Manuel Garcia to everyone who knew him in California. It had been years since he heard someone call him by his real name.

José hesitated looking up at the young man. "*Sí*, I used to go by that name. Yes." He stepped out on the front porch. *Could this man be from the INS or the police? Will they deport me back to Mexico? It has been seven years since I have seen my young ones and my beloved Elmira.*

"I am your son Miguel. I will be seventeen years old soon." He flexed his muscles to show his father how strong he had become.

"*Grande* muscles. You are so tall. And a mustache? Like mine. You can't be my son. You would be shorter, like me, like your mother." José was now dazed.

"*Mi abuelos,* your parents, bought us two cows after Pedro Castillone stole our other two, and it was my job to milk them every morning and every night. I drank some of that milk each morning and each night. I didn't use a cup. I just squirted *la leche* into my mouth while I was milking. I am a perfect shot. Remember how good you were at squirting milk in my mouth when we milked together at night. *La Abuelita* in our village told me milk gave me long, strong bones." He licked his lips as he remembered the flavor of warm cow's milk.

"Is it really you, my little Miguel?" José peered closely at him. And with his fingers he examined the spot on his son's forehead where he had fallen against the table edge when he was ten months old. *Yes, the scar has faded and has moved back toward his hairline.* "The scar is still there," he said aloud.

José threw his arms around Miguelito's slender, muscled waist in a bear hug like he had done every morning of the young boy's life until that fateful day he was forced to run away to America.

"I know it's you, *papá*. No one else could ever hug me like this." Miguel wrestled his father to the floor right there on the front porch and pinned him down.

José lay there huffing and puffing. *I must be out of shape for this young man, my son, to hold me down like this.*

"You are so strong," murmured José feigning more exhaustion than he felt.

"That is what they tell me. I work out, and I wrestled and boxed in Mexico City to earn money to get here. I told them I am twenty years old, so they believed me."

José's thoughts became scrambled words as he spoke rapidly from sheer emotion, "Tell me about your mother. *Mi blessed Elmira.* I have almost enough money to send for her and the children at long last. Why hasn't she answered my fumbling letters? Each time I called the store over the years, Pablo refused to let me talk to any of you. He told me it was not safe. To leave my family alone."

Miguel's face reflected his confusion. Surely his father knew his wife Elmira and Miguel's mother had died six years ago. Miguel had been almost twelve years old when he watched her cross over to join the saints. Surely Pablo had told his *papá*. Miguel lifted himself to his feet and offered his hand to his father to pull him up. He and his father needed to talk.

"*Gracias,* my son. Let's go into the house. We have much to say to each other."

Miguel followed his father and sat down at the kitchen table where his dad gestured for him to go. "Let me get you some food and drink."

"Give me orange juice. I have learned to like it during my long search for you," Miguel said.

"Please tell me about your mother. I still ache for the sound of her voice," José said as he poured the juice.

"*Papá,* didn't Pablo tell you when you called? My mother was dying the first time you must have called. I have been angry with you for not writing, calling… something."

"She is a healthy woman. She can't die yet."

"*Papá!* She had the dreaded disease, *the secret disease, La Abuelita* called it."

"Dying? What are you saying? Elmira is there waiting for me to send for her. She would not leave you children. She waits for me." José could not believe his ears.

Tears rushed to his cheeks as José repeated in a hoarse voice, "She waits for me!"

"*Papá,* my mother's buried in the village cemetery. Only we children wait for you. We live with our mother's parents. They took us in and your parents bought us the two cows and more goats after the other cows disappeared to the Castillone house. Pablo kept me working at the store until a year ago when I trained Francisco who is now fifteen to take over the cleaning. And… and I came to find you. Eleven months ago I left home."

José cried silently, his shoulders shook as he listened to his son. "I should have known. I should have known," he whispered over and over, "Pablo tells me she is alive."

Miguel explained, "I called Pablo on the telephone to tell the family I am safe when I reached San Diego. He always told me you were dead and I cannot find you. To stay home. He became angry when he knew I was going north to find you. I came anyway. I looked for *Tio* Miguel and could not find him."

"I was never able to find him either, my son," said José sadly.

Miguel looked at his father whose head was in his hands on the kitchen table. "Father, I am sorry to give you such sad news. I thought you had forgotten us. If it had not been for wanting to find you, I might have run away to another village. The people call us the murderer's children. Do you know how much that pained us?"

"Maybe the sins of the father are visited on the children. I did not mean to kill Enrique. I was protecting myself when I struck out at him. He had his strong hands around my throat squeezing, squeezing. I thought I would die," José said passionately.

"*Mi mamá* told me you would never hurt anyone unless it was an accident. She told me over and over, before she died, how gentle you are. How loving and so kind."

"She was the one who was gentle and kind and good. God blessed us for those ten good years. This world is a hard place, Miguelito. Some men never find one woman who loves them the way I was loved by your wonderful mother. I was blessed."

"I am the one who should have died. It seems killing Enrique hurt all of you. Your mother was cursed because of what I did," said José. "Over the years I pushed it down in my mind so I couldn't recall the pain of that day."

"*No, no, mi papá. Mi mamá* told me you were good. *La Abuelita* told her in her last days that wicked Enrique gave her the *secret disease.*"

"What are you saying? Enrique cursed your mother? I don't understand."

"I don't either. I don't remember Enrique ever coming to our home. Even though I was young, I would remember."

José's eyes widened in shock suddenly recalling why he had been so angry with Enrique. Elmira had told him about the rape, but he wanted to deny the pain in his memories, even when he talked to Yucca Joe about it. He pulled his hair with both hands. "Now I know how he could have given her the *secret disease.* Enrique was an evil man. He forced himself on your mother. Enrique confessed to me he raped her, but I thought he was trying to make me jealous. I didn't want to believe him... or her."

Miguel replied, "I should have known. She spent so many hours crying. I have so many good memories of my childhood before you left home. I knew all would be right when I found you."

"If I was so easy to find, why didn't Pedro and Pancho find me to kill me?" asked José.

"They are lazy men. They sit around drinking, especially Pedro who won't work. After hunting for you for a couple of months when you left our village, the brothers came back home. Pedro, once in a while, upsets everyone by starting a fight. He is thin and wasting away…no energy. Some say he has the *secret disease.*"

"And Pancho… what about him?"

"He is different since Enrique died. He kept visiting Maria with the limp foot, and one day her father told them to marry. And they did. They have three little ones. He even works some in the garden with Maria. I hear that Pancho will not let Pedro come to see him and Maria. Only their mother, Juanita Castillone, goes to be with them. Every day she prays in the little church and thanks God for Pancho changing his life. She burns candles all the time thanking God for Pancho. Their father, the drunk, is almost dead. The old man and Pedro sit and drink together every day, all day long. The men of the village gamble on which one will die first."

"Which one did you bet on?" asked José with the twinkle in his eye that Miguel remembered from long ago.

"I bet the next nanny goat's kid that Pedro will die first. You haven't seen how thin and wasted away he is. I can put one of my big hands around his upper thigh – if I wanted to."

"I will have different prayers in the future. I thought I would have to avenge these years I have spent away from you, but now I find God's own vengeance in the Castillone family has been at work."

CHAPTER 36

T HE FOLLOWING WEEK MIGUELITO asked, "Do you know how I found you, *Papá*?" He had become Miguel *grande*.

"Tell me," said José.

"I followed your way north. Your goodness went with you and you didn't try to hide. The villagers you befriended and helped told me you were going by the name Manuel Garcia. You helped an old woman named Rosa rebuild her well. She died in her own bed in her sleep last year, but the neighbors remembered you."

"In her own bed...*gracias* to God. That was her wish." José looked toward Heaven.

"To find out where you were going, I had to trade some strange things. I came upon this one farm where they had such ugly daughters. The father made me sleep with the youngest two girls for a whole month before they would tell me about you. By the time they let me leave, I began to think the youngest who is 19 was pretty. Can you imagine?"

José looked at him grimly and said, "*Sí*, I can imagine. He was desperate to have grandchildren to carry on the work of the farm."

"Well, when I arrived in San Diego, *mi nuevo amigos* I met there sent me to investigators who help our people to find family members. I called Pablo and sent him money to mail back old photographs, anything offering clues to your whereabouts."

"I'm surprised they could find me," said José.

"They warned me that not everyone wants to be found. Some come here to start a new family. Others just don't want to return to Mexico. I worried you would keep changing your name."

"I only used the name Manuel Garcia. It seemed to keep me out of trouble. I tried to stay out of sight and not talk too much. I learned if someone has friends who cause problems, it would get me into serious trouble."

"*Papá*, why didn't you send us money?"

"Miguelito, I did send money once a month when I could, many pesos. For years I sent money and small gifts. I always found a post office."

"We never got anything. Whom did you send it to?"

"The mail always went to the general store. It is like a post office in the big cities. I sent it in your mother's name. Pablo had to have seen it. Pablo is my friend. I worked for him and knew he would care for you. He tells me he gave the money to your mother."

"Pablo? He gave us money only because I worked for him. Sometimes he gave me a little extra money to help the family, but he never said it was from you."

"Perhaps he was protecting me by not telling you. He was afraid of Pedro and Pancho as much as the rest of us."

Miguel looked at his father thinking out loud, "Pablo built a bigger store. He now has the biggest house in the village. He is doing well. Could it be on your money?"

"I would not want to think the *Señor* would do such a thing. Your grandparents needed help in caring for you. I have been saving up money to send for you, *mi familia*. It took me three years to pay off the *coyotes* the $2000 I owed them for stealing me across the border. That is a hard story to tell.

"For two years I have been saving money to send for you. I have $5000 ready to bring *mi familia* to California. It is expensive to pay the *coyotes* for a family with seven children. The young children could not do the walk you and I took on our way here to Whittier. Tell me more about the young ones."

"You should see *Josélito*. He is nine years old now. Francisco will be sixteen soon and looks much like you. And Miranda, who has straight, long hair like your mamá. She is almost eleven. The twins,

Leone and Valeria, are twelve. *Mamá,* wanted so much to live to see the children grow up and marry."

"And beautiful Alicia, my curly haired one who looks like her mother?"

"She looks more like her and is a beauty of fourteen years. The boys all want to walk with her or sit with her. I fight them off."

He saw his dad blink with tears. "That was the way it was with your mother, but she always wanted only me."

Miguel interrupted, "I will go home for them. I don't want you to miss any more time. Your Elmira would not want them to be away from you another day."

"No, Elmira would want us all to be together. It will be easier for you to go south across the border, Miguel. I could not go because I am a wanted man, but you can bring the children here. We must buy a good used van for you to go back across the border. We will buy a green card for you, so you can get back across the border when you return. That short mustache makes you look older and the children could be your children."

"So I am told. I never tell anyone my age. *Papá,* how do we get a green card?"

"We will drive to downtown Los Angeles. I know a corner where I can get you a green card."

"How do you know, *papá*?"

"That is where a friend took me to buy my green card three years ago."

****

"*Papá,*" said Miguelito. "I came north to find you because the young ones do not always have plenty to eat. We had several good years of rain and growth from the crops right after you left, but the last two years there has been another drought. I left after the early spring planting. *Abuelo,* grandfather, was to water it and keep it going. But the water in the well gets scarcer and scarcer until the next rain. This year the rain doesn't come again."

"Miguel, that is the way of life for the farmer. Feast and then famine. It's a circle."

"Francisco works for Pablo in the village store in my place. Pablo sees to it *Abuela* has enough tortillas and flour and beans with the money Francisco makes."

"Francisco? Is he big enough to work in the store? He was so small."

"Yes, *papá*. He is a hard worker when I am not around. When I am there, he depends too much on me."

José smiled, remembering....

"*Papá*, the reservoir that you dug dries up so quickly during this drought. The village must use it for drinking water. Very little of the water goes for irrigation. Some of the men and I helped to dig another reservoir, so when the rains come again we will have twice as much water as before. We did not have enough money to buy concrete to cement it in like you and the other men did on the one built 25 years ago."

"*Hijo*, son, the dirt without concrete will wash away when the rains come."

"I know that, *Papá*. I hope we can send money to *Abuelo*, your *papá*, to help pour concrete to reinforce the thick, dirt wall that we built."

"And we will put concrete on our list of things to do to help the village," said José. His list was long and money was earned only by back-breaking work. He would have to find some method for his energetic son to earn money to make that list shorter. Some of his friends played the Lotto to win money, but he noticed no one he knew ever won.

"We will load up the van with bags of cement, so the men in the village can reinforce that reservoir. When the rains come down hard, the reservoir must be ready to hold back all that water."

Miguel said, "We have prayer rituals in the little Church that the rain will replenish the reservoirs in time for next year's planting. For two years the rain does not come."

José said, "I found in my travels coming north in Mexico, the rich men who take out big loans for each year's planting have pain in the head because of the worry. Will it rain enough to pay back the loan, so they can take out another loan to buy grain and seed to plant for the next year?"

"Is it better to be poor?" asked Miguel.

José laughed and said, "The rich man has something to help him make it through the bad times, but the poor man doesn't. He watches his children cry with hunger in their bellies.

"I found it worked better when your mother and I saved some of the best seed for the following season's planting. We never had extra money, but we never saw you children cry from hunger pangs."

Miguel looked at his hands, "We always had enough milk, but since you left I have seen the little ones cry for more food. As they got older the grandparents and I made the young ones work the fields so we can have more potatoes, onions, corn – whatever we could make grow."

"Oh, my Miguel, you have had to grow to be a man while still a boy."

CHAPTER 37

"*P*APÁ, WHY DID IT take you so long to get to the American border?" asked Miguel who would turn 17 on Wednesday. They were sitting at the kitchen table eating huevos rancheros in José's triplex apartment. José was teaching his son to cook some of the dishes he had picked up from Yucca Joe who made the *world's greatest tacos*.

A wave of sadness as well as the memory of the weariness and struggle of his return from the Guatemalan border passed over José's face.

"I was foolish, *hijo*. I caught a ride to the border outside of Mexico City but believed the man and his wife were going to the same border crossing I was heading for. They tricked me. They needed me to help them drive. And then they dumped me off in the middle of the night in the jungle this side of the Guatemalan border. It took me almost a year to get back to Mexico City. Out of fear I spent too much time walking instead of getting rides.

"Then God was with me. I met a truck driver outside Mexico City, and he needed someone to help him drive melons to the Texas border. I was able to make a little money. But the driver was afraid because I did not have a driver license nor a green card. He was afraid of going to jail. He would not take me across the border in his truck, so I had to find a *coyote* to sneak me across the border." José thought it best not to tell Miguel about Joaquin the Prepared and the trouble that man caused in so many lives.

"I did not know our people could drive in the United States and not get in trouble," said Miguel.

"Miguel, this American President has a Mexican nephew and niece. He loves our people. He backs the North American Free Trade Agreement and now Mexican drivers can drive loads here in the U.S. Our men charge less per mile, so many commercial markets make more money by hiring Mexican citizens. One of my friends was beaten up last month for undercutting some California drivers, but he undercut their prices honestly."

"I'm sorry about your friend. How far do they drive?"

"*Hijo*, my friend says he often drives from the Port of Long Beach to Syracuse, New York."

"*Papá*, where's New York?" asked Miguel.

"It is 2,000 miles from California, far north and east of Whittier. At 13 cents a mile. But you get paid to bring more goods back this way, so that would be 4,000 miles."

"That is a long way, a lot of miles. At 13 cents a mile that would be a lot of money to spend. Can I study and get a license to drive those tractor trailer rigs?" Miguel asked.

"Why not? I suspect you could do anything you want. You are not having to hide from the authorities as I am for killing Enrique Castillone."

"How much could I make?" He reached for a piece of paper and tried to add 4000 thirteens. He finally gave up.

"My friend charges less so he makes 13 cents a mile after all his bills are paid. The Americans are angry because they make 32 cents a mile. They are greedy and want it all for themselves."

Miguel shook his head. "I can see why they're angry. They made 19 cents a mile more before our people got into trucking."

"Maybe you are right, *hijo*."

"Americans drive newer trucks than our Mexican people do. Do the Americans have an inspection station to inspect our trucks to make sure they share the same safety standards?"

"*No sé*, I don't know," answered José.

Miguel asked, "Did you have trouble crossing the border when you first came here?"

"Yes, we were stopped and sent back once by the border patrol. Our first *coyote* was taken away. He may be in jail to this day. I don't know. Those officials just dumped us on the streets and left us to find another *coyote*."

"That's the one who threatened to cut off your little finger. Right?"

"Yes, he gave us all a discount price of $2,000 each because there were so many of us. But he was a tyrant who took every penny he could squeeze from us as fast as he could."

"I understand, *Papá*. I ran into several *coyotes* who offered to get me across the border for $2,000. The cheapest price was $1800. A man, a truck driver, who became my friend helped me across when I was trying to find you. I offered him money, but he paid me to help him drive. He said he was happy to help me find you, because of what you did to catch the serial killer."

"Oh, that. I did what any good man would do. The wicked man was sent to prison so he could no longer torture and kill any more women."

"Weren't you afraid of what he'd do to you?"

"Yes, every minute. But I had to do what I had to do. God had been with me that long, so I knew He would keep me safe while getting me to America."

****

Miguel helped José and Yucca Joe mow lawns the next day.

Yucca Joe told Miguel, "I'm impressed how well you speak Spanglish. You're good at mixing the two languages to get your ideas across."

"After my father went north to California, I knew I would be living here some day, so I got a small English/ Spanish dictionary and studied it at night by candlelight – when *Grandmamá* and I could make candles. As I worked during the day I had pretend conversations with Americans. I would practice with Francisco who speaks better English than I do," admitted Miguel.

Then José told Yucca about Miguel's idea of becoming a long-distance driver.

Yucca Joe said, "After lunch I will take you over to my friend's home so you can see his big rig. I think he is home for a couple of days before he starts out again."

The next day Miguel was awed as he inspected the huge truck. Behind the driver's seat he saw: one 19-inch color television set, a full-sized bed, something they called a microwave oven like in his dad's kitchen, a refrigerator to keep things cold, and something Mike Brown called a satellite radio. In the front of the cab there was a regular radio, a CD player and places to set soda cans as they drove along.

Mike explained, "My wife Hannah and I drive together. She drives while I sleep and then we switch, and she sleeps while I drive. We get 5 or 6 miles to the gallon so we load up on fuel in states where diesel is cheaper."

"Do you have another truck I could drive?" Miguel asked.

"No, but we have talked about buying another truck if we could find a dependable man to drive it. Would you be interested?" Yucca Joe translated for the men as they explained.

"Yes, I would be happy to drive for you. I got my C driver license last month at the DMV."

Mike Brown said, "You will have to study and get an A license to drive these semis. Yucca Joe will get you the DMV book to study."

Miguel nodded.

His hands perspired from his longing for what he hoped for the future. But first things first. He must earn money to return home to Siempre to get his family of brothers and sisters.

CHAPTER 38

T WO MONTHS LATER MIGUEL said, "*Papá,* I think it is time for me to return home to Siempre to get my brothers and sisters. We have the old green van that I've been driving to pick up things from garage sales and sell them at swap meets. The van drives well."

José agreed, "We've added hundreds of dollars to your 'coming to America' fund. I wish I could go with you, *hijo,* but I dare not. *La policia,* if I am imprisoned, would not let me return with you."

"*Papá,* I understand. Please, you don't have to feel guilty and explain,"

"But I must tell you. I must keep my gardening accounts taken care of so we can pay the rent here in the triplex. Yucca Joe has helped me get some of my own accounts that I do after I finish my work with him. My next goal is to buy this triplex, so we can have room for you older ones. The young ones can live here with me. I am pleased here in my heart," said José crossing himself with both hands. "I pray on my knees by my bed each morning and night for the safety of all of you. I know it will be a difficult trip."

****

Miguelito found it easy to drive across the border going into Mexico. He showed his newly-purchased green card and his new class A driver license to the insurance brokers on the United States side of the border near Tijuana. He bought Mexican insurance as Yucca Joe had insisted.

Driving across the border with the green van was easier than hiring a *coyote* to get back. He planned to shave his mustache on his return to look less like his male counterparts from Mexico. He practiced the casual manner of an Americano. He didn't know what else to do.

Yucca Joe, his *papá's* boss, had helped him practice by saying in English, "Have a nice day" and "How's it going?" He then told him to work on the American slang sounds, so Miguel had practiced with Yucca Joe's tape recorder – over and over.

Driving days and into the night for eight days Miguelito reached Siempre, Mexico. He found his grandfather, Elmira's father, had died the previous month from pneumonia, called in America *the old man's friend.*

"Francisco, why didn't you tell me about *Abuelo* being sick?"

"You were working so hard to get here to bring us up there, I didn't want to slow you down. *Grandmamá* was worried too many trips back and forth would put you in danger. She told me to wait until you got here."

Miguel grieved because he missed *Abuelo*, but he didn't have time to cry now. He knew he must bring Alejandra, his grandmother, *Abuela*, to California with him. The younger children considered her like a mother, so he felt he had no choice but to bring her. He could not leave her alone. In fact she *might be an asset to help him corral* the children. *Could I negotiate with the coyote to bring so many of them across the border? What if the coyote wants me to leave some children behind? Why not be my own coyote. Why not? But if I am caught I would be thrown into jail, and Grandmamá would have to return to Siempre with the children.* He had a difficult time sleeping. He tossed, turned and worried, awaking with black circles under his eyes.

Miguel piled all of his family into the van and headed back to Southern California. The children were excited and noisy. He became irritable with them, but his *grandmamá*, Alejandra Ortiz Ramirez Armando, calmed him down:

"They are young, they miss their grandfather. Be patient, Miguelito." Her voice was soft and soothing.

"I know why I'm angry. I have something that must be done," replied Miguel.

He had one thing to do before he left with the family for the U.S. He drove to the general store where his *Papá* killed Enrique in self defense, the place where José hit and killed the bully with the flatiron and then fled on his perilous journey to America.

Pablo, the store's owner, smiled a big, nervous, self-conscious grin when he saw him. "Miguel, what are you doing here? I thought you were lost somewhere in our big country." Miguel could see Pablo was not sure of himself.

"It would be better for you if you were right and I was lost. Why didn't you tell *mi Papá* that *mi Mamá* died? He sent you money for us for many years. Where is the money?"

Pablo stammered trying to think of a good answer, "Mi...Mi...Miguel, I gave you money when I paid you each week. Remember I gave you extra food and pesos."

"Yes, you gave me a little, but you made me work very hard and many hours for the extra money. You stole from *mi Papá*. My brothers and sisters could have lived better and had better clothes if you had given us *Papá's* money. Sometimes they were hungry."

"Please forgive me, Miguel. Please forgive." Pablo's frail knees were trembling.

"I will forgive you after you get a present from me." Miguel hit Pablo one powerful blow to the belly that sent Pablo reeling to his crippled knee. "I would hit you in that bad kneecap, but your family needs you. If I ever hear of you robbing someone else, I will come back to give you the beating you deserve.

"*Papá's* parents and their two sons, *mi tios*, are not coming with me. They will let me know if you continue your evil ways, because I will return next year."

Pablo lay there groaning.

Miguel pulled him to his feet and demanded, "Where are the many gifts, more than 100 that *Papá* sent to *mi Mamá*?"

Pablo mumbled, "Forgive, forgive. Your mother died and couldn't use the presents. I gave them to my wife. Please don't tell her. She would beat me."

"I will tell your wife if ever I hear of you mistreating anyone in this village. And it is time you gave some big help to the Ramirez and Gonzalez families who remain here. Look at this store. You have done well on *Papá's* money… the next time I come I want the jewelry *Papá* sent to mi *Mamá*""

"I promise! I promise!" agreed Pablo, beginning to breathe regularly again.

Miguel walked behind the counter and picked up the phone. "I'm calling *mi papá* in California." José was out working with Yucca Joe so the answering machine picked up his message.

He tossed five American dollars on the counter to cover the phone call. "I'm not a bandit like you."

Miguel then turned around and walked to the van and climbed in. He smiled at his family and said, "Pablo will be a good friend to everyone in the village from now on. I'll explain to you more while we are driving."

His curly-haired, gorgeous 14-year-old sister, Alicia, kneeled near him at the driver's seat looking up at him adoringly. She reminded him of his beautiful mother, Elmira. Alicia missed the days when he played corncob dolls with her. He could fight any man in the village to a draw, but it was never beneath him to play games with his sisters. She loved him. Today, not wanting to share her big brother she pushed away her younger sister, Miranda, the child just older than the twins.

CHAPTER 39

FOR THREE DAYS THE Ramirez family drove until they came to the village where the ugly daughters lived. Miguel knew he had to see the youngest daughter, Benecia. She might be homely, but she was kind and had gone out of her way to please him. Miguelito had missed her. *Besides*, he rationalized, *she is the prettiest of the sisters and the sweetest. And she can do a good day's work.*

He pulled up in front of the farmhouse and told his family, "Be quiet and stay in the van. I have to see someone."

"Who? Who?" asked Alicia, his favorite sister, who had followed him around since she was born.

"I may tell you later or I may not. Now hush!" They all waited curiously.

At the unpainted but tidy farmhouse he peered in the window near the front door. He saw nothing, so he opened the unlocked door. Within, he found Benecia asleep. It was his turn to be shocked. Her belly was large with child.

"Can it be mine?" he asked himself. She looked prettier than he remembered. Her mouth was closed covering her buck teeth. Becoming a mother was good for her. Her cheeks looked rosy and glowed from the added hormones.

He leaned down and kissed her lips that parted slightly in her sleep.

Her eyes popped open with fright. Then she recognized him. "Oh, Miguelito, I knew you would come for me."

Had he really come for her? He stood debating with himself.

"Where're the others?" he finally asked.

"They're all working in the fields. They'll be here soon for lunch which I have on the stove ready for them. They won't let me work outdoors any more. I must save my energy for the birth of the baby."

"Benecia, is it my child?" he asked, and paused.

"You know it is. Our love, yours and mine, made him. Here, feel how he kicks."

He hesitated, then felt her hard, swollen abdomen and said, "One more in the van won't make much difference. We are already crowded."

"*Mi papá* won't let me go. He's so excited about the coming child. He longs for a grandson. We must run away and go back to your village." She rushed into a back room and soon came out with bags of things she was making for the coming child.

"Miguelito, take these to your car and put them in. I'll get my things. We must go now before they come for lunch."

"I knew you would come for me. I am prepared." She all but ran back to the room to get another bag.

****

When Benecia's family came in for lunch, plates were set on the table, the dinner was on the stove, cooked and ready for them: Beans and rice and homemade tortillas. They sat down to eat, thinking she had gone to the outhouse behind their large back barn.

Following a hearty meal, Benecia's father, Hector Rodriguez Generoso, rubbed his belly and asked his oldest daughter, Lucia, "Go, find Benecia. She no longer has morning sickness, so why is she gone so long?"

Lucia went first to the outhouse. She returned to say, "She's not there. I'll look in the bedroom." She rushed back, "Benecia has taken all her clothes and the baby's things."

Hector jumped to his feet. "Where could she go?"

Gregoria, the vigilant one, who was next to Benecia in age, said, "I don't know. She has probably gone for a walk. You know how lazy she has been since becoming with child." She was ashamed and disappointed that it was Benecia and not she who was now pregnant.

Cesaria, his long-haired second daughter, shouted, "Benecia always told me she knew Miguelito would return for her when he found his father in America."

"Yes, you are right! Miguelito has come for his child and my daughter. Get all your possessions. We will track them down."

Hector and his four remaining daughters packed up the wagon and hitched it up to his two ponies.

As they rode down the dusty road away from their home, he laughed, "We are going to America. We will live with our new son-in-law and our grandchild. The babe will be born in America, and we will all become American citizens. In America I will make enough money so I can buy husbands for my homely daughters."

His four daughters cheered displaying their misshapen teeth.

CHAPTER 40

J OSÉ, ALIAS MANUEL GARCIA, showed up early at the Miles Johnstone house to mow the yard for Thelma Johnstone. She had a cold and thought staying home from work would protect her office workers. As office manager she complained to her clerks that they should not come to work with a virus. So this day she took her own advice and stayed home.

She heard José mowing her yard and looked out at him. She had not had such a diligent gardener in many years. She said aloud jokingly to herself, "It is a shame Manuel Garcia don't know English. He would be able to get more accounts."

Thelma went back to reading the local newspaper, *The Daily News*, and spilled her coffee on page three. As she wiped up the liquid, she noticed the advertisement on that page recommending the Whittier Literacy Center as the place to go if you wanted to tutor immigrants from other countries. The phone number and address were printed there in bold black letters.

"Manuel is an immigrant," Thelma said aloud. "They will tutor him and he can learn English to get more accounts." She tore out the ad gingerly trying not to get the dampness on the ad.

Walking out the back door where José was mowing the back yard, she waved to him and motioned for him to stop the loud front throw lawnmower.

"Manuel, look here." He turned off the mower to see what she wanted.

"*Yes, Señora*," he said walking up to where she was standing on the sidewalk in gray slacks, blue blouse and blue slippers.

"English, Manuel. Literacy Center." She pointed to the phone number and address.

"*Yes, Señora*. English."

She pointed to him and said, "You go. Learn English."

Later she told her husband Miles about giving Manuel the ad about tutoring English as a Second Language. "I hope he will go to the Literacy Center, then I can talk to him more easily."

"He may drop our account, Thelma. We only pay him $60 a month."

"Not Manuel. He is the loyal type." Thelma defended her favorite gardener.

CHAPTER 41

S ATURDAY MORNING, JOY ENGLER picked up a box of fastfood on her way to the Literacy Center. Today was her first day of training to become a literacy tutor volunteer. She was ready to begin her new life of helping other people who wanted to learn to read.

She felt excited – the first time since she found Walt cold in bed last year. He had died in his sleep at only 43. An undetected heart defect the doctors told her had caused his heart to clog and stop. She spent months feeling guilty because she had not been aware of what was happening to him while he died beside her.

Her two young adult children, now in college, would be pleased she was getting involved in something to make her happy. She needed to regain her smile and zest for living.

Vivian Sanchez, the lead literacy trainer for the literacy center, talked to this new group of twelve men and women wanting to learn to help tutor English as a second language:

Mrs. Sanchez began, "Linguists say human beings make about 160 sounds? When you add up all the vocal elements of every language on earth, you get about 160. One of the most complicated vocal systems is our own English language. We have about 55 sounds. Norwegians have 75. The Kalahari or the Bushmen have more than 145—they have the most sounds made by vocal cords.

"To linguists it is a great loss to lose the sounds of tribal languages. Perhaps 5,000 distinctive dialects have disappeared in the past century. It is estimated 1,000 languages have faded away or have gone into extinction in the past three decades. We push everyone to be alike in our schools so the homogenization process has accelerated the loss of dialects.

"When we teach foreign born to read and write in English, we hand them a great tool to their future. It is better if they learn to read and write before they are ten years of age. It is more difficult for them if they are teenagers. Adults have the hardest time unless they are motivated and have access to an English speaker every day."

"How many young people in California are immigrants with no English skills?" asked a young woman near Joy.

"At least a fourth of all immigrants are foreign youth. We have a great challenge before us."

Vivian Walker Sanchez said, "My husband is Hispanic. He explains his parents spoke Spanish to him, but he refused to answer in Spanish as did his two brothers and two sisters. So they learned little of the Spanish language except for the brother just younger than he who spent a lot of time with his father's mother. The grandmother spoke little English so he learned Spanish. She became angry and frustrated with him if he didn't answer her in Spanish. He then found his days were more interesting when they exchanged stories of the day's activities."

One of those Californians hoping to become a tutor was Joy Engler who listened intently. She had been looking for something to do to give back to her community of Whittier, California.

When Joy had seen the small notice in *The Whittier Daily News* the previous week, she thought, "Perhaps this is what I need. Since Walt died last year, the times my two sons come home from college are rare. I feel lost. Nothing has made up for the time Walt and I had together. We worked and traveled and did community service together. Going to church and Bible classes help with my relationship with God, but there is still a void in helping other people. Maybe I need to be able to work with others, one to one. To make a difference to one other person for a while might be what I need."

Joy had picked up the phone and called the number 562 698-0000 and talked to the office manager of Literacy Center in Whittier, California.

The office manager responded, "The next training as you read in the newspaper will be the following Saturday morning from 9 a.m. to 3 p.m. We will have light refreshments but they will not make up for a nutritious meal. So bring a sack lunch. Come to Hadley at the corner of Greenleaf. We're across from the Doughnut Place. Park your car on Hadley and you'll see the sign Literacy Center and walk in that door. My office is to your left and I'll direct you to the training room."

"Will I need to bring notebook and paper?" Joy had asked.

"You probably won't need notebooks or papers with the handouts and resource books we will give you to keep. We'll give you a pen with our literacy logo on it. We encourage you to take notes and put phone numbers inside the cover of your books. Write notes on the pages as the trainers tell what you need to know. You'll use the information over and over," answered Antonia Houston, the office manager.

"Please Lord. Let this be the thing I need to be content once more. My husband is dead. My children are in college, have jobs and have flown the nest. I feel empty."

Joy did not remember the minister's admonition: *Be careful what you pray for: You might get more than you bargain for.*

CHAPTER 42

José CLIMBED IN THE old black pickup Yucca Joe had sold him and drove to the Literacy Center, not knowing if he would be able to communicate with the lady in the office. The nice lady, Antonia Houston, told him, "*Yes,* I will get you a teacher, *maestra.* Come back tomorrow, *manana,* at *noche.*" He noticed she knew more Spanish than he knew English, but he had to listen carefully because of her thick Americana accent.

José showed up early at *seis* on Tuesday evening. He was worried he might miss his tutor if he didn't get there early. He intended not to let her get away. This was his opportunity to learn. His son Miguelito's friend had told him about this wonderful place on Greenleaf and Hadley that teaches people to speak, read and write English. It was the same one *Señora* Johnstone showed him from the newspaper.

"You are early. *Espera* until s*iete hora.*" Antonia Houston pointed to a chair in the hallway, and he waited patiently for his tutor to arrive at seven o'clock.

At four minutes til seven his new tutor with dark brown hair walked in the door. She looked at him without smiling or saying a word and went into the office to speak to *Señora Houston.* He hoped she would like him. Being with a strange woman learning words was going to be something he had never done before.

"What if she doesn't like me?" he thought. "Did I stare at her too hard when she came in the door? Did I make her angry? She didn't smile once at me."

Another woman who looked about his age, with light brown hair, walked in the front door, smiled at him and walked into the office.

"Maybe this is my tutor. She smiled at me," he thought.

Señora Houston and the second lady with the light, fluffy brown hair walked out of the office door and came towards him.

"Manuel Garcia, this is Joy Engler. She will be your tutor and teach you to read and write English." José jumped up and extended his hand to take the hand she held out to him.

"What is she saying?" José thought, suddenly wishing he had stayed at home.

"*Me llamo* Joy Engler," said Joy nervously.

"*Me llamo* Manuel Garcia." He felt better. At least she used a few words of Spanish. Maybe things wouldn't be as bad as he thought at first.

But I am here to learn English, not to see if we both speak Spanish. He was suddenly confused.

He followed her along the hall to a room where two other people were reading a book in the far corner. He sat down at the table near the door when Joy pointed to the chair. She handed him some pictures.

She pointed to herself with her left hand, "*Me llamo* Joy."

She pointed to José, "Your name is Manuel."

She pointed back at herself, "My name is Joy."

Joy then pointed to herself and then to Manuel and said, "My name is Joy. Your name is Manuel."

She cupped her fingers of her left hand together in a pulling motion toward herself. With her right hand she put her hand to her ear. She must want him to say something.

He pointed to himself and said, "Your name is Manuel."

"Nooo," she said pointing to him, "You say, My name is Manuel." She spoke slowly emphasizing *My name*.

He repeated, "My name is Manuel."

"Yes, yes." She was excited. He must have said it the way she wanted.

"My name is Joy," she said.

"My name is Manuel," he said. She clapped her hands together and grinned a big smile. She had taught her student something. Would he remember for the next lesson on Thursday night? Had he ever studied English before?

She pointed to one of the pictures and said, "Chair."

She stood up in front of her chair. She pointed to the chair and said, "Chair."

She put her hand to her ear. He repeated "Chair."

She sat down and said, "I sit down."

She stood up and said, "I stand up."

She sat down and said, "I sit down in the chair."

She went over and over it while he stood up and said, "Chair."

Manuel or José sat down and said, "I si … down."

Joy repeated standing up and sitting down, "I sit down." She spoke the t in sit precisely.

José said, "I sit down."

Joy stood and sat down, "I sit down in the chair."

He copied what she said.

Then she patiently said, "I stand up." She stood up.

He did the same over and over.

Joy said standing up. "I stand up." She sat down and said, "I sit down in the chair."

She had him repeat.

Next she pointed to a picture of a door and said, "Door."

Then she walked to the door and touched the door saying, "Door."

She closed the door saying, "I close the door."

She opened the door and said, "I open the door."

They practiced closing and opening the door until she was sure he understood. But would he remember for the next meeting?

****

Thursday night José was there early again. This time Joy came right on time.

She took out the pictures she had gone over with him the first night: *Bird, boy, book, pencil, pen.*

He copied what she said. He had forgotten the words, but by reviewing he now recalled them. He hoped he would remember chair and door for next week.

Then she patiently said, "I stand up." She stood up.

He did the same over and over.

Joy said standing up. "I stand up." She sat down and said, "I sit down in the chair."

She had him repeat.

Then she walked to the door and touched the door saying, "Door."

She closed the door saying, "I close the door. I open the door." Then she opened the door.

She asked José to do it. He did as she directed.

As he was leaving, he wanted to let her know he appreciated the work she was going to in teaching him. He said, "*Gracias.*"

She said, "Thank you." waiting for him to say it.

She repeated, "Thank you."

He then recognized she was telling him what *gracias* meant. *What a wonderful word to know,* he thought.

"Thank you," he said, grinning.

****

The following Tuesday night they arrived at the same time. He brought with him a Mexican sweet bread. He handed it to her wrapped in a napkin as they walked to the table of their study room.

"Why thank you, Manuel," said Joy. She did not remember having eaten one before. "I will take it home to eat with my hot tea before I go to bed tonight."

He knew she said thank you, but he did not understand the rest. But she seemed to be pleased with his gift.

They reviewed what they had learned the previous two weeks.

The next week he brought another Mexican sweet bread. She did not know how to tell him she preferred an occasional doughnut, and she had to watch her waistline. Communication was as hard as she thought it would be, but even more difficult in simple things like weight and diet. *How do you tell a man who may never have had to diet what it is to watch your weight. .*

****

One of the well-seasoned, 50-something tutors who had taught English as a second language for several years bumped into Joy Engler.

"How is it going with your new student?" he asked.

"Slow. He really tries to learn the vocabulary, but during the following lesson I have to review and review. It is a struggle."

"By the way, what is your name? You haven't been around long."

"Joy. Joy Engler."

"Joy. Okay, Joy, I know what you mean when you say he struggles. Remember it took two or three years when you were a baby to learn to speak. Don't get down on yourself. It is a slow process."

"And what is your name?"

"Warren Smith. A plain everyday last name from my father. I know. Learning English is an especially slow process, because Manuel never learned to read and write in his own language."

"He could barely sign his name when we began." Joy agreed.

"The hard part is coming. When you try to give him enough vocabulary words and sight words that will help him hook sentences together. I have the same problem in speaking my second language that I am going to adult school to learn."

"What language is that?" she asked.

"German. I want to visit my grandparents' graves in Heidelberg, Germany. It is my lifetime dream, but my German is so sparse I will have difficulty communicating in German to the sales people."

"Warren, don't worry. Most of them speak English over there."

Warren answered her. "That I know. But I want to impress the common people on the street or knock on doors to find out about the small area where my parents came from. They escaped from the Holocaust during the war. They were newlyweds and thought if they didn't get out together they might never see one another again."

"Warren, I read that but for one vote in the Congress we would be speaking German as our first language. Is that true?"

"I wouldn't doubt it. There were a lot of influential, educated Germans who migrated to America in colonial times. Half of all Americans today have some German ancestry."

"Perhaps you can answer another question I have. Is it the Mexican Americans' refusal to assimilate or is there a glass wall between us and them?" Joy remembered lying in bed the night before thinking about Manuel and the miles she saw between them in understanding culturally. Yet she felt a closeness to the man that she rarely had felt for another human being. Was it his innate goodness? she had wondered.

"Joy, it is probably a mixture of both. There are some immigrant wives who stay at home and never venture out to the store without a husband or child who speaks some English. I would say some of them never try to learn more than a word or two."

"I would feel very much alone if I thought thousands of people spoke a language I would not learn."

"The women don't feel alone, Joy. They have dozens of relatives around like they did in Mexico. They are continuing on with their old life. Tortillas, rice and beans. Rice, tortillas and beans. Same old story."

"Then we must get them in here to the Literacy Center to learn English."

"They have to be motivated. We must give them a reason," Warren said.

"They have to think they need to work or go to school. Or.... I'm not sure," she stuttered thinking.

"That is what the next meeting of the executive board of our Literacy Council is going to brainstorm on Saturday morning at nine o'clock. Come join us while you think of some ideas to bring to the meeting. By the way we have doughnuts."

"Doughnuts. José keeps bringing me a sweetbread to each lesson. I'm going to become a fatso."

Warren looked at her appreciatively, "You look pretty good to me. One doughnut won't hurt you. I don't mind a little meat on my women."

****

Saturday morning at the meeting Joy shared half a doughnut with Warren who had already eaten two.

The president of the executive board started the discussion with "How are we going to reach more non-English speaking people in our community?"

"Perhaps we can reach out to children of immigrants who now speak English. Can they help us?" asked Kitty Brownson, volunteer from the city council.

Warren said, "Many Mexican Americans have completely acculturated, so they have nothing in common with recent Mexican immigrants. The now adult children of the second and third generation immigrants from Mexico have more in common with us than they do with their parents and grandparents' generations. But they already speak English."

Kitty replied, "Many of them know little if any Spanish."

Janice Trumball, elected secretary for the Literacy Center, stood at a chalkboard and wrote in yellow chalk:

1. Contact children and grandchildren of non-English speakers.

"What methods will we use to contact them?" asked Harriet Hillman, newly elected president of the Literacy Center.

"How about talking to the teachers at the schools?" suggested Warren.

Janice wrote under number 1:

A. Talk to teachers at the schools to get names.

Joy spoke up, "I'm not sure it would be legal to get names from the schools. Can't we send flyers home with the children. Written in Spanish, or Chinese, or Korean or Vietnamese."

Janice wrote B under A:

B. Send flyers home in other languages; get info from school.

The brainstorming continued for at least two hours. The time flew by for Joy.

She kept asking herself, *José does not speak or write his own language. Even if he had children here, they would have to read well enough to read it to him. What a great challenge we have before us.*

Joy asked, "I have read Mexican Americans and Mexicans will form an independent bloc that will separate America into two distinct cultures. Is there any truth in that?"

"I doubt it," said Janice Trumball. "My brother-in-law is Hispanic and he says he keeps seeing them assimilate with the bottom-line culture. He married my sister he says because he wants their children to be more American."

Warren Smith laughed, "I suspect there were more reasons to marry your sister than wanting children to be more American." Others in the group tittered.

Vivian Sanchez, literacy trainer, spoke, "My husband is Hispanic. I am not. He tells me he feels he has nothing in common with recent Mexican immigrants. He cannot even speak good Spanish. The illegals laugh at his Spanish. He makes so many errors."

Kitty Brownson reminded them, "Dr. Marcia Garcia from Mexico City is one of my students. She wants my help to help her get rid of her accent. Not knowing does not mean a person is uneducated."

Warren began speaking, "Perhaps the Catholic Churches in the community can help us. Once upon a time European Roman Catholic immigrants came here in the 18th and 19th centuries and they had the same prejudiced scrutiny facing the Hispanic immigrants of today. They have now assimilated. It was said then they didn't look like the others living in the U.S., that they would never assimilate. They are now part of the main culture." He paused and then continued, "It comes down to you and me. We must help them."

Kitty Brownson responded, "Children want to belong to the community at large. To belong they will make every effort to educate themselves in trade schools and college. Soon they buy into the American dream of home ownership. It is their parents we need to help."

Joy looked at Warren and said aloud, "It begins with me. What can I do here at the Literacy Center? What can I do in my neighborhood?"

"Enthusiasm!" encouraged Warren. "That's what we need. Go for it, Joy. Walk your neighborhood and tell them about it."

"I need some flyers to pass out. What do we have to hand to my neighbors who might know some people who need help with reading?"

Harriet Hillman acknowledged, "We need to make up some specific flyers. Joy, could you meet with me and we'll design a flashy flyer that will encourage others to join us as tutors and share their info with others who want to find ESL students for us. ESL means English as a Second Language in case you might have forgotten." She looked around at the group.

"I'll be glad to join you two women to plan the flyer," offered Warren. "I do great artwork on the computer as well as on paper."

****

Saturday afternoon Harriet Hillman, Warren Smith and Joy Engler met together in the Clarke Room to plan the flyer to encourage students as well as tutors to come to the Literacy Center.

"Let's each of us sketch a picture or group of pictures for the flyer and then maybe we can put our ideas together," suggested Warren.

"Sounds like a good idea. Here. Each of you take a piece of paper." Harriet handed them some blank, white paper.

They brainstormed a couple of minutes about what they wanted to do and then began their sketches. Joy felt out of her league, but the other two seemed to know what they were doing, so she would do her share. She drew balloons with information in each of them. Perhaps Warren could draw people using her bubbles, she thought.

"Okay, guys," said Harriet. "Here is mine." She had drawn stick figures reading or trying to read. "I'm not sure how to get it across that they can't read."

"Let's get the idea across that with reading and speaking in English come better jobs," said Joy.

Warren had drawn some cartoon characters who were bragging about learning to read.

He said, "Let's combine what we have into a do-able flyer."

"I prefer," Harriet responded, "a more serious flyer with balloons like Joy has with some of my information in the bubbles. You can draw life-like people instead of my stick figures or your cartoons."

"Okay. I think you're right," Warren agreed. "I'll take home these large sheets of tagboard to make several charts to put up at the schools. And I'll make a flyer to run it by the Literacy Team to see if they concur."

He gathered up some things to take home. As he picked up the felt pens from Joy, his fingers lingered on hers as he took them. She looked at his ring finger and noticed no wedding ring. *I wonder if he's letting me know he is interested in me.*

Joy walked to the restroom and found Harriet washing her hands.

"You know, Joy, Warren is a womanizer. I saw him giving you those innuendos and touching. Even if you married him, he would still be looking at other women. It will eat your guts out. I know. I dated him a while before you came. I have heard he still sleeps with his ex wife. They are only separated, but he says they're divorced."

"How sad!" said Joy. "He just lost out on a few dates with a great woman. Me. Thanks for telling me before I got involved."

"I knew you would feel that way," Harriet replied.

****

Joy Engler walked down the hall to the Hammond room of the Literacy Center to find Manuel waiting for her. He was studying a paper. She pointed to the paper and asked him, "What words are you reading?"

He handed her the paper and she read:

alopecoid	fantasist
arête	fecund
asperity	gaminerie
autochthonous	mendacious
cosseted	Cannolis
conundrum	mendicant
inveigh	mordant
invidious	nascent
calumniator	scatological
	serpiginous
	sophrosyne

Joy trying not to laugh wondered, "Where did you get these words? Alopecoid, arête, asperity...." She wasn't sure she pronounced them correctly.

Manuel answered, "Me friend gave them to me from the big book."

"Big book? Oh, you mean the dictionary."

"Yes, Mrs. Engler, the dictionary."

"Manuel, it is okay to learn these difficult words, but first, let us, you and me, work on learning all the easy words." She spoke slowly.

Manuel breathed an audible sigh of relief, "*Gracias*, I mean thank you, I worry about learning all the words in the big book... dictionary."

CHAPTER 43

M EANWHILE SOUTH OF THE border, Miguelito, his family – old and new – and his grandmother drove into the city of Piedras Negras in northern Mexico. There were nine of them, not counting the baby tucked away snugly in Benecia's swollen belly. It was mid-afternoon. They were tired and they needed to buy flour to make tortillas for their beans and rice.

They stopped at a *mercado* to buy flour, beans and rice. Miguelito was so glad his *papá* had made him bring extra money. He did not realize how expensive it was to buy food along the way for so many mouths. Money went fast if he was not careful. He had stopped buying sweets for the children even though they still begged for them.

The *Grandmamá, Abuela*, ran water from the faucet outside the store where they had bought gasoline for the van. She put the water in a large pot she had used for many years. She would take the dry pinto beans and soak them in the pot as they drove along. She would later take rice and soak it in the other big pot for a while. When it was dinner time they would stop along the road, and she would cook the food on a small stove she brought from their home in Siempre.

Inside the store the grocery clerk said to Miguelito, "Thunderstorms are on their way from eastern Mexico. I hear 21 deaths have been blamed on this big storm. More than 45 of the 150 residents of a village south of here are feared dead."

"But it doesn't rain as hard on big cities," said Miguelito.

"Whoever told you that?" asked the clerk.

"*La Abuelita* in our village south of Mexico City," said Miguelito.

"Oh, you mean the *curandera*... the one who cures."

"Yes, some people call them that. But *Abuelita* shows more respect," explained Miguelito.

The clerk said brusquely, laughing, "Ha ha! We don't believe in *Abuelitas* in the city. They tell fairy tales and keep the people in ignorance."

"But I have seen many things come true that the *Abuelita* has told us," insisted Miguelito as he bagged up his own items while the clerk pushed in the keys on the cash register.

"Think what you may. Most of what they say is imagination. Maybe they get lucky sometimes." The clerk took his money, handed him back the change and turned to the next customer.

Miguelito carried the groceries outside with the help of the push cart. He did not notice the lightning in the distance until a clap of thunder hit overhead. When he looked up he saw another bolt of lightning and began counting slowly: *una, dos, tres, cuatro, cinco.* The thunder hit overhead again.

He told his family, "The storm is five miles away. *Mi papá* taught me when I was in California to count and then I would know how far away the storm is. We must hurry."

Valeria, his smallest sister, who was now nine, began to cry. "*Grandmamá*, I am afraid."

"Now, now little one. God is speaking to the evil in the world. You will be all right." She folded Valeria into her arms comforting herself almost as much as she was the child. The other children gathered close as Miguelito packed in the items he bought at the store.

He climbed into the van and started the engine. It seemed a little sluggish, started and then stopped.

He jumped out of the van and opened the hood. An older Mexican man came over and helped him pull the spark plugs. The man dug into the supplies in the trunk of his car and found two spark plugs and gave them to Miguelito who replaced them.

"We are heading for California. Where can we go to sleep out the storm?" Miguelito asked the man.

"Go to the outskirts to a gas station near the eastern part of town." He gave Miguel the directions. "My brother, Mario, owns the garage and gas station. He will help you. Tell him Francisco sent you."

Miguel and his family followed the man's directions to his brother's garage. They drove under the carport where Mario repaired other people's vehicles. There was barely room for the old green Chevy van to park.

"I am grateful to have a place to spend the night," said *Grandmamá*. The glow from the lightning by now was all the light they had in the darkening skies.

A heavyset man walked up, "What can I do for you?" he asked.

"Are you Mario, owner of this garage?"

"*Sí.*"

"Your brother, Franco, sent us. We are traveling north and he said you would allow us to spend the night. I am willing to pay a few pesos," said Miguel.

"I know. Franco called me on the telephone. I'll take 100 pesos right now," said Mario.

"Ninety," bartered Miguel.

"Okay, 95." Mario looked disgusted.

"That is high," said Miguel.

"Okay, 85. No less. But I expect you to clean up any mess you make." Mario walked away and gathered up his things to take home. They watched him drive off.

Grandmamá spoke quietly to Miguel, "Eighty-five pesos sounds high to me. We could have stayed in a motel for not much more."

"It is too much. I wouldn't have charged a poor family anything. This man is just greedy."

"Miguel, I'm glad we got water and food at the *Mercado*. Help me start a fire and we will cook dinner."

"Please *Grandmamá*, the wind is too strong for a fire. Let's eat out of the canned goods this night."

"You're right, Miguel. I won't argue with you this time." As an afterthought, she asked the girls, "Where is the can opener?" They scrambled around and found it.

After eating canned frijoles, canned lima beans, and canned spinach rolled into the store-bought tortillas, *Grandmamá* gave each of the children a chore. When all were full, the scraps were pushed into a trash bag.

Grandmamá gathered her seven grandchildren around her.

"Let me tell you a story about a time your parents were children." They listened intently almost forgetting the thunder and lightning overhead. *Grandmamá* was a great storyteller. She often told the children tales about the desert monster, but tonight was not the time to tell scary stories. She told about the cuddly make-believe friend who visited your bed to help you sleep.

Before she finished telling the stories the young ones were asleep.

She whispered to Miguel, "Fear and sleep make wedded companions on a night like this. I am not far from falling asleep myself." Soon they were all asleep.

About midnight a flash of lightning woke up Miguel. Before he could count to one the metal carport roof over them split into pieces. Sparks were flying everywhere.

He looked out and realized lightning had hit the roof and the sparks that kept flashing around them must be on the roof of their van.

Grandmamá yelled at him, "Is it safe to stay in this van? What must we do?"

"Jump. We must jump from the van. Do not put one foot on the ground and keep one in the van. You will die. *Mi papá* taught me that about metal and electricity."

He opened the van's side door and jumped to the ground. Francisco followed.

"*Grandmamá*, do not hand the children to me. Throw them or have them jump."

Benecia jumped clumsily holding her belly but landed on her feet. Francisco and Alicia followed.

Grandmamá took each child and lifted the smallest to the oldest and tossed them to Miguel, one at a time. He set each one behind him and turned around for the next. Miguel did not know where she got the strength to lift them, but she did.

Then it was *Grandmamá's* turn to leap. When she jumped, she slipped on the wet floor and twisted her foot and landed with it under her heavy body. They all heard the bone snap.

The children began crying as they heard her cry, "Ahhgh!"

Miguel rushed over to her, carefully lifted her up and carried her over his shoulder as he earlier had carried a 25-pound sack of potatoes out of the *marketa*.

"Please Miguel, get the children to safety. Forget about me." *Grandmamá* feared the sparks that continued to flash around.

Still carrying the old woman, Miguel herded the children to the bushes alongside the store next to the garage. "Stay here! Don't move while I look for something to cover us," he said.

Miguel rushed back to the van. The roof of the garage was hanging in shambles. He had to jump so his body would not become the *ground* and electrocute him. He made sure one foot did not remain on the ground. He landed in the van. Searching until he found *Grandmamá's* homemade blankets, he took an old sheet to tie up his grandmother's broken foot.

He jumped back out of the van. As the lightning flashed he saw a large plastic tarp.

"That will be a roof for us under the bushes." He ran back to his family with the supplies he had.

Grandmamá told him, "I'm all right. I feel no pain."

"Good. I won't have to pull it into place." Neither of them wanted the children to hear her scream again.

"Please, let us find an *abuelita* when morning comes. I will hold the pain for now." *Grandmamá* prayed she would be able.

****

Miguel and *Grandmamá* placed the six children and the very pregnant Benecia in the middle of the tight circle they formed under the plastic tarp. They shared the blankets as best they could, so the warmth from their bodies and the blankets spread from one to another.

Ten-year-old Valeria, one of the twins, said, "We're snuggling like the make-believe cuddle friend you told us children about."

Miguel carefully felt *Grandmamá's* foot. He did not know if pulling on it to put it in place would help.

"What should I do, *Grandmamá?*"

"Let's wait until morning when *La Abuelita* can do what needs to be done," *Grandmamá* said. She occasionally winced with a wave of pain that overcame her broken ankle. She tried not to let any of them hear the moan that was forced from her lips.

Benecia said, "Wouldn't it be better if we had the plastic under us so we can sit down? I feel the cold and wetness creeping up."

Miguel jumped up and went back inside the crumpled carport to see if he could find another plastic tarp. None was to be seen. The lightning flashed. He tripped and nearly fell over a large, wide board. It appeared to roll away from him. When the next bolt of lightning flashed, he saw it was not a board but a large, long flat cart-like vehicle with small metal wheels. He later learned it was the rollcart that Mario lay on and rolled under the cars to work on them. It was larger than those used in California.

"Perfect," he said. He rolled it with his left foot while hopping on his right.

He lifted *Grandmamá* Alejandra onto the cart with her broken foot wrapped in a blanket.

"Watch *Grandmamá's* foot. Don't touch it," he said. The rest of them climbed onto the flat cart placing the little ones in the middle next to *Grandmamá*.

The wooden cart had an inch rim around the edge which was uncomfortable to their legs.

Only the old woman complained amidst her pain, "This raised edge rubs my legs, but it's better than the wet ground." Miguel folded one blanket and tucked it under her thighs and legs to prevent more rubbing. The rest of them shared the other three blankets the best they could and sat balanced against one another to find warmth. Their heads rested on one another's shoulders as they slept.

Grandmamá slept fitfully because of the dull ache that by this time persisted every few minutes. It had begun throbbing as if feeling her beating heart.

Miguel slipped into a deep sleep for a couple of hours. Suddenly he felt the swishing of water rushing around them. He responded by grabbing hold of the wooden cart.

He yelled at Benecia and *Grandmamá*, "Grab hold of the sides. Children grab hold of a person on each side of you. Something is coming."

A wall of water from the overflowing nearby river hit the backside of the building and overlapped around where they were.

They all screamed and held on to whatever they grabbed first. The water washed up around them engulfing them in a torrent of waves.

The building had taken the brunt force or they would have all been swept away. As the water hit them Miguel was on the opposite side of *Grandmamá*. Somehow he was able to stabilize the cart and they rode away on it into the darkness.

Grandmamá reached behind her with one hand and counted her grandchildren. When each one was accounted for she told Miguel, "We are all here. We are all here. Thank you, Jesus."

About fifteen minutes of riding the rough waves, they felt a bump and *Grandmamá* cried out loud, "Oooieee," in pain. The cart had stopped. She reached out to push away from where they had bumped and found what felt like a tree branch.

"Miguel, it must be a tree. Help me hold on," said *Grandmamá*.

"Benecia, shift places with me," he said. Benecia gingerly shifted her weight and Miguel crawled over her. He took off his belt and made a loop around a strong branch.

"It must not be a very large tree if my belt can get around it, but it feels strong enough to hold us from floating away. I will hold onto it until it is light enough to see what is happening."

"Thank you, God," praised Benecia. "We are all safe. Our son is kicking me."

For the next two hours he held onto his end of the looped belt and tried to doze. He awoke with a start and found he was half hanging by the loop he was holding. His hand was numb. And he was practically on his knees. The dawn was breaking slowly around them and he could see.

"Hold on to the tree branches," he yelled to Benecia who awoke with a jerk.

"The water is receding and we're up in the branches of a tree. Thankfully it's not a very tall tree."

"How far below is the ground?" asked *Grandmamá* whose foot kept throbbing. Occasionally it became numb which gave her some relief.

"I don't know, but in another hour or two we will have to climb down—I think." Miguel could see the waves gently lapping below them.

"Oh, *madre mia*," cried Benecia looking at the sky above. "I am fat with child and *Grandmamá* has a broken foot. How will *Grandmamá* and I get down?"

Miguel spoke braver than he felt, "I am here. I will help you."

The sun was high in the sky, and the water below looked like it was near the base of the tree when a motorboat could be heard.

"Over here," called Miguel but got no response from the distant boat.

"Okay, kids, Miguel and Benecia," said *Grandmamá*. "We all yell together at once when I say, "Help.""

"Help!" they all yelled as one big voice. "Help," they again yelled waving their arms. *Grandmamá* waved her soggy blanket with the red and white colors flashing against the spring sky.

Over and over they yelled until they saw the motorboat coming toward them. The two men in the motorboat were looking for people who were stranded and needed help. They expressed surprise when they saw in the distance a large family suspended in the tree branches on a large, flat cart.

They brought the boat under the tree.

Grandmamá said, "Take the children down first. It will be better for me to know they are safe."

The two men extended a ladder part way up the tree. They turned out to be policemen and helped Miguel bring down the children from the youngest to the oldest. However fifteen-year-old Francisco insisted on climbing down alone.

Miguel then half carried Benecia down the branches to the ladder and to the edge of the boat.

One of the policemen said to Benecia, "It's a wonder you haven't gone into labor."

"Our son will be born in America in a clean, white hospital. I will not let him be born here."

"What a joke!" laughed the large Mexican policeman. "Babies will be born when they want. You won't have a choice. I have four of them at home, so I know."

Miguel and one of the policemen climbed back up to help *Grandmamá*.

"Be careful. She has a broken foot," said Miguel.

As they climbed down the branches, she held on to each branch out of fear of falling, but her heavy weight became a burden to each of them. The branch she and Miguel were holding cracked as they neared the ladder. The policeman reached for her to assist *Grandmamá's* descent to the top rung of the ladder. She slipped through his hands and fell into the water below beside the motorboat.

Miguel screamed, "*Grandmamáaa!*" and jumped feet first into the water below. He came up beside her where she had come up sputtering. A policeman in the boat rushed to grab her hands as Miguel pushed her up to him struggling to lift her up and over the side of the boat.

The policeman in the tree climbed down and went to the wheel to steer the boat back to the town. This family needed to go to the hospital.

Miguel looked up towards the tree and saw the cart still entangled in the branches. He owed that cart a lot. It had saved all of their lives.

Then Miguel felt for the money-belt he kept tied around his waist under his shirt. It was gone. Only a few pesos remained in a pocket.

CHAPTER 44

MIGUEL WAITED OUTSIDE THE room where the doctor was checking on *Grandmamá* again. The children and Benecia had been checked over by the doctors and found to be exhausted and tired but would be okay with rest. The unborn baby's vital signs were good. *Grandmamá*, however, had a rough time during and after the surgery on her foot.

The doctor walked to the door and asked Miguel to come in. "Your grandmother, *abuela*, is lucky. We were able to save her foot. How she injured it over and over again and will still keep it is beyond me. That storm caused a lot of people to lose their lives. These flash floods cause much damage every year."

"*Si, señor* doctor. They tell me at least 31 people caught in that overflowing river are now dead."

"People build too close to the river and think God will protect them. It is their choice where they live. Not God's. God made the rivers to overflow so the silt would make good growing land for the crops." The doctor smoothed his short, black hair. "The wise farmers grow in the lowlands and live on higher land."

Miguel nodded. "We owe our thanks to the emergency crew who reached us in time." He paused and said, "Doctor, how am I going to pay you? I will work and pay you as soon as I can. My family is large, but *mi papá* and I are hard workers. We pay."

"I can tell you are not a user, young man. Go over the newspaper in the waiting room and you might get an idea what to do to earn some *dinero*." He saw Miguel look down sadly thinking he was embarrassed about not having money. But actually Miguel was embarrassed at not being able to read very well.

"When can I talk to *Grandmamá?*" Miguel asked.

"Soon. She won't be awake for another hour or so. She will have pain, so I'll give her drugs." The doctor left before Miguel could add his *gracias.*

Miguel went to the cafeteria to find Benecia with his brothers and sisters. Earlier he had given her the few pesos he had left to pay for their breakfast.

Benecia had been schooled some at the local schools near her father's farm. She was proud she could read and write a little, but she struggled with the menu. One of the servers took pity on her and helped her.

The server pointed to the menu and said, "The food here on the menu is *chorizo* and eggs. The sauce is great. The next one is Jalisco-style ranchero sauce with well-done eggs. Number three is *huevos rancheros* with American pancakes and sweet syrup. The children will like that one."

Benecia said, "Please give us each one of those with pancakes. I've always wanted to try American pancakes."

Miguel watched the family laughing and giggling as they finished eating. He was pleased when he saw their childish natures were still with them, in spite of their near tragedy.

"Benecia, please take the children to the waiting room after they have finished eating. They can play there and not annoy all the people in here. I will meet you there after checking again on *Grandmamá.*"

Benecia picked up leftover toast from the children's plates and wrapped the three pieces in a napkin, "Here Miguel, even if you won't take time to sit with us, please eat this. You have to keep strong for us." He took the toast and munched on it as he walked.

Miguel took the doctor's advice and went to the waiting room and found the day's newspaper. He picked it up and took it back with him to his *Grandmamá's* room where she was still asleep. He sat in the only chair and began to look at the paper.

The news of the flooded river was the Big Headline. He read and figured out some of the words. It told of truckloads of donated food and clothing that was sent to this border town of Piedras Negras about 150 miles southwest of San Antonio, Texas. He saw the town housed 200,000 people. Miguel was sure it sounded like a lot.

Then he read the caption under a picture, "At least 19 people are still missing." He felt sad for them. He continued reading with the help of a nurse in the waiting room, "The overflowing Escondido River caused flash flooding that damaged about 600 homes and destroyed 150 others. Perhaps 2,000 people are living in makeshift shelters."

He looked at the ceiling thinking, "That would be my family in those shelters if we had not been found by the police and brought to the hospital."

He read on. When he came to the classifieds, he found nothing that made sense. Too many words seemed like parts of words to him, because he didn't realize most of them were abbreviations of longer words. His teachers in the small town of Siempre had not taught him about shortening words. Or he forgot.

Then he glanced to the sports pages and found a double-boxed article about a fight. He didn't understand what was happening there.

A nurse came into the room, and he asked her, "Please explain what this is saying."

"Oh, they are having a big boxing match tonight. Anyone who has the brawn or lack of brains is invited to fight the challenger. Surely you don't think you could beat *El Torpedo?*"

"I don't know if I could win, but I have the courage," said Miguel. "How much money will the winner take home?" He decided not to tell her he had met *El Torpedo* once before – in Mexico City.

"Twenty-five hundred American dollars, it says here." She pointed to the numbers.

"That would be more than our hospital bill. How do I get there?" She told him the location of the Fight Forum.

"Nurse, please tell my family in the cafeteria that I'll be back soon." The nurse assured him she would as she watched him walk out the door.

CHAPTER 45

M IGUEL ARRIVED AT THE boxing forum in Ciudad Juarez an hour later after walking the ten blocks to the forum and getting lost twice. He opened the front door and saw an official-looking office. He approached the young, rough-looking woman who was sitting there drinking a cup of coffee and eating a tortilla with beans and guacamole.

"*Como*?" She asked what he wanted.

"I want to enter the boxing contest. I intend to win the $2500," Miguel explained.

"You and how many others!" she laughed loudly, the way men laugh.

"God has blessed me. I always win," he spoke proudly.

"I hear that a lot. What name do you fight under?" she asked.

"*El Tigre*."

Her eyes widened as she asked, "Where have you fought before this?"

"Only in Mexico City for three months. They told me I was good."

"I have heard of *El Tigre* who fought all comers in Mexico City and he knocked out everyone who accepted his challenge. And then he disappeared. They couldn't find him to finish the fights they were setting up for him. Are you that man?"

Miguel said, "I could be. I left to find my father, and I have now found him."

"*El Tigre*, please sign these papers that I have here." She pushed papers and a pen towards him. She did not dare to let this phenomenon get away. Her father needed a winner again to keep the Fight Forum open, making money. *El Torpedo* was a great champion, but he was getting older and would soon meet his match.

"My name is Alita Gonzales Gonzales Rael. When you leave here, where will you go?"

"Back to the hospital. My grandmother is there with a broken foot. My whole family is there."

"You have a wife and children?"

"Oh, no, I have no wife yet and no children yet. Not yet. I have brothers and sisters who are with me." He didn't want to have to explain Benecia and the coming baby to this stranger.

"I will drive you to the hospital, and we will put you and your family up in a local hotel near the hospital."

"That is kind of you."

Alita said, "Not kind. I want to know where you are so you can't get away this time."

"I plan to win the $2500 purse tonight. I will win for you. And for me." His confidence pleased her. She had met many winners, and they all had this surreal type of faith in themselves. Even the modest ones believed they could win.

"It will be lunch time for the others in half an hour. Wait for me," she said, "and I will drive you to the hospital."

"Thank you," said Miguel rubbing his short mustache and chewing his lip. He was hungry. He had not bothered to eat anything but the toast Benecia gave him at the hospital. He had become so excited on seeing the boxing advertisement he forgot about food.

But now his stomach growled from hunger.

Alita did not notice. She was anxious to tell her father, Adriano Gonzales Rael, about this new contender for the money. Their part of the city was losing faith in the people they had been putting up against *El Torpedo*. *El Torpedo* had only been beaten once and that was when he fought a young man named *El Tigre* in Mexico City the previous year. Could this soft-spoken handsome young man be that same El Tigre? She hoped it was the same man as he claimed. They would get a contract with this young fighter after tonight's fight.

She found herself fantasizing about this young man. "It is time I find a husband. How wonderful to be married to the greatest fighter in Mexico! I will help him succeed, and my father will be his manager. We will buy a rich home, better than my father's house."

Soon everyone began leaving for lunch. Several planned to take their *siesta* before returning to the gym to work out again. The entire city was planning to turn out early to get a good seat in the large gymnasium at the Fight Forum that evening.

Adriano had promised the newspapers that he had several great boxers to fight *El Torpedo*. He needed more than one winner to fight the great, but aging *Torpedo*.

Alita led the way to her BMW and told Miguel to drive. He was surprised. It took a lot of confidence to allow someone to drive a new car.

She gave him directions as they drove down the rough roads. She told him where to go along the streets and pointed for him to drive into a small shopping center. She then ordered him to park in front of a clothing store.

"I don't have the money to buy more clothes," Miguel told her.

"You can pay me out of your winnings," she said. He bit his tongue not wanting to discourage her from letting him fight. He must get hold of the money, and then he could head north to his father in Whittier, California.

She went to the costume section of the store and picked out a tiger-patterned shirt. "We will make you look like *El Tigre. El Tigre* will scratch the eyes out of *El Torpedo*." She had been angry since *El Torpedo* dumped her for a prettier, more feminine looking fight follower. She was hungry to see this new fighter beat *El Torpedo*.

"I must spend some time working out and boxing with the sparring partners at the gym," said Miguel.

"After we get your family set up in a hotel, I will drive you back so you can work out. How long has it been since you last fought?"

"I shadow box for an hour every day I can. I don't usually have someone to box or wrestle with," he explained. "I work out and do pushups, sit ups. I work out each muscle so I can be ready to use it."

Alita looked puzzled. "I've never seen anyone work out as you say you do. And you wrestle, too?"

"*Mi papá* taught me when I was a child to wrestle and to shadow box. All the men in our village of Siempre learn to shadow box."

****

Alita was happy to provide him all the transportation he needed. Miguel arrived two hours early before the fight. He needed to spend some time hitting the heavy punching bag with gloves on his fists. It had been a few months since he had fought with gloves.

"Miguel, leave your brothers and sisters in the hotel room," said Alita. "If you get cut up during the fight, you wouldn't want them to see you bleeding. Your pregnant sister does not seem strong enough to handle it."

Miguel did not deny Benecia was his sister, because he was concerned about tonight's fight.

Alita set them up in a hotel and could see Benecia did not trust her. She decided Benecia must be shy. Her future was in Miguel's hands. She, however, was sullen around Alita and spoke little. *Perhaps she is embarrassed about her homely looks, especially when she smiles.*

Miguel spent an hour sparring and feinting around the punching bag. Some of the men around the gym laughed and pointed. Alita heard one say, "Who is this dunce from the countryside in southern Mexico?."

"Why would he be fighting *El Torpedo*? His arms are too long and skinny."

"Yes, he is weak. Look at him, he fights with the air." They all laughed loudly.

****

The announcer stepped up to the microphone saying, "Tonight the honorable, *Grande Torpedo* will fight the heretofore unknown, *El Tigre*, from the village of Siempre, from the State of Monterrey. He claims he has fought previously in the mighty City of Mexico where he says he fought and won against all comers. We shall see if that is the truth." Many in the crowd hooted loudly.

As he spoke, both of the men climbed into the ring. *El Torpedo* waved his arms over his head and stood on tiptoes to appear even larger. He was a couple inches taller than his opponent, Miguel Ramirez.

179

El Torpedo spoke to his handler when he got to the corner, "This fighter looks familiar."

The muscled Franco Marquis de la Torre whispered to him, "He should. You fought him in Mexico City last year."

"Madre mia! Give me hints what to do. He fights as if he is fighting the air, but it isn't air he hits, but my face."

"He hits and pushes, hits and pushes," said his handler, Franco. "You must fight as if you are fighting with the air. When he pushes, disappear. Cut and run and hit him when he least expects you to be there."

"But I don't know how to fight and run."

"You must," insisted his trainer.

Alita dressed in men's clothes and acted as *El Tigre's* handler this night. Her father had argued with her but as usual lost the argument. She told her father, "If this boxer is as good as I have heard, I want to be here at the beginning of a great career."

In the first round the two boxers touched gloves often. Both found it difficult to reach within the circle of the other. The crowd went wild. *El Torpedo's* fans yelled for him to cream this stranger.

"Hey, you in kid's pajamas, you're going down."

"Take that tiger man out!"

The bell rang: *Round Two:* "*El Torpedo* feinted with a left and then a right one to the left, one to the right, backed away and feinted another one to the right and slipped one in to get a jab off *El Tigre's* jaw." Miguel felt a snap. He was sure it had broken. Later, he would be pleased to find it was just dislocated because of the good-fitting mouthpiece Alita's father, Adriano Rael, put in his mouth when he practiced with the punching bag.

Earlier Adriano himself had sparred a couple of rounds with him. "*El Tigre* is good. But is he good enough?"

Alita whispered to *El Tigre* before he left the corner for the next round, "His arms are longer than yours. Stay inside those arms and pummel him in the body and the face whenever you can. Keep those arms going. *I'm sure you can pummel in bed as fast as you can in the ring.*" She was pleased to see him blush.

Round Three: Miguel used his gloves to defend against his face. For the first time in his fighting life, he fought as if he were unsure of himself. More people in the audience bet pesos against him.

The announcer spoke quickly, loudly: "This new fighter, *El Tigre*, is well-conditioned even though he appears to be too slim. He is strong. He dances around the ring swiftly and artfully; he's smart because he boxes aggressively. Yet watch him, he fights as if he were injured, but it is too early in the game for him to be injured. No blood. Is this a ruse? It may all be tactical. *El Torpedo* is a seasoned fighter. He probably boxes in his sleep."

Round Four: The announcer continued, "*El Tigre* chases *El Torpedo* as if he is angry with him and wants to beat him up like in a neighborhood fight. This is a hungry fighter."

Round Five: "In the last round El Tigre landed thirty-three punches to only four. Has *El Torpedo* given up? Is he asleep? He is absorbing such savage assault tonight. He is being toppled by a superior boxer." *El Torpedo* stumbled back to his corner exhausted.

Round Six: "*El Torpedo* has won twenty and lost one until tonight, with nine KOs. Is he going to come back tonight and knock out this valiant opponent who won't let him hit him?"

Alita whispered to him between rounds, "When we hone your skills, you will become the world champion. We will go to the top."

"*Round Seven:* If *El Torpedo* wants to remain the champion, he is going to have to snap out of the box he has been in. This has been a slaughter tonight, ladies and gentlemen. His long arms are usually to his advantage. *El Tigre* will not let him use those long arms against him."

By *Round Eight*: The announcer jumped aside when *El Tigre* took over the fight, "He is pummeling *El Torpedo* as *El Torpedo* has never been attacked before. His face is gradually beginning to look like ground beef. It looks like we have a new winner in the grand division of boxing. Yes, the referee is announcing a TKO, a technical knockout. Yes, yes, yes it is a knockout in the eighth round."

Adriano stayed behind to tell the newsmen as *El Tigre* went back to his dressing room, "We will go to California soon. *El Tigre* and *El Torpedo* can take on all heavyweights in the U.S. The Los Angeles Staples Center is my goal for my boys."

The newsmen interviewed *El Torpedo* who said, "I tried to fight him in the first few rounds, but his hands are faster than I am used to fighting. I felt like I was feinting …boxing with ghosts. I found it better to let him chase me around the ring. Perhaps I just had a bad day."

El Torpedo's manager interrupted, "The next time they fight, *El Torpedo* will win. We will talk more later. I want to take him to the hospital to have his right ear checked, for it is oozing blood."

****

Alita was pleased with the fight. Her father had bet $100 on *El Torpedo*, and he bet 50 pesos on *El Tigre* in case the favorite lost, Alita knew he would make a lot more on the longshot. Perhaps he could clear as much as 5,000 pesos if the stranger won. He was going on his daughter's gut feelings. She had been right before.

Alita thought she would clear a lot in the future with their new fighter. She walked into the room where doctors were checking him over and cleaning up the winner, her *El Tigre*. She patted him on the shoulder and saw him wince.

"Check him for a cracked collarbone," she said to the doctor.

Looking Miguel in the eyes she told him, "You are my hero, *El Tigre!*"

"My eyes are a blur. Too much sweat and blood in them," Miguel told her.

"With the money you make, you can get your homely sister's teeth fixed and she will be presentable to bring to your fights."

"My sister? Oh, you mean Benecia. Do you think getting her teeth fixed would help her look better?"

"Of course! She could use a nose job, too. She has that rounded proboscis that many of our people carry around in their genes. With a good plastic surgeon she might even be pretty," said Alita generously.

"I think she looks pretty as she is." Miguel defended the mother of his future son.

He was being honest with Alita, because familiarity with Benecia had brought him to love her. He didn't care what other men, or women thought. Benecia was good to him, good to his grandmother, and cared about his brothers and sisters. And he appreciated her loud, raucous laugh when he told a joke, even one she had heard before.

"You've got to be kidding!" said Alita. "Sorry to offend you. You have to live with her, so you've gotten accustomed to her looking like that."

"*Señorita* Alita, Benecia is a good woman. If you get to know her, you will see what I mean." He spoke through his teeth because of the pain in his right jaw.

One of the doctors said, "Stop making him talk. Go ahead and change your clothes. That jaw is dislocated, so drink soup from a straw and try not to talk." They and Alita walked out of the room so he could change to his street clothes.

Alita called from the open door as she walked out, "I'll get your fight clothes and bloody clothes and have them washed at the laundry next door." She hoped the blood and short tears had not ruined his boxing shorts. She waited outside for him while he dressed in his old clothes.

When he walked out of the dressing room, Alita grabbed up his costume, threw it in a bag. Taking him by the arm she said, Let's go to *mi papá's* office. He is waiting for us with your winnings, and papers for you to sign.

As they entered Adriano's office, he told him, "*El Tigre*, sign these papers and I will give you your winnings."

"What are these papers?" Miguel asked through his clinched teeth, as he fingered the three pages of the contract. His jaw was aching.

"These papers are a contract for us to set up future fights. And to say you received the $2500."

"Can I sign later? Give me my money so I can go home," Miguel whispered feeling weak.

"*Papá.* You can see he is in pain. He needs to get that pain medicine one of the doctors gave him. I will take him back to his hotel and pick up the medicine with the prescription the doc gave him."

"You're right, daughter," Adriano shrugged his shoulders. "Miguel, sign this part right here to show I paid you off." He neglected to give Miguel his copy.

Miguel signed groggily where Adriano pointed and picked up the bag of money. He would count it when he got back to the hotel where his family was staying. But he insisted on stopping at the hospital for Alita to pay off *Grandmamá's* hospital bill.

Now he needed to sleep. To heal.

****

Miguel was almost asleep on his feet by the time they arrived at the hotel. Alita had made him take his medicine for pain practically the moment she bought it for him. Alita tucked Miguel into his bed and left. She planned to return in the morning to continue their relationship both business and personal.

Alita told the family, "You should have seen Miguel box. He beat *El Torpedo* who lets no one beat him. Here is the money he won." She handed the money to *la Grandmamá* and watched the old woman's eyes widen in surprise and pleasure at seeing the $2500 in American money.

Unknown to Miguel, his *Grandmamá* and Benecia used the phone and called the garage to see how things had fared with the garage and their old green van.

The owner, Juan Franco Rosales, told *Grandmamá*, "Your van is ready for you. I put in an alternator, air-dried the engine and all the parts for you. It drives around the courtyard. Will you pick it up today?" He didn't tell her about the soggy clothing still in the van.

"We will pick it up tomorrow morning," *Grandmamá* said. She had no idea how they would pay for the repairs. She knew much of Miguel's money was gone. Yet she was confident Miguel would know what to do, because they needed the van to get across the border and to Whittier, California, where her beloved son-in-law José now lived.

Miguel woke up before it was light. It was so dark he thought at first he was blind. *Grandmamá* who was sleeping nearby on a couch said, "Miguel, I hear you stirring. Are you awake?"

"Yes, *Grandmamá*. I feel like a truck ran over me."

"Yes, you look like a truck hit you."

"Let me sleep some more." Miguel was out like *El Torpedo* had KO'd him, when in fact he had knocked out *El Torpedo*.

Grandmamá and Benecia had counted the money. When she counted it after everyone was asleep, there was $2400 in the bag. The young *señorita* had told her there was $2500, but *Grandmamá* was not going to quibble about $200 when there was so much.

She gave Benecia $1300 and told her to call the garage which she did.

Benecia quietly dressed and used the telephone to call a taxi, "I want to go to Mario's Garage."

"Where?" she asked listening to the operator, "Oh, outside the city."

Within fifteen minutes she met the taxi downstairs. First, ahe drove to the hospital and gave them $1,000.

An hour later she was back at the hotel with the van. She was a good driver, she made it back without running over child or dog in the almost empty streets. Mario had charged her 200 pesos. He was surprised she had the money and took it without comment.

Benecia rushed into the apartment and said, "Come on children. Let's get packing." While they packed, she went to the manager of the hotel and paid him the $44 they owed for the room.

When they had everything in the van, Benecia gently spoke to Miguel, "Wake up, *mi* almost *esposo*. Your van is downstairs and we will be driving to America." *Grandmamá* took the warm blankets from Miguel's bed and asked Francisco to carry them to the van. She laid $20 on the dresser to cover the cost of the blankets.

Miguel slowly put on his clothes and stood up. He leaned on Francisco and Benecia while they walked him down the stairs. They opened the sliding door of the van, and he lay down on the floor behind the driver's seat.

Benecia said to the six children who were tucked into the corners, "Don't touch Miguelito. He is hurting from the fight."

Benecia drove the van. It was like back home with her *papá*. He often let her drive his very old pickup that broke down every other day. With a wrench and a screwdriver he had taught her to fix anything mechanical.

She looked at Miguel's 14-year-old sister, Alicia, wondering how she could become better friends with her. Alicia seemed distant as though she was jealous of her, even though Benecia went out of her way to include her in anything they did. Alicia had the fresh bloom of youth. She was going to be a beautiful woman.

Benecia smiled thinking, "I am lucky to have someone like Miguel to love me. He could have any beautiful girl he wants, but he wants me and our baby." She felt warm and loved. She would do all she could to deserve such a family.

CHAPTER 46

JOY HAD BEEN TUTORING José Ramirez about two months when she taught him *husband and wife, mother and father, daughters and sons.* She wanted to teach him the words for the family. Then she wanted to show the difference between husband and a friend. She knew that friend is *amigo* for a male friend and *amiga* for a female friend. The o meant male and the a meant female.

She held up the flash cards she had made.

She showed him the husband and the friend cards. She showed him the mother and father cards. She showed him the daughter and son cards.

Joy pointed to herself to show she had two sons. José smiled a big smile. She held up two fingers to show two sons and no fingers to show no daughters.

"I have two sons and no daughters," she said. He put up two fingers on one hand and showed no fingers on the other hand. She could see the calluses on his hands letting her know he worked hard.

She motioned with her hand towards him, "You have two daughters and two sons." She really didn't know how many children he had.

"No, no," he said. "I have four sons and three daughters."

She held up four fingers to show four sons and three fingers to show three daughters. He copied her.

"Very good, Manuel. You have seven children in all."

"Very good, Joy. You have two children in all."

Joy was pleased because he was so good at mimicking her. When he copied her so carefully she noticed he usually remembered for the next lesson.

"I am Joy Engler. I am a mother. I am a daughter. I am a sister. I have two brothers." She spoke slowly enunciating clearly.

"I am Manuel Garcia. I am a ..." He hesitated.

"You are a father."

"You are a father," he said.

"No, you say, 'I am a father.'"

"I am a father."

"Yes, yes," she said excitedly.

Then she said, "You are a father. You are a son. You are a brother."

"I am a father. I am a son. I am a bro...ther," he answered.

"Good, good." She smiled broadly while rubbing her reddish-brown hair out of her eyes.

"Good. I am a good," he said.

"Manuel, good is an adjective. Brother is a noun. Never use a in front of an adjective. Say, I am good. I am a brother."

"I am good. I am a brother." She printed on a paper to show him. She realized many people learn fast if they learn to speak and print at the same time. And they learn to read while learning to print.

"Good. Good," she said.

She showed him the cards *brother and sister*. "You have how many brothers and sisters?" she asked.

He looked puzzled again.

"Mother, father. Sons, daughters." She showed the cards. She showed cards with pictures of two girls and two boys.

"Brothers." She held up the pictures of the two boys and pointed to them. "Sisters." She held up the pictures of the two girls.

"I have two sisters. I have no brothers." She shook her head.

"You have... sisters?"

He smiled understanding, "I have three sisters."

"You have ... brothers?"

"I have three brothers."

She pointed to the table, motioned with her hand and said, "Manuel, please bring me a cup of coffee."

He went to the table but stopped puzzled.

She walked over to the table and pointed to a cup and to the coffee. He smiled and poured her a cup of coffee.

She said, "I like one teaspoon of sugar in it." She picked up a plastic spoon and poured one teaspoon of sugar in the spoon, dumped it in the coffee and stirred it.

Manuel beamed. She could tell he was pleased.

"Now pour yourself a cup of coffee." She pointed to the cup, to the coffee and to him motioning that he should drink.

"Yes, yes," he said. He fixed his coffee with no sugar and made a face when he drank it. She laughed, and he laughed.

"I don't think you have had coffee before." She got a package of creamer and put it in his coffee. He tasted it.

"Good," he said.

She showed him the creamer and said, "Creamer."

José repeated, "Creamer."

"What kind of work do you do?" she asked. "Work?"

"Work?"

"I am a tutor. You are a ...?"

"Tutor?" he asked.

"Tutor, maestra." She pointed to the things they had been doing and to herself.

"I am a ..." He stood up and acted like he was pushing a lawnmower.

"I see. You are a gardener."

"I am a gardener," he said.

"I am a tutor. You are a gardener," she said slowly.

José asked, "Money. How much?"

Joy laughed, "I am a volunteer. I do not get paid any money. No money." She shook her head.

He looked surprised. "No money?"

She repeated, "No money."

"Much work." He was puzzled. "No money?"

"What kind of work do you do?" asked Joy.

"I am a gardener." He showed how he pushed a lawnmower by standing up and pretended to push the lawnmower.

"I need a gardener. What do you charge?" Joy asked.

"Charge?" José asked.

"Money. How much?"

"For you. *Nada*. No money."

"*Nada*?" It was her turn to be puzzled. She was used to giving and not taking.

José leaned over and patted her on the shoulder and told her, "*Gracias*." He made her feel warm all over. Comfortable. She could tell he felt the same.

We are friends.

CHAPTER 47

I T WAS DARK WHEN the Ramirez family arrived a few hours from the Tecate border crossing, after that two hours to San Diego. Miguel had relieved Benecia from driving after two days from leaving the hotel. He now wondered how they would cross. Miguel stopped at a market and went in to buy some food with the boys. Benecia went to the restroom so she and Alicia and the little girls could use the restroom and wash up.

Benecia then hurried back to the van to help *Grandmamá* walk on the crutches the nurse at the hospital taught her to use.

"Oooh! My arms are sooo sore," complained the old woman.

"I'm happy you can walk," sympathized Benecia.

Soon they were all back in the van eating some of the Mexican sweetbreads Miguel bought for them. He was feeling better. His body was young and strong and healing quickly. Although he had lost weight from drinking soup through a straw, he was now able to chew soft food with his healing jaw. *Grandmamá* offered to chew some meat for him, but he refused thanking her, "That's okay, *Grandmamá*. I have to learn to chew for myself."

They all laughed.

Miguel looked out and saw a man lurking around the van. He called out the van window to him, "Green cards. Where do we get green cards?"

"I have a friend who will sell you green cards," the shady-looking man said picking at his short, black mustache. "Follow me. I have the silver pickup over there." Miguel strained his eyes in the dim light from the market. He looked at the pickup. It looked more rusty than silver.

When they got to the end of the pavement, they kept driving on a hard, dirt road.

The men who lived in a small group of shacks sold Miguel green cards for all of them. The green card Miguel bought in Los Angeles had disappeared along with the money and wallet he had lost in the rising waters.

"Remember," said one man, "Drive to the Tijuana border. You have a better chance of fooling the border agents with these green cards. Thousands of people cross the border there."

"Tijuana," said Miguel, suddenly tired. "Tijuana is a long drive from here."

****

Light filtered into the van when the children and *Grandmamá* stirred.

Grandmamá looked around and counted the children as was her habit. Miguel had been driving for several hours toward the Tijuana border.

"Miguel," she cried. "Where is Alicia?"

He paled. "With you. Back there with you."

Francisco expressed their fears, "No, she's back at the restroom. We left her there. I saw her go in after the little ones went in with *Grandmama*."

Miguel turned the van around. It would be a long drive to return for his sister, and they would be using up precious gas. He had no choice. However, they could never leave one of their own behind. He drove faster, often breaking the speed limit. No longer did he feel his exhaustion.

Almost six hours later a policeman pulled Miguel over for speeding. They were not far from their destination.

"Please sir," said Miguel, "I'm sorry. Forgive me. We left my sister, Alicia, behind when she went to the restroom. It was dark and we were tired and no one counted each child. Please help us?" His voice was pleading.

"Please, please," interrupted the *Grandmamá*. "My precious Alicia is not with us. Can you guide us there and help us get her?"

"Come. I'll help," said the policeman. "Follow me."

He drove the police car even faster than Miguel had been driving. He put the red flasher on. They arrived 20 minutes later at the gas station store.

Miguel jumped out of the van after pulling to a fast stop beside the police car. The policeman followed him into the market.

"My sister. We left her here by mistake last night. Where is she?"

The clerk looked up, "She was here for a few minutes, but when I left for home she was no longer around. I assumed she went with you."

The policeman stepped up close to the man and put his face in the clerk's face, "What have you done with her?"

"She went with her family, I thought," he said, beginning to shake.

"She went with those people? This is her family. What did you do with her?"

"There was a man here who was speaking to her when I went home. I thought they must be family. So I left."

Miguel yelled at him, "You mean you left a fourteen-year-old girl talking to a strange man. You are a mad man."

The policeman interrupted, "Who was the man? What is his name?"

"I think his name is Franco. Yes, I hear people calling him when he comes in here for beer. He doesn't live around here but often stops in to buy drinks for the girls he has with him."

"Girls? With him?" stuttered Miguel.

"You mean he's a seller of women?" said the officer in a threatening tone.

"Yes, sir. I suspect that's what happens to the girls." He was afraid to say the words for fear the cop would suspect he got a percentage of the money.

Miguel's eyes popped out at the man, "You left my sister with that man!"

"Yes, I'm afraid so. I didn't think...."

Miguel looked at the policeman. "What do we do? Can we follow them? How do we get her back?"

"That is what I am thinking. He must be taking her to one of the border towns." He turned to the clerk and said loudly in his most vicious tone, "Where do you hear this man sells his girls?"

"I hear him bragging he takes them to Tijuana and there he sells the women to *coyotes* who take them across the border. Then they sell them to men who use them for prostitution. The young girls bring them more money."

Miguel was in shock. "You mean Alicia will be sold for sex?" His sister was not only beautiful, but a virgin and would be in great demand. He swallowed hard, feeling strangely sick to his stomach. He stepped on the gas and went back the way they had come.

Before long he pulled the van to the side of the road, got out and threw up.

CHAPTER 48

M EANWHILE ALICIA HAD BEEN stashed in the back of a camper shell bolted onto a pickup truck. There were six other girls in the truck. Several were whimpering, now without tears. They were frightened wondering what was going to happen to them. One of the three men had locked them in the camper and would not let them out even to go to the toilet. He had given them a bucket and told them to use it.

Every once in a while, the truck stopped. They heard the man talking and then another young girl would be pushed in with them. Two more were picked up after Alicia was shoved in the pickup with four girls.

When the driver stopped at a grocery store to get gas, he got them each a drink with lots of ice.

"Here's something to drink," he said compassionately while opening the door a crack to hand them the box with seven cups. The girls drank ravenously. Then they nurtured the ice along not knowing if they would get more liquid to drink.

"I don't want these men to do bad things to me," sobbed a blondish-looking girl to the others.

"Don't be a baby," said the oldest of the girls, a long dark-haired, attractive girl about eighteen. "They will sell us for maids—to clean houses. When we make enough money, then we can look for a rich husband."

"What do men do, when they rape you?" asked a plain, dark-skinned girl about Alicia's age. She had long black braids.

"They have sex with you, that's what," said the dark-haired eighteen-year-old. "They put it in you." She grimaced and looked away.

"That is the way to have babies," said Alicia, looking puzzled. "Our cow has a calf every year that way."

The first girl began crying louder. "Please, I want my *mamá*." Then the eighteen-year-old wrapped her arms around her quieting her down.

Alicia told the girls, "My family drove off without me. My brother, Miguel, must have thought I was in the van with them. They will be back, and they will come hunting for me."

"How will they find us?" asked a red-haired Mexican girl who looked about sixteen.

"She's right," said another girl about the same age. "He won't know how to find us."

"You don't know my brother, Miguel. He loves me. He never gives up."

"I hope you're right," said the redhead to Alicia.

Unknown to the girls and Dario, the driver of the pickup, Miguel's van passed them returning to the market. Dario continued driving an hour towards the outskirts of Tijuana.

Dario stopped the truck and camper in front of a rundown house in Tijuana. He knocked on the door and spoke with the man who answered. The girls watched out the camper window where they were captives and tried to hear what the men were saying. They heard only mumbled conversation. The man at the door had long, straight black hair that reminded one of the girls of pictures of Indians in Southern Mexico called Chiapas.

Soon both men came to the pickup and climbed in the front and continued driving. About 20 minutes later they stopped at another house, a rich-looking house, and both men went to the door and knocked.

Dario looked back at the camper shell and saw the girls looking out. He screamed at them, "Get back to your seats! This is not your busness!"

The girls jumped back down to where they had been sitting on the floor except for Alicia who continued watching.

Dario glared at her until she, too, sat down. He turned back to speak with the man who came to the door in answer to their knocking.

"Be quiet, Dario. The neighbors don't want to know about your business," said the man who answered the door.

"I don't want the *puntas* seeing where we are," said Dario.

"Don't worry about the girls. They frighten easily. By the time we are through with them they will be afraid to tell anything they know."

The first man with the long, straight Indian style hair took the many bills of money the gangster handed them. He counted out some and handed the rest to Dario.

A new man came to the door and walked with Dario to the back of the camper shell. He carried a long rope and as Dario pushed each girl out the door to the ground, he tied her wrists together and then tied her to the next girl as she fell out onto the ground.

Dario complained, "Don't rough these girls up and bruise them. I'll be blamed by the others. They know I never hurt my girls. I bring them to you in top condition."

The Indian laughed, "Except for that one. I remember her."

"Oh, the blonde one," said Dario. "She tried to escape, and I had to hit her. It wasn't my fault it broke her jaw. She should have obeyed me."

It was Alicia's turn to be pulled out of the camper. She heard the men talking, so she lowered her eyes trying not to show her anger at being touched. She did not want a broken jaw. She heard the other girls talk about the bad things that could be done to women by strange men, but she still didn't know much. Her *Grandmamá* told her about her periods which started three months ago. She had watched the goats and knew how babies came. She blinked back tears of anger and fear. Alicia was determined not to let them see she had feelings. She hoped her time to escape would come.

****

The girls were taken to a five-year-old Ford pickup truck that appeared to be hauling produce across the border.

Dario laughed, "The produce stinks so much the border guards don't want to stir through it." He then helped place the girls in boxes underneath the smelly produce. The fumes from the trucks, cars and vegetables at the Tijuana border made the young women gag and cough. They had been ordered not to cough or make noise or they would be raped and killed by the American border guards who would take them.

Alicia felt sick to her stomach from the fumes of the rotting vegetables by the time they had been checked and waved safely across the border. She fought desperately to swallow. *What will they do to me if I throw up in this box?* She willed herself to swallow the sensation away. She had felt braver when she confronted the bad men, but she became fearful when they hid her away, alone. She knew the other girls were nearby, but what could they do to help? They feared for their lives.

After riding a couple of hours to the south side of San Diego, California, the Ford pulled to a stop among a stand of thick trees. The three men riding in the pickup pulled the seven girls out of their boxes and let them breathe fresh air.

"*Gracias*," said all the girls. Alicia looked at the three men and ducked her head when she saw the familiar face of a man from her village. She was ashamed and did not want him to report to her friends what had happened to her.

The 18-year-old in a teasing manner asked one of the men, "Would you like to take me as your wife? I'll cook and clean for you. And you can buy me some nice clothes."

He laughed, "I already have a wife, but let me try you out to see if I might trade her for you." He told the other men, "We'll be back in a minute. Watch the other girls so they don't get ideas."

"Don Blanco, I don't think you should be using the girl," said the short, slender Hispanic driver, Dario, who held a gun on the girls. His partner stood by eyeing the young women.

"They want virgins. It's obvious this one is not a virgin," said Don Blanco calling back to the two men as he disappeared with the 18-year-old.

The man without a gun said, "As my name is Alberto Castillone, this one right here doesn't look like a virgin either. I'll take her," and he reached for Alicia.

"Alberto, leave her alone. She's pretty, but that doesn't mean she's not a virgin. And, and she's young."

Alberto grabbed Alicia by both arms dragging her to the cab of the pickup. He forced her up onto the front seat of the pickup and ripped off her brown-stained, old panties.

"What is your name, little one?" he asked.

"Alicia. Don't hurt me, please."

"Well, little Alicia. You remind me of a pretty little girl from my village. Haven't you done this before?"

"No, *señor*. I am a good girl."

"A virgin. My lucky day!"

"Please, I'm a good girl."

"You'll enjoy what I'm doing to you." He lowered his voice to a whisper, "I know I will enjoy it." He spoke maliciously, unzipping his pants, as he leaned down on her trying to kiss her mouth. She moved away so he kissed her ear.

She kept whispering, "I'm a good girl, I'm a good girl." He forced himself into her, and then she screamed. And screamed. Then silence.

The other girls sitting on the ground behind the pickup were quiet, their faces pale with fear. Would they be next?

CHAPTER 49

GRANDMAMÁ, MIGUEL, AND BENECIA stopped for a prayer in a roadside park and to feed the children some tacos they bought at a Tijuana roadside stand.

"Please God," said Miguel, "take us into the land our *papá* promised us. We want to be Californians. And please oh God, help Alicia to be taken into California so we can find her."

Benecia felt uncomfortable and refused to eat more than a bite of taco meat. "The greasy aftertaste of the meat must have upset my stomach," she thought. She decided not to tell anyone because she didn't want to delay their crossing the border.

It would soon be time for them to get in one of the long lines to cross the American border into California. Benecia, wearing a new, pretty maternity outfit, sat in the front seat opposite Miguel. With all the excitement, he didn't notice her looking pale. Miguel had shown her how to pull her hair behind her head in two ponytails like girls wore at the beach near Pier 14 at Huntington Beach. He even gave her a razor like his to shave her legs and under her arms. *Grandmamá* shaved, too, with a lot of complaining.

"Perhaps it will make you look more *Americana*," he told her. He had shaved his mustache two weeks before and his upper lip had browned with a tan from the sun since then. He looked at each one approvingly. "I think we are ready."

Grandmamá said, "I will sit in the back, pretending to be asleep."

He had spent the last two weeks at each meal teaching them all to say, "Have a nice day" and "How are you doing?" Yucca Joe had told him over and over again that those are the two things you need to know to get along in America."

And whenever one of the kids joked with him, Miguel joked back and always said, "Gotcha!" in English. And then they would laugh hilariously.

Miguel was compassionate to the many Mexican children who tried to sell them trinkets along the lengthy lines as they waited their turn to get through the border. At first, he bought one from each child who came to their window. It attracted other children. Soon there were so many children pounding on his windows that he finally had to say, "No. No more *dinero*." He needed to keep money he had for food and gas if they crossed the border safely. Miguel had never prayed silent prayers so intently in his life. Sweat rolled down his neck, and he could feel the moisture on the backs of his arms and hands.

Benecia felt worse. Her abdomen tightened as a slight dampness spread between her legs under her dress. "What am I to do?" she worried. "My baby must not come now."

They finally approached the border agents who were letting people through the line or if a vehicle and its occupants looked suspicious, they would motion the car or truck to open the trunk for a search.

It was now their turn. Everyone was eerily quiet in the back of the van. No sounds of children's voices or laughter as was normal.

Miguel showed the agent his driver license. The border agent looked in at Miguel and Benecia and said, "I want to look in the back of your van." He walked to the van door and slid it open.

To the agent's surprise the children met the border agent with the shouted greeting, "Gotcha." And all the children, except Francisco, laughed rolling around on the van floor.

The border agent laughed and said, "Go on." He slid the door shut and waved them on as they had seen him wave on many cars before their van drove up.

Miguel drove on and said, "What happened?"

"I don't know," said Benecia. "What happened?"

"I think," said Miguel, "he thinks we are Mexican American because the children were joking with him in English slang." He realized then the border agents were not used to joking, laughing

Mexican children. Most sat so still they appeared lifeless and afraid as they tried to pass through the border."

****

An hour past the California border Miguel's ears picked up a strange sound. Was it a kitten mewing? Was one of the small children having a bad dream? He looked over at Benecia.

Then he realized the noise was coming from Benecia sitting in the seat across from him. *Grandmamá* made her sit there because she felt Benecia with her full belly needed more space than was available for her in the back of the van. She remembered how uncomfortable she was before the birth of each of her children.

Benecia was moaning slightly in her sleep.

Every morning when the family woke up, *Grandmamá* would say, "I can't believe that baby is still in there."

"This baby will be born in America," Benecia said each time *Grandmamá* said the *baby is still in there.*

After they had passed the border when the American agent waved them on through, Francisco had looked around and laughed, "Well, your baby can come now. Do you think he knows he is in America?"

"Yes, he must know," said Benecia. "He can tell I am happy. I can tell by the way he is stirring around and stretching." She reached over and took Miguel's hand swallowing hard to keep the discomfort in her abdomen from him.

"Well," said Miguel, "please tell our son he must wait to be born until we reach Whittier where *his grandpapá* lives." He was worried because they had not found Alicia. His baby was due any moment, and they had five hours to drive to their triplex in Whittier.

Benecia said, "I feel strange." She turned to *Grandmamá* and asked, "How does it feel to have a baby? I am getting wet."

"Oh, *mamá mia, mi muchacha*, your baby is coming."

Miguel pulled into a McDonalds at the edge of the town of Chula Vista, south of San Diego. *Grandmamá* checked her belly and cried, "The water broke. The baby's dropped and pushed into the birth canal."

An older Hispanic employee taking her break heard *Grandmamá* and rushed over. "You must take her to the hospital. Follow me. The hospital is not far."

And that is how the next Miguel happened to be born in America in a clean hospital.

Chapter 50

Two days later, Miguel and the family drove into the driveway of his father's rented triplex. What would he say to his *papá* about losing Alicia? The joy of his new son's birth was bittersweet. It should have been a completely joyous moment for the entire family. But it was not – until Alicia would be found.

After hugging and kissing and explaining, José settled his family into the other two apartments of the triplex. He had rented the apartments for the coming family. The owner acquiesced that it would be a good deal for him to rent the entire property to José who mowed the lawns and kept up the yard.

Miguel and José went to the police while *Grandmamá* and Benecia were fixing *burritos* for the family for dinner. They gave the police the information Miguel had on Alicia and her kidnappers. They sent Miguel to Los Angeles where he was interrogated by police detectives who were doing undercover work on two immigrant-smuggling safe houses.

Miguel asked the policeman who spoke to him in Spanish, "Please let me go with you. I want to help save my sister."

"You would be in the way. We never know when they might fight and shoot back at us. We get in enough hot water with the news media when we try to keep our noses clean. Having you along would be asking for trouble."

"I promise to stay in the police car."

"We'll see. You might help us in identifying your sister. Then she could help us with the others."

"She is only fourteen-years-old. She's my little sister. Just a baby," Miguel said.

****

Miguel accompanied the police to the second safe house. He saw them lead out the bedraggled looking men, women and children. He looked at the younger girls and could not find among them the curly-haired Alicia.

They drove back to the station with a downcast Miguel. He had looked for his sister earlier that day among those in the first safe house. She was not there.

The police psychologist came into the room and spoke to him in Spanish, "I understand your young sister is somewhere in Los Angeles and you are trying to find her. We have no curly-haired girls among the ones taken in."

"It is hard to keep your eyes off of her. She is an adorable child," said Miguel.

"The only one you haven't seen is an older girl whose hair is not curly. They shaved her head."

"Please let me see her. I cannot go home to my father and tell him I did not check out every one of these people."

"Oh, all right." She guided Miguel down the hall to the room where they kept those who were not stable. "I hope this one is not the one you are after. She will take a lot of therapy to be healthy. She keeps saying over and over, 'I am a good girl.' Something real bad must have happened to her. We can't get her to say anything but 'I am a good girl.'"

She pushed open the door and walked in with Miguel following. Miguel looked over the woman's head and glanced out around the room at the three women in the room. Two were sitting staring at the wall opposite them. The third was curled up in a ball on the sofa. He walked over to her and tried to see her face. It was pushed into her knees. She had almost no hair.

He spoke gently to her in Spanish, "Hi. My name is Miguel. What is your name?"

204

Her arms were wrapped around her legs clutching them to her chest. He noticed only her fingers moved when he spoke. She didn't say anything.

"That is the first time she has moved," said the police psychologist.

"What is your name?" Miguel repeated.

The voice from the girl said, "I am a good girl. Miguel, I am a good girl." She still did not move.

"Alicia, is it you? I have been looking for you all the way from Mexico."

The psychologist suggested, "Touch her. Maybe she will respond to you. She called your name."

Miguel reached out and touched her gently. "Alicia, take my hand. I am here. I will take care of you. I will take you to *Grandmamá*."

The girl's right hand reached up to take his, "*Grandmamá*? Will she be angry with me?"

"*Grandmamá* could never be angry with you. She loves you and worries about you. Her foot is healing the doctor says, and she will be walking again soon without crutches. She is at our *papá's* house in Whittier. He wants you to come home to him."

Alicia began uncurling her body to look at Miguel, "Is it really you Miguel? I knew you would find me. I kept telling the other girls you would come, but they didn't believe me after a while. And soon I doubted, and I gave up." He sat on the sofa beside her and cuddled her in his strong, swarthy arms. Her slender arms went tightly around his neck and would not let go.

"Alicia, what happened to your beautiful hair?"

"I cut it off with a razor I stole from one of the men. They said I was beautiful, and they did bad things to me. I made myself ugly so they will not look at me anymore."

"Oh, Alicia. You're beautiful both inside and outside. You're my sister. I love you with or without your hair."

The psychologist continued in Spanish, "So, we know who she is."

"Yes. I want to take my sister home with me. I have her green card."

"A green card. She was with a bunch of illegal immigrants, undocumented aliens. We got her in a safe house. How could she have a green card?"

Miguel looked at the woman and said, "Her father lives in Whittier. He has a green card. He has been here for over seven years."

"I can release her to her father with the green card. Do you promise to take her to a psychologist in Whittier? We can't predict how she will recover, although she seems to be able to respond to you. I was ready to submit papers to commit her to an institution."

"No, I will take her home." He picked her up and carried her to the door.

"You must sign papers at the front desk to check her out."

"Good. Our father will sign," said Miguel. "He is sitting in the front waiting room."

CHAPTER 51

José and Miguel sat watching the evening television news on the new 27-inch color television set they picked up on sale at BusyMart for $299. The newscaster announced: "Unidentified body washes on shore in Santa Monica."

> *"The body of a tall, thin man at least 25 years old washed up on the water's edge on a Santa Monica beach early Saturday morning. Authorities are asking the public's help in identifying this unknown man who appears to be Latino. He is 5-feet-9 inches and about 180 pounds, said Lieutenant John Somers of the Los Angeles coroner's office. There are a few wisps of gray in the black hair along with a short, clipped mustache, and he was wearing a white T-shirt, dark gray shorts and gray socks. His shoes were not found.*
>
> *"The man was found in the 1200 block floating in the surf along Pacific Coast Highway near San Pedro about 6 a.m. The corpse appears to have been in the water for many hours because it was bloated, and there is massive trauma to the head.*
>
> *"This is a picture, perhaps of the man, that was found in his shorts pocket along with a key."*

"Papa," said Miguel. "That looks like one of the Castillone cousins who left Siempre five years ago. What would he be doing here?"

"I don't know. But how did he die?"

"Could he have followed me?" asked Miguel.

Alicia, now fifteen years old, was sitting at the table doing her homework. She looked up at the TV, stared and then began crying, shaking with her sobs.

Manuel or José went to her and hugged her, "What is wrong, *mi muchacha?*"

"That's the mean man they called Alberto. He's the first man who did bad things to me in the pickup. He hurt me."

"Well, it looks like God punished him. He's now dead," said Miguelito kissing her cheek.

****

Manuel clumsily told Joy, his tutor, about the dead man when they showed up at the Literacy Center for tutoring on Tuesday.

She suggested they call the television station to find out how the man died.

Manuel hesitated and then said, "Joy, it is important I know more."

Joy took out her cell phone from her purse and dialed information asking for the phone number of the TV station.

When she was connected to the secretary at the station, she told her she wanted to know about the young man who had been found dead on the Santa Monica beach.

"We do not know the name of the man as yet," replied the secretary.

"What happened to him?" Joy asked.

"The police department suspects the massive trauma to the young man's head was caused by a boat propeller. He may have fallen overboard and was caught under the boat and injured by the propeller. Or he could have been swimming and the driver of the boat did not see him in the water and ran him under."

"How tragic!" said Joy. Manuel smiled sadly, after she passed on the information.

Chapter 52

DURING THE NEXT YEAR Joy Engler taught José wonderful things about English words. Not knowing English in America was like allowing a wall to stand between him and others. He had invaded their country, so he knew he must reach out and learn from them. A few Americans were learning Spanish, but most were busy with their lives so they would not reach out to learn to speak and read his language.

He must learn theirs. Ever since he became Joy's gardener, they had become best friends. He was surprised at having an American friend. When she suggested they date like Americans, he could hardly believe it. He had fantasized being with her, but the reality at times almost overwhelmed him. He felt contentment with her as he had in his youth with his beloved Elmira.

American women constantly surprised him.

"Why? You want me?"

"You are a good man. I feel here for you," she explained putting her hand over her heart."

He still found it difficult to believe that Joy wanted him. She was attractive, comfortable in herself, and was reaching out to help him. But he knew he had started it.

One day three months before, after they had worked for two hours at the Literacy Center on vocabulary and speaking in sentences, he had smiled at her. She smiled back. He took her hand gratefully for all she did for him. He knew she tutored as a volunteer. She did not get paid except for feeling good about her good deed. He tried to repay her by mowing her lawn each week. She tried to refuse him, but he insisted on doing it anyway. Pulling weeds together had built a strong bond between them.

She took his fingers with her other hand and counted them aloud. "One, two, three, four, five ..." She counted on and on until she had reached one hundred. Then on paper she showed him one hundred, two hundred, three hundred until they reached one thousand. No one had ever cared to teach him such exciting things.

Without thinking of the consequences he had leaned over and pressed his lips lightly on hers. Then he had jerked back embarrassed.

She worried a bit. *Was Manuel out of line? Should she report the kiss or keep it to herself.* She knew she enjoyed getting the kiss, but she missed her dead husband. Was any man better than no man? Manuel she could tell was a good man. He was caring and thoughtful. Who else would mow her grass as thank you for the tutoring.

Joy's best friends and next door neighbors were Pearl and Bob Bridges. Pearl told her, "You should stop tutoring Manuel. You're getting too close. I fear your two worlds are too different and you don't even go to the same church."

The next time she tutored Manuel she ignored Pearl's advice but went with her feelings.

"Don't be embarrassed Manuel. I know you like me. I like you. Would you like to take me to a movie? The movie will be in English." She hadn't had a date since her husband had died. Splitting a doughnut at the literacy meeting with Warren certainly didn't count as a date any more. Would this movie with Manuel count as a date?

"Movie?"

"On Greenleaf Avenue. *Pelicula.*" She was glad she remembered the name for movie.

"You and me? *Pelicula.* Movie. *Bueno.* Good." He grinned his best smile.

"Manuel makes me feel warm all over," she later told Pearl who shook her head and worried about her good friend's decision.

CHAPTER 53

AFTER THREE MONTHS OF going to the movies together and afterwards drinking lots of hot coffee and eating tantalizing berry pie at their favorite pie place on Whittier Boulevard, José and Joy knew they loved each other. They progressed from many a late evening rendezvous talking for hours in English. It was amazing how fast José learned when his desire to learn English combined with love and passion. And he began teaching her love words in Spanish.

José and Joy began considering the problems they might have if they married and tried to blend their two worlds. He suggested he go to church with her for a month. When he met the minister, they decided to study the Bible with him.

One day Joy suggested, "You can continue helping your children who live in the triplex. When we marry, you can move in with me and someone can use your room in your apartment."

"Yes, I can. But my little ones will miss me; I will miss them," said José. "I'm not sure that is best for them."

"They have your *Grandmamá*. We can eat over there two or three times a week, and I will help your mother cook. Your children have bonded with you again, and perhaps you can eat lunch with them each day that you work. I will have you in the evenings and for breakfast. After a while, perhaps we can buy a house for all of us."

"I see. Do you mind if we bring the little ones here on the weekends?" asked José.

"Yes, Manuel, do bring them. I would love it. They would get to know me gradually, and one day they might want to live with us. I always wanted a big family but Walt's and my finances were not a lot, so we stopped at two children."

"In Mexico, we didn't think about stopping with two children. We just took what God gave us."

Joy laughed, "You must not have known about birth control."

"Birth control? We did that for the animals. Only about inserting large fruit seeds to stop a goat or a cow from getting pregnant. But we rarely used that method because we wanted the young males for food and the females were used for milk."

"I forgot. Your Church teaches no birth control but the rhythm method."

"Rhythm method. What is that?"

She blushed and then tried to explain. She found out José and Elmira had never heard of a rhythm method where Elmira skipped sex when she would be ovulating so as not to have children.

After she explained haltingly, José said, "I see. We used the love method."

****

Joy called her two sons Steven and Edward and invited them to dinner to meet José.

"This is my new friend, Manuel Garcia," she told them when they walked in to the livingroom together. "I tutor him as I have been telling you. We are now friends."

Her sons were gracious but each called her the next day encouraging the friendship but worried about it going beyond that point.

"Don't fret over me. You want me to be happy, don't you?" They agreed and let it be. "Mother, we trust you," said Edward the younger son.

****

The day of José's and Joy's wedding was a spectacular sunshiny day.

Joy looked at José as they joined hands before the minister of the Bible church and whispered, "God planned this lovely day for us."

They stood outdoors in their wedding clothes in one of the wedding circles in Penn Park.

José smiled at her thinking back to his marriage to Elmira and *his happy years* with her. Tears flowed down his cheeks in new happiness as he looked from Joy to his children, his new grandson and Joy's sons sitting in the audience. Yucca Joe was there with his wife, Gail.

José said aloud a brief prayer in the wedding ceremony, "Please God, give us all moments of happiness, joy and blessings for our children and grandchildren."

Then Minister Mike introduced them as husband and wife to their family and friends.

CHAPTER 54

J OSÉ LAY IN BED with his new wife. His arms were filled again with the body and love of a woman. He was now able to feel deeply for another. In a corner of his mind he had painted his beloved Elmira and wrapped her up warm and cozy until they met again in Heaven. On this earth he made room for vivacious Joy. Her energy filled him with pleasure. She was delicious like a candy bar invading his senses. He found it difficult to stop touching her with his fingers.

"*Mi* Manuel. You love me like a man. God has blessed me twice with a good husband." She rubbed his tummy and kissed his navel.

He rolled her over and made love to her slowly and lovingly. Afterwards he whispered to her, "Please let me make breakfast. You lie here and relax until I call for you."

She uttered a low, "Uh huh," and rolled over covering her head.

José walked to the kitchen singing in Spanish and began pulling out eggs and salsa, beans and tortillas, rice and orange juice.

In an hour he called for Joy, his new love and wife, to come for her surprise. She wondered, "Will I have to clean up the kitchen for two hours as I did for Walt, my first husband? It will be worth it today if I do have to clean up Manuel's mess."

As she seated herself, he explained to her, "*Huevos Rancheros* must be served on a flat plate, never in a bowl. You want the tortilla crispy and it must be made of corn, not flour. You want fresh cheese, not a jack cheese. Always use ranchero sauce, never pizza sauce."

Joy rubbed his cheek and said, "Manuel, maybe we should open a restaurant. You are so good at creating tantalizing tastes."

"You may be right. We from the farm in Mexico are used to eating large meals for energy for the day. We work hard until *siesta* time—a big lunch and then sleep for an hour or two."

"What do your people do after they sleep in the afternoon?" asked Joy, giggling.

"Oh, some go home for the *siesta* and stay there if it is still hot when they wake up. I always get up and work more because the sun is cooling down and the weeds always grow – but with Yucca Joe we skip the *siesta* and mow more lawns."

"Yucca Joe promised to get you more of your own accounts. When will that be? Then you can come home at lunchtime and have a *siesta* with me," Joy whispered, flirting.

"I will speak to Yucca Joe about that," José answered seriously but with twinkling eyes. He leaned over kissing her, enjoying the moment her arms went around him.

****

Two days later on a weekday morning, José told Yucca Joe what he discussed with Joy.

"Manuel, it will take six months or so to build you a route and then you will need to knock on doors and advertise to get even more customers. Your son, Francisco, is a good gardener, and I will train him to take your place with me within a year or so."

Yucca Joe frowned, hoping he was making a wise decision.

CHAPTER 55

T HE FOLLOWING WEEK JOSÉ and Joy were in deep pre-dawn sleep. Both were lying face to face on her pillow. His down pillow had fallen to the floor. Each night he pushed that old softy to the floor, because he liked to wake up in the morning feeling her breath against his cheek.

Those first few seconds of shaking brought down fragments of ceiling plaster on their heads. Confusion poured down around them.

"God help us!" Joy cried. "An earthquake!"

José did not recognize the word she said, but he remembered the familiar movements from the strong earthquake he felt that once in Mexico City while he was there sleeping on the sofa in Elena Veracruz's apartment. He had felt as though he and the whole city were swimming in sand as the soft soil of the city moved in circular motions with the quake.

This moment, this earthquake felt different like it was shaking the cooperating ceilings up and down upon them. Later he was to learn the difference between slip thrust faults and slip strike faults.

He could hear rain out in the hallway. They slipped on their shoes, and he grabbed Joy's hand running to the hall after throwing open their bedroom door. He saw it wasn't rain but fast-gushing water coming from the water heater pushed akilter in the small closet where it rested next to the bathroom. The hot water burned their feet, which they hardly noticed as they ran.

"Looks like we'll get new carpet out of the insurance company," she yelled. "The insurance companies really take it hard each time one of these shockers happens."

They rushed to the front door and couldn't get it open. "Where is a crowbar when I need it?" he yelled.

Going to the window he threw the heavy stool through the large picture window. He continued hitting the remaining glass with a chair until there was room enough for them to get their bodies out and into the front flower bed of azalea bushes.

Ignoring a bleeding cut on her arm from the window glass, Joy rushed to the van, found the key under the hood and opened the van doors for them. They sat and listened to KFI, 640 radio to the information. José found a towel hanging nearby and patted her arm until the bleeding finally stopped. Then she poured bottled water in a pan to soak their sore feet from the hot water they ran through.

The news station gave out suggestions where to go to find the Red Cross, city parks and what to do if houses seemed too dangerous to go back inside. They reminded people that "traffic signals will not be working in most cities, So be careful."

"Is our house going to fall down with the aftershocks?" asked Joy who was surprised at how long this quake had lasted.

"What is an aftershock?" asked José.

"It's another earthquake that happens after the first one. There always are quite a few aftershocks. Some people will be sleeping in the parks tonight for fear their houses will come down on them."

"I hope the house won't come down."

"Usually not, but maybe we should sleep here in our van tonight. I'm glad I washed all these blankets and bedding after returning from our honeymoon at Glen Ivy Campground last weekend in *Corona*."

His fear had subsided some. "In Mexico City in their big earthquake I found buildings came down all around us. I was sleeping on a couch in an apartment when it happened. We went out rescuing the injured as well as women and children all day. We were afraid but acted like we weren't."

"My poor dear Manuel. My poor dear." She rubbed his forehead and kissed him hoping to ease her own concern.

****

A few minutes later Joy said, "Oh, no! I almost forgot. We have to turn off the gas near the kitchen door. We don't want a fire." They changed their night clothes into clothing Joy had hung in the van closet.

Joy suggested José take the wrench from the toolbox in the van, and the two of them walked around to the kitchen door to turn off the gas at the meter. They also shut off the breaker switches to the electricity.

"Last year my neighbor at the end of the block died in her kitchen when her washing machine flooded over. A small split in the electric cord going to her refrigerator shorted out and caused her to be electrocuted when she stepped in the water to mop it up."

"You mean she died?" asked José.

"Yes, she died. We had a big funeral for her," added Joy.

"What about the neighbors' gas meters?" asked José. "We should turn theirs off if they don't have a wrench."

"You're right, Manuel. Someone needs to turn off the gas at the neighbors' homes, so their meters won't explode if there is a leak." Then they walked up and down the street shutting off the gas for each of the neighbors who had not already turned theirs off.

The elderly neighbor two doors down from them met them outdoors, "My television is broken. It shot off the chest of drawers in the bedroom and hit the floor."

"You're lucky it didn't hit you in the head. Didn't you have it anchored down so it couldn't move?" asked Joy.

The neighbor said, "No. We never thought of it."

Joy continued, "Well, you know for next time. Have your son Carl tie it down for you. You could have been killed…. My water heater broke and my carpet is ruined I'm sure."

"Oh, I must check my water heater." The elderly woman trotted back into the house to see if hers was all right.

Joy called to her, "Be careful."

She looked at José, and they continued on to the next house. He smiled.

Neighbors kept walking over to them and asking, "Should I go to work or remain with my family? Is it safe to leave them alone?" Others who had motor homes or vans were staying in them like José and Joy.

"Better to stay off the streets 'til we know what to do. I wouldn't go to work today until the radio tells you to do so," suggested Joy.

"You're right. People won't want me there."

Joy suggested, "Save the parks and schools for people from apartment buildings."

Manuel added, "Park away from any trees. They might come down on your vehicles or tents with the next aftershock."

Bob and Pearl, Joy's best friends, were on vacation, so they turned off the gas meter at Pearl's and Bob's and checked to see if there was any apparent damage before returning to their own home.

"We'll turn the gas back on for them when the aftershocks have eased to under 3.0. The radio will tell us." When they had completed checking each house on both sides of the street, they walked back to their van to turn on the battery-operated radio again. She always kept the radio in a box for their camping trips.

She turned on the radio to find the newsperson saying, "A soccer field of sleeping bags will be spread out at the schools and parks where people will be sleeping tonight. You are asked to take tents with blankets and tarps if you are setting up at the parks outdoors. The Salvation Army will be furnishing bottled water and some food. There will be milk and disposable diapers for babies and small children."

Joy said to José, "We can probably stay safely here in our van. And tomorrow you can see about getting back to doing your gardening route. That is, if the streets are drivable."

Strong aftershocks sent waves of renewed panic throughout the cities. Telephone poles swayed like palm trees in a typhoon.

The radio described the latest warnings from helicopter news observers, "The freeway system is shattered. The overpasses may be weakened so take side streets unless you know the freeway near you is safe."

"Here in California," she continued, "we have so many medium-sized earthquakes we rarely get upset for long. This one is stronger than normal, but we know the 'Big' one is coming. I usually have water and some canned food stored in the garage but after four months I start drinking the water and eating the food. Soon I have to buy more. With this van we can keep stored water and food because we can go shopping after each trip. I haven't gone shopping since our trip last weekend, so we only have what we didn't eat at Glen Ivy."

"We can go to the market," Manuel suggested.

Joy laughed, "Do you know how many people will have that idea?"

"Why are you laughing at me?" he asked.

"I'm not laughing at you. I'm laughing at what you said," she tried to explain. She had to spend some time comforting him before he understood the difference between laughing at him and laughing at a statement. So much of his life was disrupted by life situations, he felt fear of yet another change coming his way. Now he was afraid of losing Joy because of their differences.

Before long they ended up under the covers in the overhead bed of the van. When another aftershock came along 30 minutes later, they were under the covers involved in pleasing one another. He was teaching her to climax one after another like he and Elmira had learned so many years before. They soon were exhausted and delighted with his longevity.

Joy whispered to him, "This aftershock is a 4.0 or less. Don't worry, this feels like a light aftershock."

José commented, "You Americans take life so casually."

"Hey!" exclaimed Joy. "You used the new word we were working on – casually."

"I did, didn't I?" He hugged her and continued their romantic episode, casually.

CHAPTER 56

A COUPLE OF MONTHS FOLLOWING the earthquake, Miguel answered the soft knocking at the door of the triplex one night. Standing there were his young, former neighbors in Siempre, Mexico, Marco Andres Castellone Huerta and his sister Adriana. Miguel gulped, remembering she followed him around when she wasn't playing with his sisters.

Francisco, the brother just younger than Miguelito, stood behind Miguel and pushed forward saying, "Marco, Adriana. I knew you would join us,"

Miguel spoke up, "Join us? Why are you here?"

Marco said, "We want to make a better life for ourselves just as you do. Francisco told us where to come when he called the general store. I worked for Pablo after Francisco left for California."

Francisco put his arm around Adriana and took her to the living room where he sat down and pulled her down beside him.

"Adriana, *mi mujer,* I have missed you."

"How are you and Miguel?" Confused at Francisco's words she glanced over at Miguel where he continued to talk to her brother.

"Miguel is good. He and his wife Benecia have a baby son."

He couldn't help but notice her shocked expression.

"You didn't tell us Miguel is married and expecting a child."

Francisco continued, "They named their new son Miguel. A new Miguelito." How could he explain to her how much he wanted her to come? Would she be angry when she knew all the truth?

"Francisco, I've missed you, too. When Marco told me you wanted us to come to Whittier, I knew I had to come with him. But it has been a long, hard trip. Marco stole all our papa's *dinero* to help us get here. Before we ever dare to go home again, we must pay him double the *pesos* we took."

"Who is your *coyote*?"

She lied. "We don't have a *coyote*. Didn't have enough for a down payment, so we hid in the back of a pickup when it stopped for gas in Mexicali. Marco and I crawled in the back under a bunch of smelly trash. We buried ourselves deep and almost got caught, because they searched the truck. The stuff had a terrible odor."

Marco interrupted her from across the room where he spoke with Miguel. "It stank like puke, like decaying garbage." The memory almost made him gag.

"So they didn't search but a minute." Adriana held her nose to emphasize the odor.

"How did you stand the smell?"

"It was bad, but I had caught a cold and couldn't smell much. Marco is the one who really got sick from the stinks."

Marco who had been talking to Miguel turned to his sister and said, "Don't speak too much, *mi hermana*. There is time."

"Okay," agreed Francisco. "We still have plenty of time. We have our whole lives to plan and prepare for the future."

Miguel who was now seventeen going on eighteen added, "We must decide where you will sleep. Adriana can share Alicia's room. She lives in our apartment. My wife Benecia and I and the baby have our own room in the triplex and the young ones live in the third apartment with *Grandmamá*."

"Marco can sleep in my room," said sixteen-year-old Francisco, "here in the front of the triplex where our papa lived before he married his new wife."

"Your papa is married?" questioned Marco.

"*Si*, he married an *Americana* who teaches him to speak English."

"Strange," said Adriana. "I thought Americans didn't like Mexicans."

Miguel said, "That is not true. Some Americans don't like and trust us, but many of them do. There are a lot of Americans. They are like people in our village of Siempre. Some are good, some are bad. Remember the three Castillone brothers when Enrique was alive?"

They nodded.

****

Marco and Adriana sat at the kitchen table following dinner the next night. Miguel, Benecia, Francisco and Manuel along with his wife Joy had enjoyed the meal and the conversation. Joy was happy for José and his sons, even if she couldn't understand all that was being said. She could pick up a lot from their tone of voice and expressions on their faces. They were happy to be together.

"We have something serious to discuss with you," said Marco. Adriana who was sitting between Benecia and Alicia looked down at her hands.

"What is it?" asked José.

"Adriana was forced by one of the *coyotes* before we escaped from them. We luckily found the trash truck that saved us…, and… she is pregnant. We want to know about her getting an abortion."

Everyone was quiet. The word *a b o r t i o n* hung in the air as if it were a poison gas.

Joy finally asked José, "What is it? What is wrong?"

José explained to her, "Adriana is going to have a baby."

"Oooh. Who is the father?" Joy was almost afraid to ask.

"They say it is one of the *coyotes*."

"Well, she can have the baby. There are a lot of mothers here in Los Angeles County who will help her. The churches in America do not punish innocent children."

"They want to abort the baby?"

"Please, no," gasped Joy. "If they don't want it, there are hundreds of American women who will adopt the baby and raise it as their own. Explain that to them."

José looked at Adriana and Marco and repeated in Spanish to them what Joy had said in English.

Adriana looked at Joy and said in Spanish, "I don't want to give my baby away, but who will marry me now that I am no longer a virgin? Too hard to raise the baby with no man to help me."

José translated to Joy, and she spoke to José again and said, "Churches and fire departments take babies less than three days old. They take them with no questions and give them to a hospital that will then look for parents to adopt the baby."

Francisco who was shorter than Miguel and built more like his father, José, spoke up, "I would be pleased to marry you Adriana. I am still a boy according to the Americans, but I am a man in many ways. I have loved you for many years, but I thought you loved Miguel. He now has a wife and baby."

Everyone looked at Adriana who said, "Francisco, I have always liked you, but this is a big decision. The baby will not be born for almost six months. Maybe you will not like the baby after it is born."

"How could I not like the baby? The baby will be part of you. I will love it."

"But what if it doesn't look like me. It might look like the fat man who forced me."

"So far as the family is concerned," José disagreed, "that baby will belong to all of us as much as any who would be born to you and Francisco."

Francisco said to Adriana, "What do you want to do? As they say here in America, 'It's your decision.'"

****

José and Joy drove back home after all the new guests settled into beds in the tri-plex. Tired, they headed right to bed. Joy turned out their bedroom light and climbed under the covers with him as he asked, "You told me women dump newborn babies. Why?"

She explained, "In the year 2001, a law was enacted in California to save babies that were being dumped in the trash by women who don't want them. I hear about one hundred babies have been surrendered to health and law enforcement officials. And only two dozen have been found dead since the law began."

"But why would a woman dump her newborn baby?" asked José not understanding.

"Most of them are born to very young girls. Some to foreign women from other countries, like Adriana, who are afraid of what their families will do to them. You can guess some of the other reasons. I think it's all from fear."

"But what happens if the mother changes her mind about giving her baby away?" asked José.

"Well, she has fourteen days to reclaim her baby before the state puts it up for adoption."

José was quiet.

Then Joy mused in the darkness, "I wonder what Adriana will decide to do?"

****

In the coming weeks Francisco took many walks in the evening with Adriana when he and his *papá* got home from gardening. He was tired from working all day in the hot sun with Yucca Joe. Yet he was energized about being with Adriana. The young people talked and learned about one another. She insisted they go to church together every Sunday morning. He agreed.

After a month Adriana told him, "Francisco, you are young, a year younger than I am. But I see in you a man and not a boy. You put in a good day's work. I believe I could be a wife to you. You are good. I see you are a hard and willing worker when you go to work for Yucca Joe. You would take good care of the baby and me. We will have other children that are yours."

"Don't worry, Adriana. The first baby will be mine as much as any others we will have. There is no reason for the child to know I am not his father. I will treat him as mine, because he is yours."

She hugged him and kissed him on the mouth. The first time she had shown him such affection.

"I love this baby and it's not even born," she said. With each kick I feel more love for it. I could never give him up if we can give him a good life."

CHAPTER 57

I T TOOK TWO MONTHS for the insurance company to replace the old carpet from water damage caused by the broken water heater. Joy also replaced two chairs caused by damage of the 6.5 earthquake. Joy and José were settling into their newly repaired home when she answered the door. She jumped up before José could get up from his chair in front of the TV. He was resting from a hard day of gardening with Yucca Joe. It was a Monday.

There were two armed policemen and a plainclothes officer looking at her. The third one spoke for them.

"Mrs. Joy Engler?"

"I was. I am now Mrs. Manuel Garcia. Can I help you?"

"You called a news station about a man whose body was found in the Long Beach Harbor."

"Yes, I did." She swallowed hard and looked at the three men still standing on the porch. "Do you want to come in?"

They thanked her and walked into the newly decorated living room.

She looked at the recliner where José was sitting. "This is my husband, Manuel Garcia."

"Pleased to meet you," Manuel said.

"We need to follow up on your call," said one of the officers in uniform.

"Why were you interested?" asked another uniformed officer.

226

Joy interrupted, "I just wanted to know if it was an accident or if it was an on purpose." She knew police don't waste their time on nothing.

"We have to follow up on all leads, even if they lead to nowhere," said the dark-haired uniformed officer.

"I also know that most people don't call a news station if there is no reason. So what was your real reason," the officer in the suit inquired.

José spoke up in English, "My wife called because one of my children said she recognized him. We wanted to know if he was of the Castellone family."

"Castellone? You think that is the man?"

"Possibly," said José.

"We want to talk to your...?"

"My daughter."

Joy interrupted, "She is recovering from an injury. Please don't disturb her. She's suffered enough mental trauma."

"We must talk with her so we can identify this man. Please, we will be careful of your daughter. What is her name?" The dark-haired uniformed officer took over.

José said, "Her name is Alicia."

"Alicia what?"

"Alicia Ramirez. She has a green card. Please don't hurt her." José was afraid.

****

In the following days Alicia was interviewed and told the police about her kidnapping, her sale to *coyotes* on one side of the border, the rape after she crossed over the border and her subsequent rescue in Los Angeles County. Following investigation they discovered the dead young man was involved in Alicia's rape and sale.

Then the L.A.P.D. discovered her father, Manuel Garcia, was actually José Ramirez. Joy was shocked to find out her married name should be Mrs. José Ramirez and not Manuel Garcia.

The police through further investigation found José Ramirez was wanted for the murder of Enrique Castillone in the small village of

Siempre, Mexico. Then José was arrested, waiting to be returned to Mexico.

"José," Joy asked him in the Los Angeles jail, "why didn't you tell me that you changed your name?" She was hurt because he had kept his name a secret from her.

"I was afraid. Afraid that you might be arrested if ever I was arrested. And I think I believed I would never be found out while using the name Manuel Garcia on my green card. It had been so many years. Now I know nothing is kept secret forever," he looked at the floor where he was standing by the bars.

"José, do you have any other wives or children? What other secrets have you hidden from me?" Her words stumbled over one another.

José looked shocked. "There is nothing else. Since I left *Siempre*, I have not been with a woman. No sex. No more children. Until I met you, I did not think of a woman as I once thought about Elmira. She was the love of my youth. You are the love of my middle years. I cannot imagine life without you and my children, my grandchildren. I even love your sons and their girlfriends."

Sadness flowed from his words to her. Joy began to cry.

As José reached over to comfort her, a guard yelled at him, "No touching. Leave her alone." Tears came to José's eyes, and they wept together.

CHAPTER 58

THE NEXT MORNING JOSÉ awoke in his cell in the Los Angeles County Jail. He knew he would be returned to Mexico to be tried for the murder of Enrique Castillone. Because he was a Mexican citizen, the U.S. would not get involved. He tried not to think about what would happen to him in the Mexican jails.

In this jail he even had a soft blanket, heavy but soft. The bed was not like his in his home with Joy, but it was more comfortable than the one when he was imprisoned in Chihuahua, Mexico. It seemed a lifetime ago when he thought about his experiences with the serial killer.

He prayed, "It looks like I must pay for my sins. Would it have been better if I had turned myself into the authorities in Mexico when I first hit Enrique on the head? I didn't plan to do it, but I fought back. Should I have let Enrique strangle me? God, please give me some answers. I am so ignorant."

His crime had occurred in Mexico. If it had happened in California, he knew he had been told by American lawyers that he would have had a trial in California and most likely would get only a few years. Most of the sentence would be for running away and not for the murder itself, because it was self-defense – if that was proven. But in Mexico if he could not prove himself not guilty by reason of self-defense, he thought he could easily be shot at dawn one morning when the guilty verdict of murder came in.

One of the Hispanic American guards befriended José. "Why're you in here?" he first asked him in English.

The guard was surprised when José answered him in English. "I was fighting with a man who raped my wife, Elmira. My beautiful Elmira who is now dead."

"You're in here just for fighting?"

"No, I hit Enrique on the head with a flatiron when he was strangling me. It killed him. I am guilty."

"Was he an American?" asked the guard.

"No, he was Mexican like me," admitted José.

"You illegal aliens make the U.S. government spend money on you we don't have. We spend up to $100 million on you criminals a year. Why? Did you kill him here in our country?"

José answered, "I didn't come here to kill someone. I killed him in my village in Mexico. He was choking me."

"In America we have leniency for those who defend themselves. Sounds like you should get a good Mexican lawyer when they send you home," the guard suddenly sounded sympathetic.

"I'm doomed. There are evil things in Mexican jails. The smells make me sick. When I was in the Chihuahua jail, I saw guards beat one prisoner to death. There were others who were injured, and we never knew who did it. Guards looked the other way for a few dollars."

The guard frowned. "My family comes from Ensenada, Mexico. That is why I know so much English. They brought me here when my mother was pregnant with me. I was born on this side of the border so I am an American citizen."

"Then we are brothers," said José.

"Hardly. But I believe you. My cousin practices law in Tijuana. I will see if he can do something to help you. Will your friends help you pay some good lawyers to help you?"

"I don't know. My sons are young. My new wife owns her own home, but I could never ask her to sell it to help me. I am guilty."

"Stop saying you're guilty. You were defending yourself."

"I know it, and you believe it. How do I prove it?" asked José.

"That is what good lawyers are for. They know the legalese."

"But I am poor."

"I see the people who come to see you at visiting hours. You're rich in friends. Perhaps they will help you," said the guard.

In the following days José found out the guard's name was Gregorio Ortiz Perez. He was distantly related, he claimed, to *el*

Presidente of Mexico. José had his doubts about his new friend because Greg's people were not poor but neither were they rich.

Greg the guard came to work complaining one morning to another guard outside José's cell. "We need more money to incarcerate you illegals," he said looking at José.

The other guard said, "You're right. There is no funding in the budget sent to Congress for the State Criminal Alien Assistance Program."

"You mean SCAAP, don't you?" said Greg.

"Yes, those are the initials for the program. The U. S. President keeps crossing out the funding for the program. I hear our California Senators have requested $850 million for the program." José walked up to the bars and peered at the guards, listening.

"There is more chance if our Governator gets involved. He has promised to be the Collectornator for things we need. We need at least $700 million, most of which will come to California to help us care for the incarcerated illegals."

"I hear in 2004, California got $120 million of the $300 million directed to SCAAP."

"Am I included in those who use that money?" asked José.

"I don't know. You committed your crime in Mexico. I think this is for illegals who commit crimes in the U. S. of A."

"Will they make my family pay the government back for feeding me?" asked José.

"Americans should be so lucky," laughed Greg. "It's nice of you to volunteer." The other guard joined in the laughter.

"I didn't volunteer any money. We don't have much. Just my wife's house. Please don't take it from her." Panic was written on José's face.

"Calm down, José. No one is going to take your wife's house away from her. She can take out a loan. When you are free, you can work to help her repay the loan to the bank."

The other guard said, "If you are ever freed." José looked at the floor of the jail cell sadly.

CHAPTER 59

The Mexican American guard, Gregorio Joséph Ortiz Perez, talked to José through the bars of the jail cell one morning.

"The first lady of Mexico wants to run for the office of *el Presidente*. She is interested in the numbers of women who were murdered outside Ciudad Juarez over the past decade. My cousin, the lawyer, in Ensenada contacted her when he found out that you were the one who helped capture Joaquin Mercado. He's the longtime serial killer of hundreds of women thrown into the desert between Ciudad Juarez and Chihuahua. Since his imprisonment copycat killers have taken over, but they have been easier to capture.

"She's agreed to help my cousin, the attorney, in your trial in Mexico when you get there." Gregorio, nicknamed Greg, was fired up.

"Would she really help me? I am nobody. She is a great lady." José's eyes opened wide in surprise – and hope.

"You may be nobody to a lot of people, but the first lady is grateful for your help in solving the serial killer murders. And her helping you may get her a lot of positive press as she runs for office. An emotional issue such as murdered women might be something to help her win over the opposition."

"*Mi* wife, Joy, will be so happy. I will tell her today when she comes to visit."

****

At visiting hours Joy came to visit feeling depressed and sad, but his news about the first lady of Mexico thrilled her. Perhaps there was hope in his coming trial in Mexico.

"I'll call the newspaper in Whittier when I get home. They will want to interview you to let all of our neighbors know you acted in self-defense when you killed that monster, Enrique Castillone."

"You won't want them to know I killed a man," José protested.

"I only know the more publicity you get, the more protection you might have when you are sent away from our safe jails. I fear for your safety, Manu... I mean José."

She was still unused to using the name José.

"I will be fine," he said. He didn't want to tell her he, too, feared for what could happen in prison. Those Castellone brothers had long fingers that often maneuvered the law in southern Mexico. He kissed his fingers and touched her fingers with them. She did the same.

He told her, "I can smell your perfume and will take that memory with me."

CHAPTER 60

I T WAS TO THE Eastern Prison José was sent soon after lawyers from Mexico became involved.

El Presidente's wife and the lawyers went to visit José Ramirez in the sprawling prison outside of Mexico City called by everyone, The Eastern Prison. At first he was so embarrassed by her presence, he sat tongue-tied.

She spoke, "Please let us know the truth." José bowed his head, said a prayer and began speaking of his past. She listened and soon tears came to her eyes.

The trials are now open to the general public. The power of the police and judges also have been given new independence and investigative authority at all levels. The capacity of the judges has been reduced in an effort for the individual to have due process of law.

There are many prisoners who languish in jails when they are not able to show their innocence. Good lawyers are expensive, and most Mexican people are poor.

CHAPTER 61

M EANWHILE AT HOME IN California, Joy read the morning paper and found a letter written in the editorial section.

Letter-to-the Editor sent to the Los Angeles Times:

Presidente Vicente Fox of Mexico makes sure his undocumented immigrants to our country have Matricular Consular documents so he can keep tabs on his people in our USA. Those documents are used in many American cities to obtain library cards, water privileges, to visit incarcerated kids in prison, etc. Soon they will get green cards with them if some American legislators have their way.

Green cards are the first step to driver licenses to show I.D. Then they can open a checking account and be able to vote – all the while being non-citizens.

I have a fair suggestion. Billions of taxpayer dollars are used to care for these illegals. Let us consider accessing Baja California all the way through Cabo San Lucas. Soon we can vote on it to become our 51st state.

Vicente Fox, do you hear me? Send us your illegals and we want Baja as dowry for this illegitimate bride you insist on pawning off on America. Your government has it set up that these people are allowed dual citizenship and can vote in both Mexico and America. Someday, later if not sooner, they will vote to annex Baja to the U.S. to become its 51st state. President Fox, do you hear me? Listen up!

SIGNED, *The Average California Citizen*

CHAPTER 62

B ENECIA WAS TENDING HER newborn son in the bedroom she and Miguel shared in their apartment of the triplex. Miguel was away – driving with Mike Brown as his co driver to learn the route to Chicago. Mike Brown had purchased on credit the new truck he had told Miguel and Yucca Joe about. He knew he would double his profits with two trucks, one traveling to New York and one to Chicago.

Benecia heard loud knocking and a blaring, familiar voice. "Daughter, answer the door. I know you are here. Your friends working in the yard next door tell me you are in there."

"*Papá*," she yelled happily even before opening the door. There on the porch were her father, Hector Rodriguez Generoso, and her four sisters. "I'm so glad to see you." Benecia threw her arms around her father's neck and then one at a time, each of her sisters.

"Where is my grandson?" Hector, *Benecia's papá.* demanded before the hugging had stopped. He stepped past them all looking for his grandson. "Did you name him after me?"

Lucia, the oldest daughter, grinned around her protruding teeth, "Benecia, it has been a long, hard trip – but we made it." She held her sister away from her and looked closely, "What are those ugly plastic things on your teeth?"

"Yes," said Cesarea. "What have they done to you?"

"These plastics are called braces. They are straightening my teeth."

Gregoria, the vigilant sister, who was next to Benecia in age, said, "Can you do my teeth, too? Your mouth is pretty even with the coverings. I want to be beautiful."

Benecia laughed, "None of us will ever be beautiful except to those who love us, but we can all look better. You should see the strange surgeries they do on people here in California to make women look more attractive."

Cesarea, the very long-haired second daughter, said sadly, "They will never have surgery that will cure my eye that moves by itself so I find it hard to see." She pulled her long hair away from the eye she kept covered.

"Cesarea, I have heard them say, for a lot of money, they can make both eyes move together," said Benecia.

"Where is your husband?" asked Hector interrupting his daughters.

"He is driving on the road. He needs a co driver soon, and you will be the perfect one until the children are big enough to travel. Then I will travel with him again when I learn to drive the big trucks."

"Benecia, you, a woman, would drive the big trucks?"

"*Si, Papá*, in America women do everything they want. I already have driven the truck a few times with Miguel. *Papá*, I have strong wrists from helping you in the fields."

"Oh, woe is the lot of man if women do everything they want." Hector buried his face in his hands. All his daughters smiled big *revealing* smiles and dreamed of great futures, handsome husbands and straight teeth.

CHAPTER 63

J OY ENGLER GARCIA, WHO now knew her name was Joy Ramirez, found herself trying to think positively. She prayed each day that José would come home from the Mexican prison. She planned their future and what would make them both happy.

She continued attending the small nondenominational church around the corner with her best friends, Pearl and Bob. She knew she needed faith in God's plans for her life to give her strength. Her sons tried to be a comfort to her, but she knew she needed more.

She kept asking God, "Will you answer our prayers and give us back José?"

One Saturday morning, she read the morning newspaper and found an article on "Multi-Generation Households."

She said aloud as she thought about the idea, "Would we be too crowded?"

This kind of household is what a lot of Hispanic households do – live together - grandmothers, parents and children. Why can't José and I do this and save money for all? We will split expenses and build up equity in a big house.

I have taken out a loan to help José. The rest can be a down payment on the house I will look for.

****

Joy planned her future and that of José's family. She checked with several real estate companies in Whittier to find the perfect house for her and the household she planned to have. She was aware that José would want to have all of his children and their future families in one house—at least the ones of the family who wanted to stay and grow together. She didn't want to think about what would happen if José never came home. She reached out and took God's hand in faith.

All José's children welcomed her and constantly gave her many hugs. Of course, she knew it might not be so easy after the extended families moved in together. Joy was struggling to learn Spanish. Yucca Joe recommended they all learn Spanglish which the children were picking up quickly.

The tri-plex where José's mother-in-law and the six children were living was not adequate. Miguel, his wife, and child were living in José's old rooms. His widowed *Grandmamá* was in the second division of the tri-plex with the younger two girls and little *Josélito*. Francisco and the other brother, Mario the tenacious, had the third division. It was costing Francisco a lot of back-breaking work to earn enough to pay the rent for him, Adriana and the expected new one for their third of the tri-plex. Hector, Benecia's father, worked some when he was not attending adult school, but Francisco pushed him to do homework which took time.

Francisco told Benecia and Adriana, "No man is going to live in our home and not pay his own way and that of his family." The two women nodded in agreement.

Driving long distances Miguel was absent a lot from Benecia and his young son, now one year old. She and the baby went on an occasional trip delivering pasta with him to Chicago and Colorado. He noticed how tired she was since she recently became pregnant again. He thought it better she remain with the family, since driving had become an ordeal for her. He decided to hire another driver to help him drive.

Joy saw a documentary about a Greek family who came to America and bought a big house. It gave her an idea which she explained, "Miguel could pay me $1,000 a month of what he earns, and we could have a big house with lots of bathrooms for all of us. There would be privacy when they wanted it, yet there would be family. If Francisco gave $500 a month, we could make it on what I could pay by getting a part-time job tutoring at The Learning Center. And the young ones could all finish school with diplomas and go on to college."

She called three realty companies and told them what she wanted in a house. The house needed to have three different floors, for three different generations. She and José, when he came home from the Mexican prison, would live on the first floor; the family of Miguel and his wife and son and soon-to-be daughter, according to the sonogram, would have the second floor. Francisco and Adriana would be on the other side of the hall of her and José. The other two brothers and three sisters would live on the upstairs floor with *Grandmamá*. When *Grandmamá* got older and was unable to climb stairs any more, they would make a room on the floor where she and José would live.

Finally, Falstad's Realty called her back and told her they had three houses for her to look at. Margie Falstad picked her up in mid-afternoon and they drove to each of the houses.

The first two houses did not impress Joy, so they drove in silence to the third home. Margie Falstad doubted if she could sell Joy on a house she didn't want.

As they rounded the curve of bushes and eucalyptus trees to the big house atop a rounded hill surrounded by tall pine trees along Sycamore Canyon Road, Joy Engler Ramirez felt like she was going home. A doe with a hopping, skipping fawn calmly walked along the side of the road beside them, unafraid. Soon she walked with her fawn following into the shadows of the large trees and shrubs and disappeared.

The three-story mansion suddenly loomed into sight. Margie Falstad looked at Joy's face and knew immediately Joy had found what she wanted in a home.

"This home is up for sale because the parents of the new owners died and the adult children want the money out of the house. Their parents lived here for over 50 years. They are willing to let you have it for less if you can buy it immediately." They drove into the wide, circular driveway up to the beckoning pale yellow and white mansion.

"Let's go in the house and see what we can see," said Joy. "I will have to bring my stepsons up here to make sure this is what they would want. They will need a few days to get used to the idea of moving again."

"Look at the first floor on this side of the landing. These actually were built to be servants' quarters. That is why you will see the drop chute from floors two and three delivers the laundry into that room over there."

"With reorganization *Grandmamá Alejandra* would enjoy living here in this section. She loves my washing machine and dryer and they would fit here perfectly," said Joy. "I can hardly wait to show her the drop chute for dirty clothes. We can build her a kitchen nook and her own bathroom."

"Just a kitchen nook. There is already a bathroom right over there," Margie Falstad pointed out.

"We'll let *Grandmamá* do her own planning." Joy paused and asked, "Can you put a hold on it so no one else is ahead of us?"

"I will do that as soon as we get back to the office and you make arrangements for the down payment." Margie beamed. She wanted the commission to pay for her next trip to Europe.

That evening when Joy told Miguel about the house, he hugged his wife Benecia and said, "Benecia and I want to have more babies after this one is born. We will have plenty of babysitters like the Americans do, but our babysitters will be family and in the same house."

Joy beamed. "Sunday morning after Church and lunch would be a good time to see the big house. We must put a definite hold on it so we can buy it… if José and his other children agree."

CHAPTER 64

THE MEXICAN GOVERNMENT AND government lawyers found José Ramirez, alias Manuel Garcia, had not only helped capture the serial rapist/killer of Juarez' many victims but had killed Enrique Castillone in self-defense. The aging *Abuelita* of José's hometown in Siempre testified that Enrique gave José's wife Elmira the severe case of venereal STDs that had killed her.

Enrique's own mother, Juanita Castillone, testified of the evil things her son had done over the years. Pedro and his father, Jorge Castillone, both had recently died, a month apart. Pedro from the secret disease and Juan from drinking that destroyed his liver. There were no living persons who could or would testify in favor of the man Enrique Castillone. He had hurt so many in Siempre and surrounding villages leaving a legacy of fear and disgust for the Castillone men.

The Mexican judge had no choice but to rule for José Ramirez and declare him not guilty in first and second degree.

"This man is innocent," the Judge said. "I find no fault in him. His family needs him. For running away from the law, he is released for the time served while he waited in prison." He ordered the guards to release him that same day.

Joy rushed from her seat in the courtroom – tears streaming down her rosy cheeks, flushed from the heat of the day – to touch this man she had given her trust to. José took her hands and kissed them over and over. "God has been good to us. He has never let me down."

CHAPTER 65

One year later.

J OSÉ'S GRANDSON MIGUELITO, THE youngest, was now well over two years old. He climbed out of his bed where he slept in his parents' room in the big house up the hill. Benecia and Miguelito and the new little sister were still sleeping in the big bed as dawn broke filtering sunbeams through the tall pine trees that surrounded the three-tier home. He glanced at them quickly while he stood on tiptoe pulling the bedroom door open.

Miguelito traipsed down the hallway, down the stairs to his abuelos' bedroom. The door was open slightly waiting for him. He pushed it, dashed to the bed and climbed in between José and Joy.

"*Grandpapá, Grandmamá*," the little boy yelled happily as their arms went around his small body to hug him. They were ready for him, the cute little tyke with his father Miguel's black Elmira-like eyes. When he spoke to Joy and José, he spoke in English. When he spoke to his parents and aunts and uncles, he spoke in Spanish. He spoke easily with no accent Joy noticed, probably because he copied her. She often took long walks with him around the large yard looking for the wild life that often were there – so they could talk.

Joy basked in the pleasure of a loving little boy. She said to José, "We did the right thing in buying this multi-generational home." He hugged her hard, making her squeal. Miguelito laughed and hugged her, too.

Since José had been released and returned from the Eastern Mexico Prison, he had been a major hero in the city of Whittier. The U. S. of A. had granted him amnesty, and he was enrolled in adult school studying on Tuesday and Thursday evenings to become an American citizen. He studied now with others like himself who wanted to become part of this amazing land of America.

The daily newspaper in Whittier wrote success stories and pictures of José and Joy, the Literacy Program and their wedding pictures; the exoneration of José from The Eastern Prison in Mexico City. The children and grandchildren played a lower profile in the news stories, because they were still working on becoming real citizens instead of using green cards purchased through fraud on street corners.

****

Joy had another great idea – she thought.

The *Grandmamá* had cooked a Mexican meal of tacos with steamed meat, rice, salad and refried beans to go with corn tortillas. Sweetbreads were for dessert. She was happy to be teaching Joy her secret recipes. Benecia, Adriana and the granddaughters were willing learners, too. Her life was full.

Joy announced at dinner that evening, "I am going to teach all of you English every night after dinner. José translated to Spanish. "Joy is trying to learn Spanish from me and you, and now she wants to help all of you speak English."

Everyone was silent.

Finally, Miguelito spoke up in Spanish, "I am willing to learn. When Benecia and I travel from here to Chicago in my big semi-diesel truck, I find I need to speak more English words."

Benecia agreed. "I want my young son to know English. He will be able to get a better-paying job. His sister who is asleep in the other room will go to college and one day teach English."

Adriana said looking at Francisco, "Our son will be a businessman. He will go to college."

Francisco said, "He will have his own business. If he is smart as I think he is, he will make a lot of money to pay a lot of workers."

Benecia smiled contentedly showing her straight teeth, where the plastic braces had been, and said in broken English to Joy, "We send Mexico for more *primos*, cousins, to work with us."

Joy saw her happy expression and didn't dare tell her that among many of Joy's American friends *the primos* would not be welcome. Hospitals were shutting down because so many immigrants flooding America from around the world could not afford to pay for their emergency care, many Americans cannot get jobs for their own children graduating from high school. And college graduates were being told they were over-qualified for the available jobs on the market. And the illiteracy rate was going up instead of going down. For every tutor like Joy who worked her tail off trying to teach English to non speakers/ readers, there were many who did not care to continue working as tutors after they were trained. Tutoring was hard work. Tutors often quit too soon. And many immigrants began the school but dropped out after a few weeks.

Problems were ahead of them, but for now all were happy. Joy and José glanced at each other and smiled. Then he winked, flirting.